# Praise for
## Babylon 5:
## Dark Genesis: The
## Birth of the Psi Corps

"A solid, stand-alone novel . . . A fascinating spotlight on the enigmatic, deadly telepaths."
—*USA Today* (recommended reading)

"*Dark Genesis* is the kind of rare tie-in book that equals, or even bests, the franchise whose world it borrows. If you've heard the ravings of *Babylon 5* fans . . . then this book is for you. You'll get a glimpse into the world they enjoy so passionately."
—*Cinescape Online*

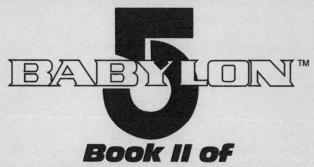

# BABYLON™ 5

## *Book II of*
## *Legions of Fire*

**Armies of Light and Dark**

**By Peter David**

**Based on
an original outline by
J. Michael Straczynski**

A Del Rey® Book
THE BALLANTINE PUBLISHING GROUP • NEW YORK

A Del Rey® Book
Published by The Ballantine Publishing Group
TM & copyright © 2000 by Warner Bros.

All rights reserved under International and Pan-American Copyright Conventions. Published in the United States by The Ballantine Publishing Group, a division of Random House, Inc., New York, and simultaneously in Canada by Random House of Canada Limited, Toronto.

Del Rey is a registered trademark and the Del Rey colophon is a trademark of Random House, Inc.

BABYLON 5, characters, names and all related indicia are trademarks of Warner Bros. © 2000.

www.randomhouse.com/delrey/

ISBN 0-345-42719-X

Manufactured in the United States of America

First Edition: May 2000

10 9 8 7 6 5 4 3 2 1

## *Legions of Fire*

# Armies of Light and Dark

**EXCERPTED FROM *THE CHRONICLES OF
LONDO MOLLARI—DIPLOMAT, EMPEROR,
MARTYR, AND SELF-DESCRIBED FOOL*.
PUBLISHED POSTHUMOUSLY. EDITED BY
EMPEROR COTTO.**

**EARTH EDITION, TRANSLATION © 2280**

**Excerpt dated (approximate Earth date)
December 14, 2267.**

My "masters" are pleased with me this day.

In retrospect, it is rather difficult to believe. Today, I stood in opposition to the Drakh who calls himself Shiv'kala. He ordered me to kill Vir Cotto, my former aide and, according to the predictions of Lady Morella, the future emperor of the Centauri Republic. Quite probably one of the few individuals in the galaxy whose continued existence gives me any fragment of joy whatsoever. Shiv'kala wanted Vir dead because Vir spoke his name, indicating that Vir has obtained knowledge he should not possess.

Such a coward, Shiv'kala. Such a damnable coward. But then, that is the way of creatures that live in shadow, as anyone who has ever lifted a rock can attest, having watched the bugs beneath scurry away. As for Shiv'kala, he lives within the shadow of a shadow, and so is even more likely to fear the light.

Not that he would admit it, of course. Those who are the most afraid are also the quickest to speak with the air of confidence. They believe that, as a result, observers will not detect their fear.

Just once—*just once*—I would give anything to see the fear I know he carries within him appear on that monstrous, craggy, blue-grey face of his.

I do not know where or how Vir learned the name. Nor do I have any idea what prompted him to sit here, in the great palace of Centauri Prime, and ask me about Shiv'kala. Obviously Vir has some sort of hidden allies, although I could not say whether they hug the shadows as assiduously as do my own associates. They sent him in, asked him to speak the name, and in doing so, used him. It was a rather reckless thing, and I can only hope that Vir will take the time to castigate them severely for placing him in such an untenable position.

So when Shiv'kala ordered Vir's death, I stood up to him. Yes, I did. I waved a sword around and spouted threats. I had no idea if I could carry off those threats, mind you, but I made them sound most sincere. And Shiv'kala— somewhat to my surprise, I admit—did not press the matter. Truthfully, I don't know what I would have done. Would I really have attacked Shiv'kala? Tried to butcher him, knowing that his death would only have unfortunate consequences for me, and potentially lethal repercussions for my beloved Centauri Prime? After all, the Drakh still have their fusion bombs in place, ready to wipe millions of my people out of existence with the simplest press of a button.

The Drakh possess the ultimate trump card.

But they will not be quick to use it, I think. It is my belief that Shiv'kala views me as some sort of experiment or project. He seems interested in seeing whether he can break me in some way. Break my spirit, break my soul—presuming I still have such a thing. If I do, it is very likely so blasted and blackened by now as to be unrecognizable.

I am not entirely certain why that would be of such importance to him. It could be that if I am completely broken, I can be of greater use to the Drakh. On the other hand, for all I know, he has a side bet with his fellow Drakh as to whether I can be broken. These Drakh enjoy playing their little games, and I am simply a pawn to be moved around from square to square.

Not even a king. Just a pawn.

Vir came to this place to help me, as did Timov. It is truly amazing how one's perceptions can turn around. When I was young, I thought so much of the position of emperor. I thought so little of Timov. When I first journeyed to Babylon 5, I met Vir and thought very little of him. Oh, and I thought *very* little of myself, which was why I was so quick to drown my sorrows in drink.

It is amazing how much things change. Now I consider Vir to be the last, best hope that my beloved Centauri Prime has for a future. And I consider Timov, whom I held in such disdain, to be one of the noblest women it has ever been my honor to know. As for myself . . .

Well . . . I still think very little of myself. It's interesting how many things change, while many other things remain exactly, depressingly, the same.

The Drakh have some sort of new plan brewing. I can always tell when something is going on. Shiv'kala, the Drakh who is my primary keeper, has a way of comporting himself when there is some particular scheme afoot. I have no idea, however, what it might be.

It is my understanding that many captors and their keepers develop a love/hate relationship with one another. I suppose that Shiv'kala and I have that, to some degree. I love to hate him. It was Shiv'kala, after all, who insisted on putting that bastard, Durla, into place as my minister of internal security. Durla, in turn, has placed his own people in other key places, and I am slowly becoming isolated from any potential allies. I am both the most and least powerful individual in all of Centauri Prime.

The only person left in this entire palace who brings any joy to me is Senna, the young girl who is the daughter of the late Lord Refa. I took her under my wing, educated her, and made her my personal project. My sentiment was simplicity itself: I felt that if I could save this one girl, then perhaps I would have that much better a chance of saving all of Centauri Prime.

Yet the girl is a liability, even though she does not know it. She is yet another pawn in this great game of power and revenge that Shiv'kala and the Drakh have continued to play. By keeping her close at hand, the Drakh continue to remind me of the control that they have over me. Apparently, having a small one-eyed creature called a keeper permanently affixed to my shoulder is insufficient to do the job.

I think of what might have been. I think of all the possibilities that lay before me in my youth. I always promised myself that I would make no compromises, if power were ever given to me. Yet I have lived my life making nothing *but* compromises. No . . . it has actually been worse than that. At least when one compromises, one gets something in return for making a concession. I have been given nothing, nothing at all. My power is an illusion; my efforts to safeguard Centauri Prime a waste of time . . .

*Bah.*

I am doing it again. So often, I find it easy to slip into self-pity. Wallowing is my most comfortable state of being, be it either in an alcoholic stupor or a psychologically induced state of despair. Instead of being designated emperor, I should be called "head wallower" out of a sheer sense of accuracy.

There is still much to do. There are still things that I can accomplish. Shiv'kala wanted to dispose of Vir, and I threatened him in such a way that he actually backed down. It was the closest thing to a triumph that I have had in quite some time. It gave me a small measure of hope. That is most dangerous, of course. Once hope sets in, who knows what could happen next? Hope might lead to a belief that all will work out for the best.

Perhaps it will. Perhaps it will at that.

If only I knew what the Drakh were planning. If only I knew whether Vir might be able to stop it.

Such a thing would seem beyond credibility. Vir has his better attributes, certainly. I could not have asked for a more loyal friend and follower. And the prediction by the Lady Morella, that Vir will follow me as emperor, gives me—oddly enough—a sense of comfort. Of all the individuals I know, he probably has the best chance of doing a good job.

But if the Drakh have some sort of revenge-driven plan in the offing, it will require a true hero to prevent it. For all that I respect Vir, for all that he has grown up under my "tutelage," a hero most definitely he is not.

And I, of course, cannot even warn anyone. If there were to be a strike against the Interstellar Alliance, it would be impossible for me to alert President Sheridan or any of his people. The only possible means of doing so would be to use Vir as a go-between, and Shiv'kala has seen to it that Vir has been exiled from Centauri Prime.

I shall have to find a way around that.

My keeper stirs—the alcoholic stupor into which I've placed him is starting to wear off. As always, I must secure this journal and make certain that the dangerous game I am playing is not detected. In a way, this historical record is a small bit of rebellion, which helps to keep my soul and spirit alive.

But a small bit of rebellion is all that it is. Truth to tell, I am no more a hero than Vir. That is quite a shame, for Centauri Prime could very much use one at this point in our history. Let us hope that a hero steps forward.

And let us hope I do not have to act as the instrument of death when and if he does.

# — chapter 1 —

*Vir stood before the giant, crackling energy gate. The ground around him was littered with bodies. On the other side of the gate loomed something so dark, so evil, that he was paralyzed with fear, and then he remembered a time—days, even hours ago—when he had been convinced that he could never, would never, be afraid of anything ever again. He would have laughed at his arrogance were he not too terrified to laugh, and his thoughts spun back to that period a short time before . . .*

It seemed to Vir a lifetime ago that he had stood before the techno-mages and trembled. In fact, it had not even been the techno-mages themselves. Instead he had quivered as shadows in a darkened corridor had loomed around him in a most threatening manner.

Vir had been going to speak with the techno-mages on Londo's behalf. The mission had seemed fraught with peril at the time. Londo had required him to inform the techno-mages that he, Londo, wished to meet with them.

That was it. That was all. Tell them that Londo wanted to set up a meeting. Beginning, middle, end of the assignment. But oooohh, how his knees had knocked, and oooohh, how the breath had caught within his chest, all because of an assignment that had involved nothing except acting as Londo Mollari's messenger boy.

He reflected upon that incident, and found the man he was at that time to be rather amusing, even buffoonish. What a charming, amusing individual he had been. He had always acted out of concern for everyone's needs.

That person was dead.

His death had not been abrupt. Instead it had been an agonizingly slow process, as he died by degrees. The final death-blow had been when he had slain the Emperor Cartagia . . .

No. No, on second thought, that wasn't it at all. No, the deathblow to the man that Vir Cotto had once been had come on the day when he had waggled his fingers cheerfully at the severed head of Mr. Morden, as it adorned a pike outside the imperial residence. Oh, certainly, he had once commented how much he looked forward to such an event, but he hadn't really meant it. The truth was that it hadn't been all that long ago that seeing a bodiless head would have been enough to make him physically ill.

Yet there he had stood, *reveling* in the death of an enemy. Granted, Morden had been the incarnation of evil, but even so . . . it had been a truly hideous punishment. And the Vir of old would never have taken such personal joy and satisfaction in witnessing its aftermath.

But that was the Vir of old.

Vir had been struck by fear over many things in his life. Those huge Shadow ships, or the techno-mages, or the sight of Londo sliding toward darkness while he, Vir, could do nothing to stave off the inevitable.

However, the single most frightening thing he had ever had to contend with was pondering the future. If a few short years had turned him into the current incarnation of Vir Cotto, what in the name of the Great Maker would he be like years further down the line?

Casting aside these thoughts, the Vir-of-the-moment, however, was determined not to dwell on such things. Instead he tossed restlessly in a small vessel belonging to the very beings from whom he had cowered in fear, only a few years before.

On some level, he knew that he should be afraid of even entering a vessel belonging to techno-mages. However, in the past week alone, Vir had discovered that the new, deliriously joyful love of his life, Mariel, had actually been stringing him along. She had been playing him for a fool, using him simply to position herself so that she would have greater access to assorted diplomats and ambassadors on Babylon 5. He could only guess why, although he suspected that espionage very likely had something to do with it. Then he had learned that Londo was involved with beings that were servants of the long-gone Shadows, creatures called the Drakh. One of them was named Shiv'kala, and the mere mention of the name had been enough to get Vir thrown into a Centauri Prime dungeon. If Londo had not interceded and freed him, Vir would already be dead.

He wondered just what it had cost Londo to purchase Vir's freedom. What had he promised to do in exchange? What further piece of Londo's soul—presuming there was any of it left—had been traded away so that Vir could continue on the twisted path of his own destiny?

He couldn't remember the last time he had slept soundly. Once he had entered the techno-mage vessel, however, the female named Gwynn had led him to a seat and told him in no uncertain terms to go to sleep.

"Sleep," he had said bitterly, the stink of the dungeon still heavy in his nostrils. "You can't be serious. Sleep, my dear woman, is absolutely the last thing that I'll be capable of. Thanks anyway."

Whereupon Gwynn had touched two fingers to his temple, and suddenly the room was swimming. Vir's eyelids had been unable to sustain him, and in an instant, he had passed out. It was not, however, anything remotely resembling a peaceful dream state. Images of Mariel, Londo, Timov, Durla, all tumbled one over the other, fighting for dominance in his mind. There was Londo, white-haired and tired, many years hence, with a glass of some sort of liquor clutched in his hand. He appeared to be waiting for someone.

And then someone was approaching him. It was Vir, and he had his hands out, and they were around Londo's throat, strangling him. Suddenly Vir's hands were transformed into Narn hands, and Vir was cast outside of the moment, watch-

ing as G'Kar stood over Londo with murder in his eyes . . .
no. In his eye.

Durla was there as well, and he was dancing . . . yes. He
was dancing with Mariel, while Chancellor Lione plucked
away an aimless tune that Vir could not identify. Curiously,
both Mariel and Durla were covered with blood.

There was a full-length mirror standing nearby. Vir stared
into it, and he saw himself clad in the imperial white. He
turned back and there was Londo, with no G'Kar in sight. He
looked as he had when Vir had first met him. He looked so
young. Only nine, ten years had passed since that day, but
Great Maker, what a decade it had been. Londo, who had
seemed so burdened with his crushed expectations of what
the Centauri Republic should be, nevertheless seemed relatively carefree compared to what he would eventually become. He raised a glass to Vir and tilted it back.

Blood poured from the glass and splattered all over Londo's
face. Then he placed the glass down and reached toward Vir
with a blood-covered hand. Vir stepped back, back, then
bumped against a wall. There was nowhere for him to go, nowhere for him to retreat. Mariel and Durla waltzed past, onto
a balcony, and then went over the railing and vanished from
sight. Vir opened his mouth to cry out, but his voice was not
his own. Instead it was the cry of millions of souls issuing
from his single throat. Outside the balcony off which Mariel
and Durla had just plunged, he could see Centauri Prime . . .
and it was burning. Great tongues of flame were licking a sky
thick with inky black smoke.

Vir startled himself awake. He realized, in a distant way,
that he should probably have cried out when he woke up.
He did not, however. It was as if nothing could scare him
anymore.

"—foolishness," he heard a voice saying. It was the female, the one called Gwynn. "Foolishness, Kane. That's the
only word for it. This isn't what we're supposed to be doing."

"It is an adventure, Gwynn. If we were not interested in adventure, we would be better off using our abilities in some
truly appropriate manner . . . like standing on street corners

and pulling rabbits from hats while people throw money." That was Kane's voice. Vir knew it all too well. Although Kane had saved his life, Vir had already come to hate him. For it was Kane who persisted in telling Vir the truth of things, and these truths inevitably served to make Vir's life all the more difficult. There was something to be said for the bliss of self-delusion.

"Finian, tell him we should turn away from this course," Gwynn demanded.

"I don't know that we should," replied Finian, the third of the techno-mage trio. "A situation needs to be investigated. We're on the scene. We should investigate."

"You always agree with Kane! There's no point in talking to you."

"If you know that for a certainty, why did you bother asking me in the first place?" Finian replied reasonably.

"Because I'm as great a fool as you, that's why."

"Then it's fortunate that you're with us. Who else would want to be seen in the company of such a fool?"

Gwynn made an impatient noise and turned away from them. Her gaze went to Vir and she blinked in surprise. "Oh. You're awake. He's awake, gentlemen."

"I thought you said he'd be asleep for at least another hour," Kane said as he moved to stand next to Gwynn.

"So I thought."

"Sleep," said Vir, "is overrated." He looked at the three of them, struck by the similarities and yet also by the differences.

They all had their hoods back, and Vir could see that they all wore their hair, or lack of same, in an identical manner. In all three instances, what little hair they had was trimmed so close that it might well have been done with a razor. Starting at a point just above their foreheads, the hairstyle angled back in two strips like a "V," with a third band starting at the same point and running straight back.

Gwynn was the tallest of the three, and certainly carried herself with the most imperiousness. She seemed the type who not only did not suffer fools gladly, but also gladly made fools suffer. Vir found himself hoping that he didn't fall into her personal definition of a fool. Kane's jaw was pointed, as if perpetually outthrust in challenge, his skin dark and his eyes deep set and unreadable. Finian, by contrast, was the shortest of the three, with a round face and remarkably pale blue eyes that seemed sad . . . or amused . . . or perhaps amused by the sadness of it all.

"So, Vir," Kane said briskly, rubbing his hands together as if he were anticipating the start of a truly engaging game of chess. "Are you ready to help save the galaxy?" Gwynn rolled her eyes and shook her head. Kane pretended not to notice.

"You mentioned that before," said Vir, "without going into any detail. I don't suppose you'd, ah . . . care to tell me now, would you. Just how, specifically, we're going to be doing the rescuing of the galaxy."

"We are heading to the Centauri dig on K0643," Kane told him. "And there—"

"There what?" Gwynn interrupted him. "I think it best we get that settled here and now, Kane. When we discover the true nature of the dig—or, I should say, when we confirm our suspicions—what is it your intention that we do? You say 'save the galaxy' in a way that could only be considered blithely overconfident. You *are* aware that you're exceeding the parameters of our assignment, are you not?"

"As are you," Finian pointed out.

"Be quiet, Finian. I'm simply here to make sure that he," and she stabbed a finger at Kane, "doesn't get into any trouble."

"Oh, of *course* not."

Gwynn looked up, startled. It was Vir who had spoken, and he was making no effort to stop the sarcasm dripping from his voice. "No, Kane never gets into trouble. Just me. I'm at the forefront of every one of his efforts." He rose from his seat and, as he spoke, shook his head, as if he were having trouble believing what he had been through. "There was an assassination attempt on Sheridan, and Kane could have stopped it with no trouble. Instead he let me almost get killed before he stepped in. Then Kane wanted to convince me that there is a 'great darkness' on Centauri Prime and set me up so that I got myself thrown in prison."

"And yet, here you are," Kane pointed out.

"No thanks to you."

"Actually, I seem to recall—"

"All right, all right, yes, on at least one occasion, it was thanks to you," Vir allowed. "And maybe there were more occasions that I didn't know about. The point is this: I don't mind throwing myself into danger at this point."

"You don't?" Finian raised one nonexistent eyebrow. "I wouldn't have fancied you the heroic type, myself."

"No, I'm just tired, and I'm fed up," said Vir. "Sometimes I think a hero is just a coward who's too tired to care anymore."

"There's something to be said for that," admitted Gwynn.

"As I was saying, if I'm going to throw myself into danger, this time you're going to be right beside me, Kane. You, too, you two. I know that Kane is only a cloister techno-mage. That he's been kind of . . . of stashed away all this time, off in your hiding place. That he hasn't really spent much time in the outside world, so he's not as proficient . . . no offense . . ."

"None taken," Kane said calmly.

". . . he's not as proficient," continued Vir.

Kane cleared his throat loudly. "You didn't have to repeat it," he informed him.

"Oh. Sorry. Anyway, he's not . . . well . . . you know, it's what I said. That way . . . in the whole techno-magic and -mage thing. But with you two along, we—"

"Actually, I am only a cloister as well," said Gwynn.

"You—?" He couldn't quite believe it.

He turned and looked at Finian, who nodded sheepishly. "Guilty as charged."

"Oh, *perfect,*" said Vir. "We're going into a dangerous situation, and none of you is an upper-echelon techno-mage." He rubbed the bridge of his nose. "Perfect. All right, then, remind me: Why are we going to K0643?"

"Because the Drakh are interested in something that's there, which is probably Shadow-related. Oh, and because diggers have been dying, trying to get to it."

"Oh, well, of course. Naturally. If there's someplace where

evil is hovering and people are dying, that's certainly the *first* place I'd want to be."

"Then you're in luck," said Kane.

"I was kidding."

"So was I."

Vir shook his head and—not for the first time in his life—the words "Why me?" echoed within it. As always, no answer was forthcoming, although he fancied that he could hear Fate laughing deliriously and rolling on the floor somewhere, amused by his predicament.

*Laughing. Yes, he could hear the fates laughing at him. He stood before the energy gate, his thoughts pulled momentarily from the past to the present, and not only could he hear laughing, but also he could detect an eerie howling. It was the voices, the voices that were crying out their contempt for his ambitions, as if to say, "Pathetic little creature . . . thinking that you—you of all people—could save the galaxy? What makes you more worthy of living than all those around you, who died in witnessing the power before you?"*

*"Nothing. Nothing makes me more worthy," said Vir, and he knew it to be true.*

*The howling increased, and Vir felt himself being lifted off his feet, dragged toward his death. He was surprised to discover that his death was, in fact, something he wasn't looking forward to . . .*

# — chapter 2 —

Vir hadn't been entirely sure what he was expecting to find when he arrived at the dig site, but whatever he *did* fancy he'd see, it didn't match up with what they actually found down there.

Empty buildings. Lots of them.

The entire dig had a ramshackle feel about it, as Vir and the techno-mages made their way through the narrow streets. Actually, "streets" might have been too generous a word. There were assorted pathways that ran helter-skelter through the settlement, but nothing had actually been paved. At some points the paths became so narrow that, if Vir and the others had encountered someone coming in the opposite direction, there would have been a considerable problem in dealing with it. However, that situation never actually presented itself.

There were others around. They heard them more than they saw them, and voices floated to them, carried upon the breeze. It was a very stiff breeze, almost a steady chill that Vir could feel slicing through right to his bones. Occasionally there were people congregating at street corners and in makeshift pubs. Vir caught scattered words here and there, and the words were quite disturbing. They were words such as "disappeared," "dead," "quit," "afraid."

"Dead." That one was said quite a bit.

There was only one other word that Vir heard with any greater frequency, and that word was "haunted."

Haunted.

Once upon a time, Vir would have laughed derisively at

such a word. But his time on Babylon 5 had served as a serious education into the realm of the supernatural . . . or, at least, it had given him an introduction to the notion that there was more in heaven and earth than was dreamt of in his philosophy. He had lived in a place where people who captured souls and nightmare beings from unknown realms of space had been all too real.

For the men he passed in the settlement town of K0643, it seemed, the line between truth and fiction, between the easily understood and the incomprehensible, had become blurred. For Vir himself, the line had long ago been completely erased. Anything was capable of happening to him. He felt that this was the only possible mind-set for him to maintain, since anything—more or less—generally did have the habit of happening to him.

"I know you."

The voice startled him. He turned and saw a fairly unremarkable, but nonetheless instantly identifiable Centauri who had just emerged from one of the pubs.

Months earlier, a Centauri citizen had been used as a helpless pawn in an assassination attempt on John Sheridan, the president of the Interstellar Alliance. He had been unaware of the part that had been assigned him, and it had only been intervention on Vir's part that had prevented the citizen from carrying out the murderous design that had been thrust upon him. The individual's name had been Rem Lanas, and it was Lanas who was now standing in front of Vir, with clear astonishment on his face.

Before Vir could say another word, Lanas grabbed him by the front of his heavy coat. Vir thought for a moment that it was an attack, but then he realized that Lanas was, in fact, imploring him. "Please," he said, "Don't take me back to Babylon 5. You . . . you said we could keep it between us. Don't tell anyone I'm here. I'll . . . I'll leave if you want, I'll—"

"Calm down! For pity's sake, calm down!" said Vir, gripping him firmly by the shoulders. "Will you take it easy? I have no more intention of turning you over to the authorities now than I did then. What are you doing here?"

"Working," Lanas responded, appearing surprised that Vir would even have to ask. "Why? What else would anyone be doing here? For that matter . . . what are *you* doing here?"

"Well . . . we're here to check into some . . . things. We've heard that this place was, well . . . haunted. And we felt that it would be in the best interests of the Republic to look into it, as ridiculous as the whole haunting thing might sound." He forced a laugh to underscore the alleged absurdity of the notion.

Lanas was looking at him oddly. "Who is 'we'? Is that the imperial 'we'?"

"What? Oh! No, no, 'we' as in myself and my—" He turned and gestured toward the techno-mages.

They weren't there. There was only empty air behind him.

Vir stared dumbly at his open and gesturing hand for a moment, and then said, "—myself and my . . . fingers. Yes, that's right," and he waggled them to display them properly. "That is to say, my fingers and I. I have names for each of them. Would you like to hear—?"

"No. No, that's . . . quite all right," said Lanas carefully, clearly not wanting to offend the man, quite possibly a lunatic, who was standing in front of him.

Suddenly switching his tone of voice, Vir inquired, "There seem to be fewer people here than I imagined there would be. Why is that?"

Lanas seemed to give great thought to what he was about to say. Ultimately, he glanced around, as if concerned that someone might be eavesdropping, and then he said, "Not here."

"Not here? You mean there are people not here?"

"No, I mean we shouldn't talk here. Come."

Turning, he started quickly down the makeshift road. Vir followed, pausing only a moment to glance over his shoulder and confirm for himself that there was no sign of those who had been accompanying him.

Within a few minutes, Vir was sitting in the small quarters

that had been assigned to Lanas. To say it was unadorned was
to understate the matter. A few sticks of furniture in a one-
room domicile in a large, prefabricated building—that was
the entirety of Lanas' living quarters. "I'm sorry I've nothing
to offer you to drink. I wasn't expecting company. Not that I
would have been able to provide anything even had I known
you were going to be here. Minister Durla keeps us on a fairly
restricted regimen around here."

"Does he."

"Yes. He doesn't want us spending his time and his money
drinking. He believes that eating, working, and sleeping
should constitute the entirety of our existence here."

"And you put up with that?" Vir was appalled. "But there's
more to life than that! There's . . ."

"Oh. And he keeps prostitutes supplied in abundance."

"Ah." Vir bobbed his head in comprehension. "He, uhm . . .
he does?"

"Yes. He believes they provide a necessary release." He
shrugged. "Apparently they fit into the budget more easily than
liquor. Less expensive, too."

"That's very frugal of him," Vir said.

"They actually have an incentive bonus program, where
they—"

Vir quickly put up his hands and forced a grin. "That's . . .
that's quite all right. I get the idea. I don't really need to know
more than you've told me. In fact, I wouldn't have been upset
to know less." He cleared his throat, and then said, "So, you
were going to tell me about . . ."

"Yes." Lanas nodded. Despite the fact that it was just the
two of them in the room, he still lowered his voice. "Between
the mysterious disappearances, and the people who have quit,
the workforce has dropped by seventy percent. The advantage is, those of us remaining are being given sizable raises
just to keep us here. The disadvantage, of course, is that we
might not see our loved ones ever again. That would probably
be more disturbing to me if I actually had loved ones." He
shrugged. "I know it sounds insane. But somehow you just

wind up adjusting to the idea that people disappear around here."

"Yes, I can guess that you would," Vir said, thinking about the abrupt disappearance of the techno-mages. "And do you have any idea what might be causing it? Any clue?"

"None at all. All I know is this: We've a primary excavation area in which we've managed to get deep beneath the surface of this misbegotten world. A number of men have disappeared along the way, some mysteriously, some running away. We have no idea what we're searching for, or what's going on here. But I will tell you what made an impression on me. Minister Durla came here once to inspect the facilities. I saw him several times during his stay here, and every time I did, there was something in his eyes."

"You mean, like an eyelash?"

"No," Lanas shook his head in exasperation. "I mean a look, a . . . sensation. As if he was pleased over the existence of this dig, for some reason that none of us could fathom. I certainly know I couldn't."

"And he's given you no clue as to what you're looking for."

"No. The only thing I know is that he increased the shifts. We're working around the clock now. Day and night. Right now the Odd Squad is on."

"The . . . what?"

"That's what we call them. The Odd Squad. A group of particularly aggressive diggers that sort of ended up working with one another. Word is that they're all former criminals or some such. Used to hard labor. They thrive on it. Enjoy doing it better and faster than anyone else because they somehow prove something to themselves." He stopped and shrugged. "Ah, but I shouldn't be second-guessing other people's motives. When you get right down to it, who ever knows why anyone does anything, right?"

"Oh, I can, uhm . . . definitely agree with you on that one," Vir said.

"In any event, if anyone gets down to the bottom of whatever it is that we're digging around for, it's going to be the Odd Squad. They claim they can smell danger and then run screaming toward it. One of them . . . Ciril, I think his name is . . . says he's looking forward to meeting Death so that he can punch Death in his privates and then assail him with a string of off-color remarks. I'm not sure why anyone would want to anger Death; but then again, it's not my fantasy. In any event, at the behest of the Odd Squad—men possessed if ever I saw them—lights were rigged to provide illumination. That was something I oversaw, actually. Electronics is my field of expertise . . . although considering the circumstances we keep meeting under, I wouldn't be surprised if you thought I wasn't much good at anything. Whenever the—"

Suddenly, a severe rumble rippled up from below them. Vir was utterly disconcerted. The sound was so deep, so all-encompassing, that for a moment he thought a fleet of Shadow vessels was soaring through the sky, their sheer weight causing vibrations as they passed. Lanas, for his part, didn't seem especially put out. "And we're getting those more often, too," he said as the trembling subsided.

"Quakes? Why? Is this area built on a fault line?"

"Not to the best of our knowledge, no. But it keeps happening just the same. No one knows what causes it."

*We do.*

Vir looked up, confused and surprised when he heard that. "You do?" he asked.

"No, I just said we didn't." Lanas looked utterly confused. "Was I somehow unclear?"

*We know. Get out of there, Vir. Matters are moving faster than we anticipated.*

There was no longer any need for hesitation on Vir's part, for naturally he knew just who was most likely to be projecting commentary directly into his skull. In an instant, he was on his feet, and through clenched teeth he said to Lanas, "I have to go. Thank you for your hospitality."

"But I wasn't being particularly hospitable . . ."

"You didn't try to threaten me, terrorize me, or toss me into prison. These days, that's enough for me to consider myself ahead of the game. It's been charming. Have to go. Bye."

Rem Lanas stared in confusion as Vir bolted out the door

so fast that it barely had time to slide open for him. Then he just shook his head and murmured, "I've heard that Babylon 5 does strange things to a man. But until I met Vir Cotto, I never realized just how strange."

When Vir stepped out of the building, he looked to his right, then to his left. At that point he was tapped on the shoulder with enough force that it caused him to jump slightly, startled. Then he glared at the three techno-mages who were standing exactly where Vir had been looking, moments before. "How do you do that?" he demanded in exasperation.

"A magician never reveals his tricks," Kane informed him.

"Yes, but you're not a magician. You're a cloister."

"True," Kane admitted.

"Have no fear, Kane," Finian said brightly. "I suspect once we are finished with this business, we will no longer be looked upon as cloisters."

"I'm so happy for the both of you," Gwynn responded sarcastically. She turned to Vir and said, "Vir, you're an ambassador. You're a high-ranking official for the Centauri. You *must* tell them to cease the excavation immediately."

"Excellent idea," said Vir. He paused. "And what reason should I give?"

"That if they continue on this course, they will enable beings of great evil to obtain power that should not be theirs. This they will, in turn, utilize for wholesale death and destruction."

"They may not buy that," Vir said.

"Vir," Kane said urgently, "time is not our friend."

"Then why don't *you* stop this excavation! Conjure up some ghosts to scare the people away; they think the place is haunted as it is. Or just . . . just magic everyone back to Centauri Prime, to buy some time. I don't know, something, *anything.*"

"Our mandate is clear—we can only observe," Gwynn said. As urgent as her plea had been, clearly she was the most aggressive stickler for protocol of all of them. "We act on behalf of each other, for mutual protection, but that is all we are supposed to do, unless we are otherwise instructed . . ."

"As I was instructed to take steps to save Sheridan's life, for example," said Kane.

"Okay, okay, fine," said Vir with a growing lack of patience. "So if that's the case, then why don't you manage to go get some new instructions, okay? Just wave your . . . your magic wand, or whatever, to find out whether you can do something about the current situation. You know, the one involving all sorts of evil that could be unleashed on the galaxy while we're standing here discussing the fine points of Techno-maging 101."

Kane did not seem amused. "My associates and I are endeavoring to inform the techno-mages of the present situation, but in the meantime—"

"Endeavoring?" Vir looked at them questioningly. "What do you mean, 'endeavoring'? Is there some problem?"

The cloisters looked at each other with a combination of annoyance and uncertainty. "Our initial attempts to contact them have . . . fallen short," Kane admitted.

"Fallen short? How? How fallen short? How short, I mean?"

"We've been unable to reach them," Gwynn said flatly. "There is something about this place that interferes with our communications spells."

"Forget the spells! Pick up a phone! Use some standard means of communication!"

"The techno-mages cannot be contacted through any 'standard means.' "

"Oh, right, right," Vir said sourly. "That's a sign of just how advanced they are; you can't reach them at all."

"We'll keep trying," said Kane. "In the meantime, you do what you can."

"Fine, fine, whatever," Vir told them. "I'll find out who's in charge and use whatever authority I can to get things shut down, at least for a while. But I'm warning you right now, whoever's running the dig probably isn't going to take me all that seriously. Most people don't."

Kane stepped forward and put his hands firmly on Vir's arms. "We do. We take you most seriously, Vir. We have every confidence in you. If you can't get this done, then no one can."

"No one can tell me what to do," Renegar said.

Renegar was the most jowly Centauri that Vir had ever seen. He was large and beefy, his hair cut unfashionably and defiantly short. He had thick lips, small eyes, and arms so powerful that they looked capable of snapping Vir in half with little to no difficulty. And when Renegar spoke, it was with a deep raspy voice that seemed to originate from his knees.

He was, quite simply, not someone with whom Vir wanted any difficulties.

Renegar sat behind his desk in his office, both of which seemed too small for him. There was a good deal of clutter about. Vir would never have known, to look at him, that this fellow was in charge of anything of any importance, let alone an excavation mandated by someone as highly positioned as Durla, the minister of internal security.

"I'm not telling you what to do," Vir assured him quickly.

"That's a relief," said Renegar. He did not, however, sound relieved. He just sounded as annoyed as he had been when Vir had first come knocking on his door.

"But certainly," Vir continued gamely, "you must know that there's something wrong on this world. You've had people disappearing from this project in alarming numbers."

"Centauri are soft." There was clear disgust in his voice. "That's always been our problem. Whenever any sort of difficulty is involved, we fold up. Call it quits. In some ways, you have to admire the Narn. Say what you want about them, but we conquered them and they still never quit. Took them years and years, but they fought for their freedom and obtained it. We wouldn't fight for freedom. Someone conquered us, we'd roll over and die, and that would be that."

"I'm so pleased we're having the opportunity to discuss this," Vir said, "but it's not exactly what I wanted to focus on right now, if that's okay. People aren't just leaving because they're tired or bored or they've had enough. There is a great evil here, and your men are in terrible danger. Terrible, terrible danger."

"And you know this . . . how?" inquired Renegar.

"Sources."

"What sort of sources?"

Vir endeavored to remember just where Renegar was on the social scale. He drew himself up haughtily, or at least as close to haughtily as he could get, and informed Renegar, "The sort of sources who choose not to be identified at this time."

"So you can't tell me."

"That is correct."

"And this great danger facing us . . . you can't tell me about that, either."

"I'm afraid not."

"But I'm just supposed to halt work on this project, on your say-so. Tell me, Ambassador Cotto, do you know Minister Durla?"

"I've . . . had some dealings with him, yes," said Vir somewhat wryly.

"Minister Durla, he's not vague at all. He tells me exactly what he wants done, and exactly when he wants it done by. Because of that, I tend to listen to him. Have you taken this matter up with him?"

"No."

"What do you think would happen if you did?"

Dissembling was not one of Vir's skills, learned or otherwise. "I doubt that he would be particularly amenable to listening to me."

"So why should I be more so?"

"Because," Vir said with unexpected vehemence, "you're here and he's not. Because he," and he pointed in the general direction of Centauri Prime, many light-years away, "is not going to care about the lives of the people here. And I thought that perhaps, since you are directly in charge of them, you just might care. Look, while we're talking here, going back and forth and around and around, the risk is growing with each passing minute. We're running out of time. In fact, we may already be out of time. Don't you understand? People aren't just disappearing. They're dying."

For just a moment, Renegar seemed slightly uncertain. Then his face, and hearts, hardened once more. "I have no proof of that."

"You have my word and the evidence of your own eyes: your populace is dropping. What else do you need?"

And at that moment, lending support to Vir's long-held notion that the Great Maker had a fairly perverse sense of humor, there was a sound of an explosion. It came from the direction of the excavation, but it was far more than just an explosion. It was as if the entire planet had been struck by a massive object, and nearly shattered by the impact. The office shook so violently that Vir didn't have the slightest chance of retaining his footing. One moment he was standing, the next he was on his back. Renegar fared no better: his chair tilted backward and spilled him to the ground.

Oddly enough, there was some benefit to that happenstance, for a huge chunk of the ceiling came free and crashed down right where Renegar had been. It might not have been of sufficient weight or impact to kill him, but it certainly would have been enough to give him a concussion—or worse.

Renegar, moving with surprising grace for one so large, tumbled out of his chair and scrambled to his feet. He looked at Vir with confusion, and Vir was pleased to see that—for the first time since they'd made each other's acquaintance—Renegar didn't seem smug or self-satisfied. Apparently Vir's predictions of imminent disaster carried a bit more weight when disaster suddenly presented itself.

All of Vir's instincts told him that now was the time to get the hell out of there. To head back to the landing point where the techno-mages had surreptitiously landed their vessel, and get as far away from this world as humanly, or inhumanly, possible. Vir knew, however, that he had reached a point in his life where his instincts were going to be of no use whatsoever. The impulses for self-preservation, for acting with caution, those were going to have to be tossed aside. At this point, not only did Centauri Prime need more than that, but Vir needed more than that, as well. For there was no way, absolutely no way, that he could bring himself to follow his instinct and return to Babylon 5, hide in his quarters, pull the blanket over his head and ignore the darkness that had fallen upon his world and threatened his people. That was the trouble with knowing what lurks within the shadows, he realized. One can't figure out where to look anymore. If you gaze into the shadows, you blanch at whatever may be in there looking back at you, and you jump as the shadows move. If you look into the light, not only are you blinded by its intensity, but also it serves to remind you that you should be doing everything you can to expunge the darkness. Light does not allow for excuses.

"What's . . . happening?" Renegar gasped out. The tremors were continuing, becoming more pronounced with each moment.

And Vir began to detect a scent in the air. The smell of energy having been released, perhaps, or the aroma of ozone as if a massive lightning strike had occurred not far away. His back against the wall, Vir pushed with his feet and shoved his body to standing. He was surprised that, when he spoke, his voice was steady.

"What's happening?" Vir called over the rumbling, keeping himself standing upon unsteady feet. "I'll tell you what's happening. Exactly what I warned you would happen. Get out of here, if you know what's good for you. Get off this planet. And you haul yourself back to Centauri Prime"—His voice became louder, more strident—"and you tell Minister Durla that this entire business was a disaster. And you remember that Vir Cotto was the one who tried to warn you. Remember who your friends are, Renegar. It might save your life someday. Now go! *Go!*"

Renegar's head bobbled so loosely that for a moment Vir flashed back to Morden on the pike. Then, without another word, Renegar stumbled from the office. Vir followed him, but whereas Renegar headed in the direction of the spaceport, staggering as the ground bucked beneath him, Vir headed in the other direction.

He had to see for himself. He had to know, firsthand, just what it was he was up against. So while his senses screamed at him to run the other way, he forced himself to head toward danger. It wasn't difficult to figure out which way to go. There was a glow not far distant, and he could see discharges of energy flitting through the air, like static electricity.

And there was a structure.

He couldn't quite make it out. It was, after all, in the heart of an excavation. But he could make out the upper reaches of it, and it seemed curved and . . .

. . . and it was rising.

Vir froze in his tracks, but not from the sight of the structure. Instead it was from the Centauri he saw lying on the ground nearby. To be exact, all he saw was the man's upper half; the lower part of his body so horribly charred that it was almost unrecognizable as anything that had once been living. The man was basically dead, but he hadn't fully come to terms with that fact yet. Through one good eye he saw Vir and he reached out in mute supplication.

Vir realized that this was the very first test of his new bravery and resolve. For there was a large rock right nearby, and all hope was gone for this poor bastard. If Vir had any compassion within him, he would pick up the rock and use it to crush the head of the agonized Centauri.

He reached for the small boulder, gripping it firmly, and stood over the prostrate form of the dying man. He raised his arms high over his head, looked down into the terrified expression of the fatally crippled Centauri.

"I'm sorry," whispered Vir, as the rock slipped from his suddenly nerveless fingers. It thumped to the ground next to head of the Centauri, who had no idea what Vir had been about to do, or indeed not too much of an idea about anything at that point.

Vir stumbled back and away as the ground continued to tremble. He stepped over a small outcropping of rock that had blocked his view moments before . . . and there were more

Centauri in various states of dismemberment. There were
also more, far more, who were simply charred corpses. Vir
shut his ears to the agonized cries all around him and
kept moving, trying to convince himself that the immediate
danger was past. That whatever had happened to these unfortunate souls had occurred at the instant that the energy had
been released.

What had released that energy, however, or what had set it
off, he could not even begin to guess.

Then there was more rumbling beneath Vir's feet, but he
suddenly realized that its point of origin was, in fact, overhead. Something was dropping from the sky, something
huge. At that moment there was so much smoke and fog, released from the energy discharge, that he couldn't quite make
out anything beyond large, nebulous shapes. They were drawing closer, however, with each passing moment. *Drakh ships,*
said a voice in his head, and he had no idea how he had known
it. But once the thought was there, he knew it to be true.

Vir looked around, hoping that one of the cloister techno-
mages would suddenly pop into existence, stepping from the
corner of his eye into full view. They weren't forthcoming,
however, and a panicked thought went through his mind.
*What if they're gone? What if they were too near the site
and somehow they were killed when the . . . the whatever-it-
was . . . was released?*

He tried to tell himself that such a happenstance was impossible. That these were techno-mages, after all. Then he reminded himself that they were, in fact, cloisters. That they
weren't necessarily possessed of all the learning and knowledge of a techno-mage. A genuine techno-mage, after all,
need not fear anything . . .

*If they're not afraid of anything, why did they run away?
Why did they leave known space?*

For Vir, who was seeking so many answers to try and make
sense of the universe around him, this was the most easily answered question of all.

*Because they're smarter than you are.*

Though he knew full well the stupidity of his actions, Vir

kept moving. It was almost as if he had been seized by a compulsion to prove something to himself. He had, after all, failed that first test. He'd left a fellow Centauri to go through the last dregs of a tortured death. But there were others like him; what was he supposed to do, bash in all their heads? Since when had he become the lord high executioner of Centauri Prime?

This, though . . . this he could do. This was something he had to do. Just keep one foot moving in front of another, keep going, see what's ahead, and ignore what's above. He kept issuing orders to himself. *Just keep going. One doesn't have to be exceptionally brave to keep moving.* At least, that's what he told himself.

There were more vessels coming in from overhead, and in his mind he actually swore he could hear something that sounded like . . . singing. Many voices joined as one, and he couldn't understand the words on any sort of intellectual level. On a gut level, even a spiritual level, the voices and words chilled him to his soul. They seemed to be coming from everywhere and nowhere, all at once, and somehow he knew that they were originating from those rapidly approaching vessels.

There were large arrays of rubble ahead of him, and he realized that they were the remains of buildings that had been at the edge of the dig. He clambered over them, trying not to think about people who might be buried beneath, knowing that there was nothing that he could do for them other than prolong their agony. He had never felt more helpless.

Once again he felt as if he was simply a pawn in some greater game that he could not even begin to imagine. A slow anger began to build in him. Under ordinary circumstances, it was the kind of feeling he would have tried to bury entirely, for to acknowledge such feelings or—even worse—act upon them could lead to disaster. He had acted on behalf of others before, particularly during the crisis with the Narn, but he had done so in secret, praying that he wouldn't be caught, and the risks that his actions had entailed were in the abstract. *If* he had gotten caught aiding the Narn, *then* there would be unfortunate consequences. This danger, however, was in the here and now, and it might very well have been that the greater immediacy further inflamed Vir's emotions.

He wanted to be angry, because emotional fatigue could only carry one so far. He wanted to be angry enough to see the day through, to put a stop to whatever this . . . fearsome, loathsome influence over Centauri Prime was. It was anger that carried him over the rubble, though he fell several times and thoroughly banged himself up. It was anger that drove him to ignore the fact that the techno-mages appeared to have vanished. It was anger that made him look up and curse at the dark vessels, which he did not recognize, as they skimmed lower over the planet's surface. It was anger that ultimately brought him to the edge of the excavation.

It was a violent surging of stark-staring fear that bolted him to the spot.

"A jumpgate," he whispered.

Which was true as far as it went. It was a jumpgate unlike any Vir had seen before. The thing was massive, having now risen out of the ground, apparently after being buried deep beneath it. The structure itself was so dark that it seemed to absorb the light from overhead. Rather than the smooth, even edges of a standard jumpgate, this was jagged and irregular, as if the architect had embraced chaos over symmetry and elegance of form.

Energy crackled around the gargantuan structure. There appeared to be three of the black ships, although they were so huge that Vir had no idea of what the crew complement might be. They hung above the jumpgate, just hovering there, as if they were communing with it somehow.

Then the power of the jumpgate flared, greater than before. And Vir fancied that, somewhere in the back of his mind, he could hear something cry out, and the cry was in turn answered. Never in his life had he heard—and not heard— anything quite as eerie. The energy in the gate grew greater still, and the ships began to tremble in sympathy with it. It was as if, in some bizarrely perverse manner, they were making love to one another, energy building upon energy until a release would be achieved.

*What a time to think of sex,* Vir's mind scolded him. In a sick sort of way, he might actually have found it mildly amusing.

That was the moment when Vir was yanked off his feet.

The gate let out a roar then, like a great pouncing beast, and Vir wondered if he were about to witness another unleashing of the gate's power and energy. He considered two things, rather belatedly. First, if that was genuinely what was going to happen, then Vir had put himself squarely on the firing line, and might well be incinerated within seconds. And second, he remembered the predictions of Lady Morella, which stated that Vir would rule after Londo. Londo himself had said that the predictions as much as made Vir invulnerable. Vir, however, wasn't feeling especially invulnerable at the moment.

He began to tumble toward the gate, rock and debris being pulled all around him. There was a twisted girder sticking up from the ground, and it seemed fairly well embedded. In any event, Vir certainly wasn't in a position to be fussy. He threw his arms around the girder, held on for dear life as the newly opened gate continued to roar with animal fury. Beyond the coruscating energies that the gate was unleashing, Vir thought he could see . . . hyperspace? Or something else? Yes, yes, definitely something else. He had gone through jumpgates enough times, and knew what to expect. This was like nothing he had ever seen.

The incredible draw of the gate started to lift Vir's feet clear off the ground, yanking him horizontal. His legs thrashed about, seeking purchase, and he managed to snag the toe of one boot around the girder. With all his strength he pulled himself to a vertical position, wrapping his legs around his anchor.

There were more ships than just the three he had seen before, more and more descending every moment. Five, six, ten . . . he lost count. They entered the giant, crackling energy gate, and with each passing, he once again heard that uncanny, frightening cry in his head, as if something within the gate was welcoming home the ships that were passing through it.

The ground around him was littered with bodies. On the other side of the gate was something so dark, so evil . . . Great Maker, how could he have thought, for even a moment, that he was too tired to be afraid?

He knew that the definition of a brave man was one who did what needed to be done, despite his fears. But he had no definition for a man who was not only paralyzed with fear, but also in fact had no idea what to do at all. The only term he could come up with was "out of one's league."

In his fevered imagination, he thought he could hear the voices deep within the gate actually speaking to him. They were laughing, laughter mixed in with the words, and they were crying out their contempt for his ambitions as if to say, *"Pathetic little creature . . . thinking that you—you of all people—could save the galaxy? What makes you more worthy of living than all those around you, who died in witnessing the power before you?"*

"Nothing. Nothing makes me more worthy," said Vir, and he knew it to be true.

And with that admission, the planet seemed to give up on him. The gate suddenly appeared to increase its efforts, determined that Vir would no longer defy it. The bits and pieces of body parts that lay strewn about the area were sucked in. The girder was torn loose from its moorings, and the jolt dislodged Vir's grip . . . not that holding onto the no-longer-anchored girder would have done him a bit of good. Vir tumbled over and over, limbs flailing, and the roaring of the gate reached out to him in triumph.

When suddenly there was another, smaller hole, directly in front of him.

He realized at the last moment that it was a small ship, and the exterior hatch was irised open, hanging squarely in his path. Tumbling end-over-end as he was, he was unable to see anything clearly, although he thought he caught just the briefest glimpse of Finian, standing just inside the hatch.

Then he was in the ship, his forward momentum carrying him to the far bulkhead, and he slammed against it.

For a long moment he couldn't move. He lay there in a tangle of arms and legs, twisted like a contortionist. And sure enough, there was Finian, except he wasn't taking the time to determine how Vir was holding up. Instead he was dashing toward the front of the ship, shouting, "Kane! He's in! We've got him! Let's go!"

Kane said something Vir couldn't make out, and he heard both Finian and Gwynn exclaim in shock, *"What?!"* Suddenly the ship lurched once more. As tossed around as Vir was, he knew with utter certainty which way they were going: toward the gate.

It was obvious that Gwynn and Finian were also aware of that, as Vir stumbled into the front section of the ship. They were standing on either side of Kane, who was calmly manning the controls. At least, that's what Vir thought he was doing, but he couldn't be quite sure because the controls were unlike anything that Vir had ever seen. Everything was utterly smooth, with simple, glistening, black panels. He couldn't see any separation between anything. He wouldn't have had a clue as to what to touch where, but Kane was operating with apparent sure-handedness.

"This is an information-gathering mission, Kane!" Gwynn said for what sounded like the hundredth time. "We're not supposed to be heroes!"

"Or martyrs," added Finian. His customary defense of Kane seemed to have been abandoned.

"I've no wish to be either one . . . but I'm doing what I must," said Kane.

Gwynn drew back her fist, looking ready to do something rather unmagical with it, such as caving in Kane's head. If that, however, was what she was going to do, she waited too long. Because then the gate was right there, right in front of them, and there was simply no way to avoid it.

The ship spiraled through, elongating, and then collapsing back on itself, as Vir heard the voices laughing at him . . .

\* \* \*

A deathly silence fell over the dig site of K0643, broken
only by the occasional howling of a less active wind, and the
distant sobbing of one legless Centauri who was watching the
blood seep out of himself. Miraculously, he had not been
hauled away by the force of the gate, having been wedged
against an outcropping and unexpectedly held there by the
natural formation of the rock.

His name was Ciril, and he had looked forward to being
able to defy Death, punch him in the guts.

His enthusiasm for that meeting waned, along with his life.
And when his crying finally stopped, only the wind was left.

# — chapter 3 —

Vir knew perfectly well what a trip through hyperspace was supposed to be like, and this wasn't it.

There were great similarities in the look and the feel. But even to Vir, who wasn't exactly a battle-hardened veteran space jockey, it felt different. As opposed to a journey through hyperspace in which one guided oneself via the use of carefully mapped pathways, this voyage felt as if the ship was somehow being propelled in a specific direction. If they had been in a planetary atmosphere, he would have said that they had a strong tailwind.

"Where are we going?" Vir said.

Gwynn didn't even bother to look at him, but Finian cast a glance and muttered, "Not just where. Why?"

"Because we're supposed to," Kane said. He sounded rather detached from the entire matter, even though he was nominally guiding the ship.

"We're supposed to?" Gwynn looked to Finian in obvious hope of some sort of explanation, but his helpless shrug indicated that he was as in the dark as she. "Are you saying you've been given some sort of . . . of separate instructions?"

Not for the first time, Vir was struck by the difference between these cloisters and the techno-mages he and Londo had encountered in the past. His current companions didn't maintain the constant air of superiority, the portentousness that usually accompanied a techno-mage's every word.

Of the three of them, Vir suspected Gwynn was the closest to having the requisite arrogance down pat. But her inexperience was allowing her obvious frustration to bubble over, most likely due to the unusual circumstances into which they had been thrust.

"Well?" she prompted when she decided Kane hadn't replied quickly enough.

Kane turned and looked at her then, and there was something in his eyes. His voice sounded as if it were coming from another time and place, perhaps even another dimension, as he said, "I have seen it."

At that moment, Vir was reminded of what Kane had once said to him, after one particularly nebulous comment: "I was going for cryptic."

"You succeeded," Vir had said to him. Now, after all this time had passed, he couldn't help but feel that Kane had succeeded once more. For once again, Vir had no idea what he was talking about.

Of significance, however, were the reactions he prompted from Gwynn and Finian. The comment obviously had meaning to them. It truncated all discussion, brought the entire disagreement to a screaming halt. Instead, all Gwynn asked—sounding not unimpressed—was "Are you certain?"

"Yes."

"Very well." It struck Vir as a bit amusing; Gwynn was acting as if she was giving permission for something in which she had no actual say. Or perhaps . . . perhaps she was just saying to Kane that she understood a bit more what had led him to propel them into the jumpgate, rather than attempting to get safely away.

Finian likewise was nodding. Vir just wished that he could be as sanguine. He wanted to ask just precisely *what* it was that Kane had seen, but he had the distinct impression that any such inquiries wouldn't be welcomed.

Suddenly, the ship lurched, and for a moment Vir was certain that they had been struck by some sort of blast attack. But Kane said with confidence, "We're coming out of the funnel."

"Funnel? What funnel? I never heard of a funnel," said Vir.

"You wouldn't have. It's theoretical," Kane told him.

"Ah. Of course." Vir didn't have a clue to what Kane was talking about.

Finian, however, saw fit to take pity on him. "It's Shadow tech," he explained. "Think of it as a sort of wormhole within hyperspace. A subsystem or subroutine, if you will. One beginning point, one end point, no detours. When you use a funnel, it renders you undetectable to any other ships that might be traveling through hyperspace at the time. Limited utility, but handy if you want to build a fast path to somewhere."

"And where would the somewhere be? At this moment, I mean?" said Vir.

"I don't know," Kane admitted. "It will take a few minutes to determ—"

His voice trailed off. He was looking ahead through the main viewing port, and Finian and Gwynn were doing likewise. Vir turned to see just what it was that had grabbed everyone's full attention. He had no idea what he was supposed to see, but—considering the reactions of the mages—what he did see certainly wasn't at all what he would have expected.

"Nothing," he said. "I . . . don't see anything."

And indeed he did not. They had dropped into normal space, but there was absolutely nothing ahead of them. A good deal of nothing, in fact.

"Nothing is what you're supposed to see," Gwynn informed him.

"Ah. Good. Then I'm right on top of things, I guess."

"Take us in slowly, Kane," Gwynn continued, as if Vir hadn't spoken, and indeed for all Vir knew, she hadn't even heard him. "We're a relatively small ship, and it's not as if they're expecting us. With any luck, we can escape detection entirely."

"And without any luck?" Vir asked.

The look they shot his way was all the response he required. Unfortunately, he still didn't know what was going on. Clearly there was some sort of imminent threat, some immediate danger . . . but he wasn't seeing it at all. Furthermore, the dark vessels that had preceded them had vanished entirely. Where could they have gone? And what was this threat? Nothing seemed to be presenting—

Then, after a moment, he looked again . . . and he saw it. Or rather, he didn't see it.

The stars were there . . . but they weren't.

The area of space ahead of them was—there was no other way to express it—interrupted. It was broken by a patch miles across, where the stars didn't appear to be shining. There was, indeed, nothing ahead of them, but it was a nothing that was most definitely something. It didn't have any sort of geometric shape to it. It was so large, so irregular, that even though he could detect the outline with his unaided eyes, he still couldn't get any sort of mental image as to what it actually looked like. But at least he knew it looked like something. Or nothing.

His head was starting to hurt.

"You see it now," Finian said with faint approval. Vir might have been imagining it, but he felt as if Finian was actually rooting for him in a way.

"What is it? Or maybe that should be, What *isn't* it?"

"It's a null field," Finian replied. "Think of it as almost a sort of portable black hole . . . except you can go in and out. It absorbs all light and all manner of sensory or energy probes. It can utterly convince instrumentation that it's not there. And people who encounter it won't bother to see with their own eyes, because they've become so heavily dependent on technology . . ."

"So says the techno-mage," Vir commented.

There was silence for a moment, then Finian said with a small smile, "Touché."

"So do we go in?" Gwynn asked Kane. Vir was mildly surprised; until that point everything from Gwynn's attitude had given him the impression that she felt she should be in charge. Yet now she seemed to be deferring, however nominally, to Kane.

Kane simply nodded.

Vir wished at that point that he had a weapon.

"Here."

As if reading Vir's mind, Kane reached into the folds of his cloak and extracted something solid and round, about the size of Vir's fist. Vir turned it over and over, trying to discern some hidden meaning. Nothing immediately presented itself.

"It's a rock," Vir said.

"That is correct."

"Is there any particular reason you've given me this?"

"I thought you might need a weapon. I suspect you did, as well."

"Yes, but I . . ." He stared at it in confusion. "A rock? Why a rock?"

"Nature's weapon. Really, the only weapon that nature intended humankind to have," said Kane. "You will do well with it."

"Thanks. And here I didn't get you anything," muttered Vir, shoving the rock into his coat pocket and reminding himself, not for the first time, that hooking up with the techno-mages might not have been the brightest idea he'd ever had.

There was silence as they approached the null field. The techno-mages didn't appear to be especially concerned, but Vir was reasonably certain that it was simply a facade they had adopted. They simply had no intention of coming across as apprehensive when an outside observer such as Vir was present.

"Time to null field . . . eleven seconds," Kane announced. Vir glanced around the control board and saw no sign of a chronometer. Yet somehow he didn't doubt the accuracy of Kane's time estimate. "Ten . . . nine . . . eight . . ."

Vir steadied himself and, for a moment, thought about requesting that they turn the damned ship right around and head back to the excavation world. They had discovered something hidden by the Shadows; something that would likely have serious consequences once the technology therein was employed. Rather than risking their necks, perhaps the intelligent thing to do was get out safely and alert . . .

Who?

Alert Londo? But Londo had evicted him from Centauri Prime. It was possible that, after a period of time, tempers would cool and relationships could be normalized, but that time certainly wasn't when Vir was still dusting off dirt left over from his stay in a Centauri dungeon.

Tell Sheridan? The Alliance? This Shadow technology had been unearthed as a result of a Centauri dig. Vir knew exactly what the perceptions would be: that he, Vir, was acting as an informant against his people. And that the Centauri themselves—particularly the government—had, in fact, allied themselves with fearsome creatures who had served even more fearsome masters. The problem was that all of that might very well be true. But Centauri Prime certainly didn't need that information getting out, causing even further deterioration of their relationships with every other sentient race in the Alliance.

No, the Shadow influence, whatever it was, had to be expunged quietly, from the inside. If the Alliance even suspected that the Centauri were in league with servants of the Shadows, they might show up to bomb Centauri Prime once more, and this time they might not cease their efforts until the Centauri Homeworld was nothing but uninhabited rock.

Centauri Prime had to be kept clear of this situation. Vir could take no chance that this . . . this whatever-it-was might be linked to the Centauri Republic. The consequences might be fatal and he, Vir, would be responsible.

But neither could he simply turn away and ignore what he was now a party to. If this *was* Shadow technology, about to be employed against other races, how could anyone of conscience stand by and do nothing? And, he realized with a shudder, there was no guarantee that this technology wasn't going to be used against Centauri Prime itself.

He muttered something and Gwynn glanced at him, even as Kane continued the countdown. "What did you say?" she asked.

"Something my mother used to say," Vir told her. "An old saying: 'One choice is no choice.' "

She nodded. "A good saying."

"Three . . . two . . . one . . ."

Space seemed to elongate around them, as if they were pushing through a gigantic wall of clear gelatin or squishy water. Vir prayed that the null field simply provided limited invisibility, rather than some genuine offensive means of beating back intruders.

Then, just like that, they were through.

This time, even the techno-mages gasped. It wasn't a sound Vir liked. The concept of startled techno-mages wasn't one he happily embraced. On the other hand, he certainly couldn't blame them.

The structure that hovered within the confines of the null field was massive beyond Vir's imagination. It would have dwarfed Babylon 5. For that matter, in terms of sheer mass, it might very well have dwarfed entire planets.

The Shadow Base—for that was what Vir had come to think of it as—reminded him of nothing so much as a gigantic coral reef. It seemed to stretch almost into infinity, with numerous entrances pockmarking its craggy exterior.

"Xha'dam," breathed Finian.

Vir looked at him in polite confusion. "What?"

"Xha'dam," he repeated. "It's nearly legendary . . . mythic. Reportedly a Shadow base to end all bases. So huge that—"

"They named it?"

Finian rolled his eyes and looked away.

There was some sort of activity at the far end of Xha'dam, and Vir tried to figure out what it was. The Drakh ships had reappeared, and had converged there. To Vir's confusion there seemed to be some sort of planet there as well. But something didn't . . .

Then he realized. "Great Maker," he breathed. "That's . . . not a planet."

"It's a Death Cloud," said Kane.

"A what?"

"A Death Cloud. Theoretically, it envelops a world and rains destruction down upon it."

"Like a . . . a mass driver or something?"

"A Death Cloud is similar to a mass driver," Finian said, "in the way that an adult with heavy artillery is similar to an infant with a toy hammer."

The comparison was horrific. Londo had been present

when mass drivers had been used on the Narn homeworld, and the description he had given had been so ghastly that Vir had wondered about the minds of the people who had come up with such a weapon. Now, upon witnessing something that was infinitely worse, Vir thought of the Shadow creatures, and knew that they were more than mere alien beings. The Shadows were incarnations of all the darkest and worst impulses that the mind of sentient beings had to offer.

"You said 'theoretically,' " said Vir. "You mean it was never actually used . . . ?"

"Our understanding is that it was close to completion when the Shadow War actually ended," said Finian. "Naturally, our information was hardly comprehensive. We're technomages, not omniscient. We didn't know the where of it, for example, or how close to completion it actually was."

"From the look of it, the answer is 'Very,' " observed Gwynn.

"That's why we took such an interest in the Centauri excavation," Finian said. "We thought that the Drakh might be seeking out lost Shadow technology, and suspected that this might be part of it."

"The Drakh. Their servants."

"Yes. But even in our wildest suspicions, we never thought . . ."

"I did," said Kane in that same oddly distant tone.

Yes, of course. He had "seen" it. Vir still felt, rather wisely, that pursuing an inquiry along those lines would likely be folly. "So what do we do? How do we stop it . . . ?"

And then they heard it.

Even though sound didn't travel in space, they still heard it. Whether there was some sort of atmosphere attached to Xha'dam, whether the null field was capable of transmitting it, Vir didn't know, nor would he ever know. What he *did* know, however, was that there was a massive rumbling that seemed to envelop everything around them.

It was as if they were trapped within a massive hurricane. They weren't being spun about, but the pounding all around them made Vir feel as if his teeth were going to be jarred loose from his mouth. No . . . it was worse. It was as if his skull was going to be jostled out of his head.

The Death Cloud was moving.

"In answer to your question, Mr. Cotto," Gwynn said grimly, "we don't stop it."

"That thing wasn't near completion," Finian said, unable to keep the sound of horrified realization from coloring his voice. "It was complete. All they had to do was turn it on. If the Shadows had unleashed it during the war . . ."

"We'd have been ready for it!" Vir said with rising alarm. "And we would have had the Vorlons backing us up! Better that it should have been used then. We'd have had a better chance against it! Now, we've none!"

"Vir . . ."

"I'm sorry, Kane." Vir pulled himself together. He took a deep breath, reminded himself that this was absolutely the wrong time to come unraveled. The simple fact was that Gwynn was right. There was no way to stop it. Already the Death Cloud was moving off, out of the null field, surrounded by several Drakh ships that acted as an escort. "They're going to test it," Vir said suddenly.

"What?" said Gwynn.

But Finian nodded. "Yes. Yes, I bet Vir's right. Whatever they're planning to use that thing for, they're not just going to take it right into battle. They're going to run a test on it first. Kane, have we got the area tracked yet?"

Kane nodded, looking over star charts that he cued up on a nearby screen. "We're near the Daltron system. There's one inhabited world there . . . the seventh planet out, with a population of three billion. Minimal space flight capacity."

"We've got to get word to them," said Vir.

Gwynn was shaking her head. "Never get there in time. And if the Drakh intercept our message, they'll know we're here. We'll lose the element of surprise."

"We can't simply not warn them! We have to tell them to—!"

"Tell them to what?" said Gwynn coolly. "Abandon their planet? A world isn't a cruise ship, Mr. Cotto, where everyone can just jump into lifepods when things go badly. Besides, you heard him: minimal space flight. They have no defenses, and they can't get away. Even if we manage to alert EarthForce or the Alliance, we're too far out here. Too remote. No one will get here in time."

Vir didn't know which he found more upsetting: the reality of the situation or Gwynn's icy, dispassionate assessment. *"Don't you care?"* he finally exploded.

"Care? About things I can't prevent? No, Mr. Cotto, I don't. What I care about are those things that I *can* prevent. Such as the chance that another planet destroyer might be built."

"Another . . ."

"Yes. Like that one." And she pointed.

Vir felt his gorge rising. For there, still at the far end of Xha'dam, he could see the skeletons being erected already for a second and third Death Cloud. With the finished model as an indelible mental template, he immediately knew the constructs in progress for what they were.

"They learn fast, the Drakh," said Finian humorlessly.

"Possibly some construct 'bots, or similar machines that they've put into place," Kane guessed. "There may be some Drakh remaining behind, though, overseeing it." He paused, and then said, "I'm taking us in."

It took a moment for Vir to register what he was saying, and then he comprehended. They were heading into Xha'dam, for a very obvious purpose: to destroy it.

"I'm picking up several key energy sources," Kane continued.

"I thought our sensory devices weren't working."

"Outside the null field, Vir, that was correct. But now that we're inside the null field, we're not hampered anymore. I'm bringing us into the closest entry port . . . or at least what looks like one. That should still keep us a fairly safe distance from whatever Drakh might be here. With any luck, we can get in and out without any problems."

"But what about safeguards?" Vir asked. "Certainly the Shadows would have built in—"

"Not necessarily, Mr. Cotto," Gwynn responded. "The null field would certainly have served as a means of avoiding discovery. And in the unlikely event that someone did stumble across it, certainly the Shadow vessels themselves would have been more than capable of dispatching any intruders. It is indeed more likely that they saw no need to integrate any sort of traps into the base's design."

"And if they have?" Vir couldn't help but ask.

"Fortunately, we have a plan to deal with any traps that may be lying in wait for us," Finian told him.

"Oh? Really?" Vir felt somewhat encouraged at that news. "What's the plan?"

"We send you in first."

Vir stared at Finian and saw a slight twinkle of amusement in his eyes. It was, however, only slight, and then deftly covered up. Vir only wished that he could find it remotely comical.

"I am concerned," Kane said abruptly. "Going on the assumption that we survive this . . . in the unlikely event that any Drakh are on Xha'dam, it would not be wise for them to see Mr. Cotto's face. What one Drakh knows, he can relay to others with the speed of thought. But they need not know the face of their opponent. Vir . . . I shall have to conceal your features. Are you prepared?"

Vir paused for a moment, then nodded yes. And then, a bit nervously, he added, "Will it hurt?"

"Unlikely."

Kane pulled a black mask with string ties from within the folds of his garment and handed it to Vir. Vir looked at it, somewhat crestfallen. "Is that the best you've got?"

"Would you prefer a bag over your head?" Kane inquired.

"Is this a vote?" Finian asked. "Because if we get to choose what he should wear . . ."

"Never mind." Vir sighed as he pulled the mask on and decided that, yes, definitely, he was not enthused with what passed for humor among techno-mages.

\* \* \*

The fact that the entry into Xha'dam went as smoothly as it did should have been enough to still some of Vir Cotto's fears. It did nothing of the kind. Instead all it did was heighten Vir's concern that disaster was imminent. As he reasoned it, each passing moment increased the likelihood that they would be discovered, and the fact that they hadn't been found out only brought them seconds closer to the inevitability of being spotted.

However, the techno-mages moved as though with full confidence that they would not be detected. And Vir had to admire Kane's sure hand at the controls. He guided the small vessel down an assortment of progressively smaller passages, before finally determining that they had gone as far as they could go. Despite Finian's earlier jest that Vir was going to serve as a walking decoy, the trio of cloisters offered Vir the opportunity to remain aboard the ship.

Vir shook his head vigorously. "I'm going to see this through," he said firmly. "Besides, if the Drakh show up and come after whoever's in this ship, well . . . I'd rather take my chances with you than without you."

"Very well" was all Kane said.

The exit door irised open, and Vir almost choked on the air. As absurd as it sounded, as ridiculous as the notion seemed, even in his own head . . . the air smelled of evil. He knew it was absurd. Atmosphere couldn't possess abstract concepts of morality as part of its chemistry. Of course, Vir could ascribe to the stale air just about any virtue he desired. In point of fact, though, there was no way that the air itself could be evil.

And yet it was.

It wasn't that it smelled particularly foul. But even as it filled his lungs, he felt as if darkness were filling not only his body, but his very soul. He wanted to suck down oxygen. He wanted to vomit up whatever it was that was getting into his circulatory system. He wanted to seize control of the ship somehow, and send it hurtling out of this abysmal place of shadow, as quickly as he possibly could.

Instead he forced himself to follow the three cloister

mages and hoped that he wasn't making the worst, and last, mistake of his life.

The walls weren't dissimilar to those of a series of caverns. As Vir walked, he would rest his palm against them now and again, and whenever he did so he would quickly yank his hand away. The walls felt incredibly cold. No, it was more than that. It was as if coming in contact with the walls allowed them to suck the heat out of Vir. Yet, if he didn't touch them at all, they had no immediate effect.

Kane, Gwynn, and Finian moved forward purposefully, so much so that Vir felt hard-pressed to keep up. The passages formed a virtual labyrinth, and yet they found their way through with ease. Vir felt tremendously envious of them. Part of him wondered whether he hadn't missed his calling. Perhaps he should have become a techno-mage himself. Rather than fighting off panic at the very thought of the science-based magic users, he would be one of them and instill trembling fear in . . . well, in people like himself.

For just one moment, he allowed himself to become preoccupied with this rather pleasant reverie. As he did so, he turned a corner . . . and discovered that the techno-mages were gone.

"Oh, not again," he moaned softly.

This time, however, he was quite certain that they hadn't simply vanished to avoid being noticed. Instead it was probably something far more pedestrian, namely that he'd made a wrong turn and become separated from them. But all was not necessarily lost, for he had a general idea of where they were going.

The concept was that they were going to head for a major power source and, presumably, blow it to hell and gone somehow. With any luck, that explosion would in turn take out the entire Shadow Base . . . while, ideally, giving them enough time to get the hell off the base before it went.

And locating the power source didn't seem as if it was going to be that much of a chore. He could hear rather distinctly a steady, distant thrumming sound, a slow pulse that beat so regularly that he felt as if he were somehow inside a living body. He made his way toward the source, at first tentatively, then becoming more and more self-assured. It appeared that the techno-mages had been correct. He didn't set off any alarms, nor did he run into any unexpected traps. Obviously, the Shadows had been overly confident.

He thought that, right up until the moment that he turned a corner and ran into a Drakh who was heading in the opposite direction.

Vir remembered being a child, wandering about in the woods once during a camping expedition and suddenly finding himself face-to-face with a wild animal. It hadn't been an especially fierce one, but nevertheless, young Vir knew that they were on the animal's home territory, and that carried with it an advantage. But his father had seemed to materialize at the side of his petrified son, and had said with confidence, "Don't worry. He's just as startled to see you as you are to see him."

That was certainly the case now. The Drakh was caught completely flat-footed. Any notion that Vir had that he might have tripped some sort of alarm disappeared when he saw the expression on the alien's face. Clearly the creature had had no idea Vir was going to be there; he had simply been going on about his business and found himself face-to-face with an intruder.

Vir, however, had a momentary advantage. After all, he at least had known that he might run into trouble, whereas the Drakh had been wholly unprepared. Vir drove himself forward off one leg, summoning all his strength and bravery and swinging from the hip as his father had taught him, back when young boys were routinely beating him up. His right fist connected squarely with the Drakh's head, and Vir felt a shock of pain that ran the length of his arm up into his shoulder.

The Drakh rocked slightly back on his heels, but otherwise didn't seem to feel the blow.

Realizing that he was in trouble, Vir took a step back as the Drakh advanced, and the grey-toned creature let out a horrifying shriek of anger that rooted Vir to the spot. Then suddenly the Drakh froze in place, his eyes going wide in astonishment. He was looking at a spot directly over Vir's shoulder.

Had he been thinking fast, Vir might have chosen that moment to press for an advantage. Instead he turned and looked to see what the Drakh was staring at. Instantly, he felt his blood turning to ice water in his veins.

It was a Shadow.

Vir had never actually seen one, except in the outermost periphery of his darkest nightmares, and yet he knew the Shadow warrior for what it was the moment it scuttled forward from the darkness. He could hear a scream in his head like a thousand souls being thrown into damnation, and there was a scrabbling sound as its pointed feet moved across the rocky surface of the floor.

A mixture of amazement and joy appeared on the Drakh's face, as he clearly waited for the Shadow to issue some sort of order. And suddenly the Drakh's head snapped around, as two hands touched either side of his temples. His eyes went wide in confusion when the Shadow warrior failed to leap to his defense.

Then the Shadow disappeared. It didn't fade into the darkness from which it had sprung; instead it simply vanished. The Drakh didn't comprehend what had just happened, but neither was he capable of staying conscious long enough to find out. Instead he simply sagged to the ground, and as he did so, Vir saw Gwynn standing behind him. Her long, tapering fingers released their hold on the Drakh's forehead, letting the Shadow servant collapse with a most satisfying *thud*.

"I . . . I got separated," Vir stammered out.

"Obviously," she said, with the air of one who did not suffer fools gladly. Feeling very much the fool, Vir could understand her impatience. "Come."

He followed her, staying so close on her heels that he nearly stepped on her a couple of times.

The tunnels seemed to be widening out around them, and the sounds ahead of them were getting louder. Vir squinted against an increasingly bright light, and as he did so, he commented, "Kane said that he 'saw' that we had to be here. What did he mean?"

Gwynn said nothing.

"Did he have some sort of . . . of psychic vision? Is that it? Some sort of look at the future?"

"Do not," she warned him, "inquire too closely into the affairs of wizards. You may not like the answers."

"Don't inquire?!" It was all he could do not to stammer. "In case you haven't noticed, I'm up to my *neck* in the affairs of wizards! So you'll forgive me if I make an inquiry or two!"

"Very well," she said archly. "You are forgiven."

Vir rolled his eyes and wondered why he had even bothered.

They approached an archway that loomed high ahead of them, and went through it. The sound clearly emanated from the other side, so loud that Vir couldn't have missed it even if he were deaf. Considering the volume that was engulfing him, he began to worry that he might indeed wind up without hearing, at that.

The place was huge, as Vir had suspected it would be. But it was like no power core that he had ever seen. There were towering columns all around him, except there was no sense of symmetry. Structures appeared to come together, then split apart from one another. It reminded him of nothing so much as a gigantic spider web made entirely of stone . . . except it wasn't exactly stone. It was some sort of porous, black material, which glowed from within with a blue fire.

He didn't have a clue as to where to look first. Gwynn, meantime, called out, "Kane! Finian!" Her two associates stepped out from behind different parts of the power room. "Vir ran into a Drakh. They're apparently not all at the other end of the base, as we had hoped."

"Then we must attend to this quickly," said Kane.

"Okay, so what do we do?" Vir asked. "Can you just, I don't know . . . wave your hands or say some magic words and blow this place up?"

"I'm afraid not," said Finian. "We cannot use our tech for destruction. Only for creation."

Vir's eyes widened. "You're not serious." But the other nodded in affirmation. "Okay, fine, how about this!" he sputtered. "How about you use your power to create a big chunk of empty space where this base used to be!"

"You must do it, Vir."

"Me!" He gaped at Kane. Then, realizing it was pointless to argue, he waved his hands about and said, "Okay, okay, fine. What do I do?"

"Blow it up."

"How?"

"Quickly." And then he pointed over Vir's shoulder, and Vir—against his better judgment—looked where Kane was indicating.

More of the Drakh were coming. There appeared to be at least a dozen of them, perhaps more, and they were pouring in through the entrance that Vir and Gwynn had just used, nineteen yards away.

"This could be a problem," murmured Finian.

That seemed, to Vir, to be something of an understatement. He backed up, watching what seemed like a wave of dark grey advancing on them quickly.

And suddenly Vir and the techno-mages ran in one direction.

And then another. And then another, and still another.

Vir had no idea which way to look first, but neither did the Drakh. Suddenly the entire power room was cluttered with Virs and techno-mages, and no one could possibly have known which way to look or which was which.

"Hurry! Hurry!" whispered Kane, and he shoved Vir in the back, to start him running. Then the techno-mages moved off in a variety of directions, and suddenly Vir was alone in a crowd.

The Drakh made no sound, yet seemed to move in unison as they literally threw themselves into the chaos. They carried what appeared to be small weapons in their hands, though Vir couldn't make out precisely what they were. They

looked vaguely like PPGs, but there was something different
about them.

Suddenly there was a rush of air and something small and
presumably lethal hurtled past Vir's face, missing by the nar-
rowest of margins. It made a metallic noise just beyond him
and Vir's head snapped around to see what it was and where it
had landed. It appeared to be a spike, about as long as one of
his fingers, narrow and sharp and extremely deadly. It was
embedded in a rocklike "web strand," and was still quivering
from the impact.

Vir had to credit the illusions provided by the techno-
mages, however. If the genuine Vir had been the only one re-
acting with obvious horror, he would easily have stood out.
Instead every single one of the mirages dashing madly about
had the exact same look of fear and trepidation. Several of
them were even "hit" by the spikes and reacted as if they had
been mortally wounded. The way they doubled over, stag-
gered about and such, it was impossible to determine whether
one of the lethal missiles had actually embedded itself in a
corporeal body or had passed harmlessly through an illusion.
Any technology capable of creating such instantly adjusting
holograms was beyond Vir's ability even to contemplate.

Not that he had the time for pondering. Instead he had to
concentrate on one thing and one thing only: coming through
this madness with his head still firmly attached to his neck.

He wove his way through the bizarre structure, trying to
find some sort of vulnerable point. Not that he had any idea
what he was going to do once he located it. It was most unlikely that he would encounter a large sign that read "Press
here to destroy Shadow Base."

He darted left, right, right again . . . and suddenly found
himself in what appeared to be another area entirely. There
was still the humming of tremendous power around him, but
there was something else, as well. Control panels still looked
like control panels, no matter what technology was crafting
them, and that was exactly what he had found. Even more important, he saw a holographic image floating nearby that he
recognized instantly: it was one of the Death Clouds that was

still under construction. With horror, Vir noted that the device was already much further along—it actually seemed to be nearing completion.

Small robotic drones were moving around it in a smoothly coordinated display of activity. They were not, however, acting entirely on their own. A Drakh was overseeing the entire operation, making sure that each of the 'bots attended to its assigned task as smoothly and efficiently as possible.

Vir knew this because the Drakh was sitting right there in front of him, doing his job. He turned and saw Vir, and for a moment, they simply stared at each other.

Then the Drakh let out an angry screech, and from the folds of his garment he yanked out what appeared to be one of the spike-firing weapons.

Vir's reaction was entirely automatic. Given time to reflect on it later, he wouldn't even remember pulling the rock from his pocket. All he knew was that one moment the stone was in his pocket and the next it was in his hand, and just as the Drakh brought up his weapon to fire, Vir let fly with all his strength. The rock crashed squarely into the Drakh's head, and the Drakh let out a shout of fury even as he toppled backward. Fumbling his weapon as he fell, his finger spasmodically tightened on the trigger. As a result, the spike embedded itself squarely in the Drakh's chest. The Shadow servant let out a last strangled protest, and then collapsed altogether.

Vir didn't even take the time to be horrified—the silence around him told him the techno-mages must have drawn the Drakh off in another direction. He just stepped over the fallen one and went quickly to the controls. He looked them over for a moment, trying to determine what was what. The robots that had been assembling the Death Cloud had ground to a halt, twirling calmly in space and obviously waiting for further instructions.

*"There."*

Vir jumped involuntarily at the sound of Kane's voice coming from practically in his ear. He saw Kane standing right at his shoulder, studying the controls. There was no hint of confusion on Kane's face—it seemed to Vir as if Kane understood everything. He pointed at several panels in sequence. "That one . . . then that one . . . then rest your hand on that and tell it to do what you want it to do. It will respond."

"Are you sure? I'm not a Drakh . . ."

"You do not have to be. The Shadows designed this equipment to be as simple to operate as possible. Even the most ignorant person, with a modest bit of training, can handle it."

"Oh. Good." Vir didn't exactly feel flattered by that piece of information, but this wasn't the time to take offense. He touched the panels in the order Kane had indicated, then placed his hand where he was supposed to. At first nothing seemed to be happening, even though Vir was concentrating so hard that he thought the top of his head was going to blow off.

"Just remember who is in charge," Kane counseled him.

Vir nodded, then realized he had been having trouble simply focusing thoughts, perhaps out of sheer nervousness. "Move away," he said firmly and, sure enough, the robots began to clear themselves from the Death Cloud.

The robots were not, however, Vir's major concern. He had given that command more or less as a test, in preparation for something more extensive and, ideally, more final. He took a deep breath, which rasped unsteadily in his chest, and then he ordered, "Move into position."

For a moment nothing happened, and then the Death Cloud slid gracefully forward and around the end of Xha'dam, positioning itself so smoothly that one would have thought Vir had been doing it all his life.

He steadied his nerves, focusing on the far end of the Shadow Base, and then in a quiet voice of command, said, "Fire."

No response.

Vir immediately assumed that the Death Cloud must not have been far enough along to have been given any sort of detonation capacity. Really . . . how could it be? When they had first spotted it, it had been little more than a skeleton. Even with all the advantages the Shadow tech provided, it simply wasn't conceivable that any sort of weapon of mass destruction could be brought into working order in that short a—

Then the Death Cloud shuddered slightly, as its weaponry discharged—directly into the far end of the Shadow Base. Even as far away as they were from the source of the destruction, Vir still felt the base trembling around him from the impact.

More hits, more firing upon the base, as the Death Cloud—operating in some sort of automatic program now—started to progress down the base's length. Then, on the holographically reproduced image, Vir saw more explosions, this time from within Xha'dam itself. The vibrations became more pronounced, even though the source of the devastation was still miles off.

"Now would be a good time to leave," Kane said, with such calm that one would have thought the base's destruction could have no immediate impact upon him.

Vir's head was bobbing. "Yes . . . yes, I think you're right."

He turned to head for the door, and suddenly Kane was shoving him to one side. Vir tumbled to the floor, wondering just what in the world was going on, unable to comprehend why in the world Kane would have suddenly attacked him. Then he heard a slight whisper of a noise, a *pfwwt* of air, followed by another, and he half sat up and twisted around to look behind him.

Kane was standing there, looking down in what almost seemed to be amusement. Three spikes were imbedded in his chest. The centermost one happened to be the one that he had intercepted when he had pushed Vir out of the way. The second and third were still quivering, having just been shot into him. Vir, to his horror, saw the Drakh lying on the ground, his fingers still twitching around his weapon, apparently not as dead as they had assumed him to be.

It all happened so quickly that Kane had no time to react or prepare a spell to freeze them in place. He tried to use his staff for support, but instead sank to his knees, and the Drakh focused on Vir. Vir desperately threw himself to one side as the Drakh squeezed off two quick shots. Both of the needle darts flew past him, but he tripped, hit the ground, and found himself lying there, eye-to-eye with the fallen Drakh. The creature swung the weapon around and Vir found himself staring right down the barrel.

"I can't die," he whispered. "Londo said so. I'm invincible."

Not giving a damn about fate, Centauri predictions, or Londo Mollari, the Drakh squeezed the trigger. His weapon made an oddly vacant sound—one that had a uniform quality across a variety of cultures. It was the sound of a weapon empty of ammunition.

The Drakh uttered a word that Vir could only surmise to be a curse in the Drakh's native tongue, and then the creature began to haul himself up. Suddenly the entire room shook violently, and the Drakh flopped over onto his back. This time he didn't get up. The creature emitted a sound that could only be a death rattle, and his head slumped to one side.

Kane was still on his knees, looking somewhat perplexed as he stared at the metal projectiles sticking in his chest. Vir hauled him to his feet, shouting, "Come on! Hurry! Back to the ship!"

"I do not think . . . that is going to happen," Kane said softly.

"Oh no you don't!" Vir yelled at him. "I am *not* about to go back to your techno-pals and tell them that I left you behind! And they're going to tell me that if I'd dragged you along with me, maybe they could have saved you, and the next thing I know, someone's going to be wearing my head for a hat! No thank you!"

Kane tried to say something else, but Vir wasn't listening to him. Instead, with a strength he never would have dreamt he had, Vir yanked Kane to his feet and started hauling him, draping one of Kane's arms around his own shoulder to provide support. They stumbled out of the control room and down the corridor, and Vir didn't even want to think about what was going to happen if they ran into a Drakh because they had absolutely no defense at all.

Kane sagged, and Vir thought desperately to himself—to himself, and to whatever deity might be willing to listen—

*Please. Please let us get back to the ship without any problems. Please.*

They rounded a corner, and there was a Drakh standing there. Vir froze, almost losing his grip on Kane. He saw, out of the corner of his eye, that Kane actually had a grim smile on his face, and for a moment he was certain that the technomage had completely lost his mind.

That was when Vir realized that the Drakh wasn't moving. He wasn't looking at Vir and Kane; they simply happened to be standing directly in the path of his blank gaze. Then the Drakh sagged to the ground to reveal Gwynn right behind him. "The Drakh and I were having a chat," she said.

Her dark eyes widened as she realized Kane's condition. For a moment her veneer of unflappability slipped, and then she composed herself. She moved forward quickly and brought Kane's other arm around her own shoulder. The two of them helped Kane toward the ship without a word. The shaking around them grew more violent, and Finian joined them on a dead run. He cast a glance at Kane's condition, but made no comment.

They half ran, half stumbled into the ship as the door irised shut behind them. "Where are the rest of the Drakh!" Vir called out.

"In case you haven't noticed, Mr. Cotto, this place is about to blow up," said Gwynn.

"I know. I caused it."

"Well done," said Finian, who had seated himself at the controls. But there wasn't a great deal of congratulations in his voice, for his attention was split between getting the ship into motion and glancing worriedly over at Kane. Kane, for his part, seemed to be staring at the spikes in his chest as if he were studying someone else's body.

"Get those out of him! Can't you help him? Wave a magic wand or something!" Vir shouted with increasing agitation. The frightening calm that had settled upon the cloisters was to him the most disconcerting thing.

Gwynn glanced at Vir for a moment, looking as if she wanted to explain something of great consequence. Then obviously she changed her mind, and instead crouched next to Kane, studying the spikes. Then she looked up at Kane, who simply shook his head. There was sadness on his face, as if he felt more sorry for her than for himself.

Vir started forward, and suddenly the ship shifted wildly. Finian was hardly handling the vessel with the same calm assurance that Kane had displayed. His jaw was set in grim determination and he shouted, "Hold on!"

Vir, who by this time was lying in a crumpled heap on the far side of the ship, considered the advice to be a classic case of too little, too late.

On the monitor display, he could see the rapidly receding Shadow Base, and then suddenly it vanished entirely. For a moment he had no idea why, and then he remembered: the null field. They had emerged from it, and the base had securely vanished back into its invisibility.

Just as the display showed where they had come from, it also provided a view of where they were going. The jumpgate appeared just ahead of them and, sensing the approach of a ship, flared to life.

A moment before the mage ship leaped into the gate, they saw the null field suddenly split apart. Gigantic chunks of Xha'dam spiraled away in all directions. There were pieces of the planet destroyer as well, ripped to shreds by the force of the explosions that the device itself had instigated. A fireball, feeding on itself and the continued detonation of Xha'dam, grew wider and faster, and for just a moment, Vir was certain that the thing was going to engulf them.

That was when space again seemed to stretch all around them, and an instant later they had leaped into the gate and were propelled at speeds that would have once been considered beyond all imagination.

Vir picked himself up off the floor and went quickly over to Gwynn and Kane. Kane's face looked absolutely ashen, his eyes were misting over. "Do something!" Vir urged once again.

Gwynn's detached demeanor cracked. "Don't you think I

would if I could!" she said angrily. "If I could help him . . . if any of this could have been avoided . . ."

Something about the way she said that brought realization to Vir. "What he saw . . . what he said he saw . . . it was this, wasn't it."

"Some of this," Kane said softly. "Not all. But 'twas enough. 'Twould serve."

"Do all of you—"

"See the future? Have visions of what is to come? Some. A few of the full techno-mages, full adepts . . . but a cloister?" Gwynn shook her head and regarded Kane with something approaching reverence. "Never. He is most blessed."

Vir gestured helplessly. "You call this blessed? Great Maker, at least pull those out of him!"

"It would be . . . too late," whispered Kane. "And it would simply cause . . . a bloody mess. Vir . . . there are things you should know. Must know. Things that . . . only you can stop."

He leaned in closer to Kane. "What are they?"

Kane's eyes momentarily refocused. "Don't worry. You already know them."

"What? I . . . I don't understand."

And he had to strain to hear Kane say, "Good. I was . . . going for cryptic." The faint smile remained on his face even as his head slumped to one side, and then he was gone.

Vir let out a sigh. "You succeeded," he said, as he reached over and closed Kane's eyes.

# — chapter 4 —

They emerged from the jumpgate, spiraling at high speed into the surface of the planet designated K0643. Finian barely yanked the nose of the ship up in time to prevent it from slamming into the ground, and the ship suddenly went straight up like a surface-to-air missile. He called out, "Something's wrong!"

"Oh, now what?" said Vir, not sure how much more he could take. He kept trying to tear his gaze away from the fallen Kane. He saw that Gwynn was still crouched next to him, and she was gently caressing the curve of his jaw with the side of her hand.

"It's not us! It's the gate!"

Vir immediately saw what he was talking about. Energy was crackling all around it, but far more violently than before. The thing was trembling wildly, and fissures were appearing all through it. It began to splinter, to shudder under some sort of pressure that Vir could not even guess at, and then the arch began to crumble in upon itself. Within moments, gigantic chunks of it were tumbling to the ground. Then with a roar, the gate collapsed completely.

"Good riddance," muttered Finian.

"But what caused it to happen?" demanded Vir.

"Not what. Who," Finian said suddenly, getting the ship's trajectory under control. "Look." Apparently in order to illustrate his explanation, he keyed the monitor to zoom in on a lone individual standing on the uppermost outcropping of some rocks. It was wearing immediately recognizable long robes, a hood drawn over its head, and a telltale staff gripped solidly in its right hand. Its left hand was placed on its hip in a casual manner, as if this being was impatiently waiting for a late-arriving bus.

"Is that who I think it is?" Gwynn asked.

"I suspect so."

"Who? Who is it?" Vir wanted to know.

They did not reply. For some depressing reason, that didn't surprise him at all.

Finian guided the vessel toward a convenient landing point at the outer edge of the excavation. Vir could see on the monitor screen that the cloaked figure was making its way down to meet them. Despite the rockiness of the terrain, the newcomer moved with self-assurance. Vir was certain, beyond any question, that it was a techno-mage.

In truth, Vir was still having trouble believing any of this had happened. After the business with Elric back on Babylon 5, he had been pleasantly certain that he would never see a techno-mage again. The thought didn't bother him a bit. Now he was ass-deep in them. He started to wonder grimly if perhaps he should just ask where the techno-mage recruitment office might be so that he could sign up and be done with it.

As soon as the ship's landing procedures had cycled through, Finian and Gwynn positioned themselves at the door. Gwynn laid Kane down gently and respectfully on the floor, and removed her own outer cloak to cover the fallen cloister with it. They stood before the door of the ship, waiting. Then it opened, and the hooded figure stepped through.

He pushed back his hood and Vir saw a very curious-looking individual. He was completely bald, with a strong jaw and piercing gaze. There was a bleak twinkle in his eye, as if he knew the entire universe was based on some cosmic joke, with death as the great punch line.

"Galen," said Finian in acknowledgment, and he bowed. Gwynn followed suit.

Galen took the entirety of the situation in with a glance, including the presence of Vir and the corpse of Kane. "Pity," he said. "He had potential. So," he continued, as if that was to be the end of the mourning period, "would you care to tell me what the hell you three . . . I'm sorry, you two . . . thought you were doing."

"I did it, too," said Vir tentatively.

"Yes, but you don't count. Don't worry, though. You will eventually."

"Oh. Thank you. I guess."

In quick, broad strokes, Gwynn outlined for him what had happened. The one whom they addressed as Galen might have been carved from marble for all the expression or reaction he displayed. Every so often he would glance at Kane's covered body as Gwynn continued her narrative. Most of it, of course, Vir already knew, but then Gwynn got to a point in her recitation that was news to Vir.

"As we were departing," she said, "I managed to capture a Drakh and ask him a few questions in a manner he could not ignore. They had intended to use the Death Clouds . . ."

"Those massive planet killers," said Galen, just for his personal confirmation.

"Yes. Those were going to be the centerpiece of their new fleet. The Drakh have been rebuilding their vessels, preparing themselves, but the Death Clouds were intended to tilt the balance utterly in their favor."

"And to what end did they intend to employ them?"

"The Drakh blame John Sheridan and his wife, Delenn, for the departure of the Shadows," Gwynn told him.

Galen nodded slowly. "That's probably because Sheridan and Delenn told them to go away. In the end, you have to credit the Shadows with at least having the good taste to leave a party when asked to depart." The words sounded flip, but Vir could tell there was very much an edge to them. Galen's hatred for the Shadows was palpable, and Vir could only guess what sort of personal suffering Galen had known at their hands . . . or claws . . . or whatever. "Do you think the Drakh would be willing to follow suit? Leave if we ask them to?"

"I doubt it," said Gwynn.

"So do I. Proceed, then. They blame Sheridan and Delenn . . ."

"And because of that, it is their intention to punish the species that gave birth to them. Their plan is to use the Death Cloud on Earth. By this point, they will already have tested it on Daltron 7. If it operates as I suspect it will, there will be nothing left there. Not a being, not a bird, not a bug . . . nothing. That is the fate they have planned for Earth."

Upon hearing this, Vir's spine froze, as did several of his major bodily organs. But Galen's deadpan expression never wavered. Gwynn might just as easily have told him that the Drakh intended to orbit Earth, spew harsh language, and leave.

"And what about Minbar?" he inquired.

"A plague. They intend to annihilate the seat of the Interstellar Alliance with a plague."

For the first time, true darkness of worry passed over Galen's face. It was as if he was confident that the Death Cloud could be handled, but germ warfare presented an insurmountable problem. "They have created a plague?"

"No. They don't know how to build or grow the virus. The Drakh aren't that advanced. They are superb scavengers, and can manage machinery and construction adroitly enough. But replicating Shadow-created viruses is beyond them. However, they managed to salvage enough of the virus from Z'ha'dum to accomplish their aim."

"How much?"

"Enough to wipe out an entire world."

To Vir's astonishment, Galen actually let out a sigh of relief. "We're most fortunate then."

He couldn't believe it. "Fortunate! They're planning to wipe out all of Minbar, and you call that fortunate!"

"Well . . . not if you're Minbari, certainly," said Finian. Gwynn made an angry face at him that indicated it would be best if he kept his mouth shut.

"Enough virus for only one world means that the situation is containable," said Galen. "Be grateful it's not enough for a hundred worlds."

"And are you going to just let it happen?"

"I will do what I can. *All* that I can."

"That may not be enough!"

"And what will you do, Vir Cotto?" Galen demanded abruptly. "Will Centauri Prime reveal its duplicity in this matter? Inform the Alliance of its involvement with the locating of the gate that led the Drakh to the weapons they craved? Leave itself open to charges of being accomplice to attempted mass murder? Will *you* do all that can be done, Vir Cotto . . . or will you simply do all that you can do?"

Vir looked away then. Galen was simply saying things that had already occurred to Vir, but he was loath to admit it. With billions of lives on the line, Vir's main concern still remained avoiding any threat to Centauri Prime and its largely innocent people.

"I will take that as my answer," Galen said icily. "Be aware, Ambassador . . . whatever hostility you may feel for the Shadows, their servants and their . . . technology . . . pales beside my own."

"I doubt that," Vir told him.

Galen smiled slightly. "Doubt is always to be preferred in all things. Very well, Vir Cotto. I will wave my magic wand, and poof! Centauri Prime will have no association with this business. I've already dispatched the unfortunate artifact your excavation uncovered. I've covered your tracks for you."

Surprised, Vir pointed at the fallen rubble that had once been the Shadow gate. "You did that?"

"Of course I did."

"I thought techno-mages couldn't use their abilities to destroy. That's what they told me," and he indicated Gwynn and Finian.

"That is true . . . for them," said Galen. "Then again, there are always . . . possibilities."

"And is saving the Earth and Minbar among those possibilities?" The thought that the Homeworlds of Delenn or Sheridan, or both, might be annihilated was horrifying to Vir, and the knowledge of Centauri Prime's culpability was almost too much to bear. At least, however, that would remain his burden and his alone, with any luck.

Some luck.

"It is . . . a possibility. A distinct one. And you, Vir Cotto . . . take solace in the awareness that, without your involvement, it could have been far, far worse. So much so that it would not have mattered whether Centauri Prime's involvement became general knowledge or not. For truly, there would have been no worlds in the Alliance left to care."

Without another word, Galen turned away from him and started to walk off. Vir looked around, still unsure as to what was to happen next. Finian rested a hand on Vir's shoulder then, and said, "Leave it in Galen's hands. He will attend to it, if any can. None are more dedicated to eliminating Shadow technology than he. As for you, Vir . . ." and his lips thinned. "Nice disguise."

Vir realized that he was still wearing the mask that he'd been handed earlier. Feeling sheepish, he pulled it off his face. Galen shook his head with an imperious air, and then said, "Go home, Vir Cotto."

"Home." Vir shook his head. "You don't understand. I have no home. Centauri Prime will have no dealings with me, and Babylon 5 . . . if I never see the place again . . ."

"Then it would be a waste of possibilities," Gwynn said.

"What sort of possibilities?"

"For starters," Finian said, "there is still work to do. You may feel you are no longer welcome on Centauri Prime, and you are likely right. However, you remain Ambassador to Babylon 5. They are not likely to replace you; they consider the position a waste, and so will not bother to fritter away manpower. And the ambassador of Babylon 5 can still get things done. You have contacts from the past . . . and from the present, have you not?"

Vir thought about Rem Lanas, and about Renegar, both of whom had certainly gained a degree of respect for Vir as a result of this debacle. He had warned them of what was to come. They would remember that. They would know to attend to what he said. They would know to trust him, as much as anyone trusted anyone these days.

And there had been other allies, free-minded and free-thinking Centauri—many of them rather young—who had provided aid when Vir had sought to surreptitiously help the Narn during the war.

Moments earlier, he had felt so alone, and yet he was starting to realize that such was not the case. It was just that he had tied so much of his belief in his power and influence to Londo. And when Londo had turned him away, why, that seemed to be that. But it wasn't necessarily the case, as long as Vir didn't allow it to be. Granted, his self-esteem and image among others in the Alliance had been dealt a vicious blow by his duplicitous lover, Mariel . . . but she could be overcome, as well. Perhaps even used in a manner that would be to his advantage.

There were indeed possibilities, if he was willing to see them.

"Yes," Vir said slowly, his mind racing. "Yes, I have . . . contacts."

"We will be in touch, then."

Vir nodded, the words not fully registering at first. Then they did. He turned and said, "And when you're in touch, what will you . . ."

They were gone. Finian. Gwynn. The one called Galen. And the ship.

The ship that had been his ride.

"What am I supposed to do? *Walk* back to Babylon 5?" Vir demanded. But there was no one there to reply. Then, physically and mentally, he shrugged. The bottom line was that techno-mages, even cloister techno-mages, still bothered the hell out of him. He would find other means of getting back to Babylon 5 . . . and then, why, then the work would truly begin. The work that would lead him to . . .

What? What would it lead him to?

He had told Londo Mollari that he would remain his friend . . . even if he became his enemy. He had the disturbing feeling that his continued activities would lead him to that point sooner than he wanted, and he would find out whether the sentiment he had expressed was, in fact, true.

And he had a further disturbing feeling that he wasn't going to like what he found.

**EXCERPTED FROM**
*THE CHRONICLES OF LONDO MOLLARI.*
**Excerpt dated (approximate Earth date)**
**January 9, 2268.**

I believe the expression my former friend, Mr. Garibaldi, once used was "It has been some kind of party." That, I can assure you, it very much has been.

The festivities have been progressing in a nonstop fashion. Naturally I cannot participate in them. In fact, officially I must scorn and condemn them, and such public rejection has prompted some reactions of outright hostility from my beloved people. After all, they expect uniform support from their emperor. How dare I imply that their rejoicing over the misfortune of others might somehow be inappropriate, or in bad taste or—dare I say it—shortsighted.

People have very little patience with that which they do not wish to hear.

Then again, considering the number of individuals who endeavored to sway me from the course that brought me to this cursed throne, I am certainly the last person who has any right to make such observations, eh?

As of this writing, it has been one Earth week, or perhaps two, since the unleashing of the Drakh plague upon the hapless Earth. I am not certain precisely how long it has been, since I have spent much of the time in an alcoholic haze. As always, this is partly motivated by the presence of my little friend and his intolerance for liquor. But it also represents my nominal participation in the fever of celebration that has gripped Centauri Prime and has plunged it into an orgy of rejoicing. Such actions are always risky, for they have an unfortunate habit of attracting the notice of Fate and her damnable sisters, Poetic Justice and Irony.

For years now, Centauri Prime has grown more and more isolationist. We have spun a cocoon around ourselves, posted large metaphorical signs that have instructed others to keep away from us. If the Interstellar Alliance has desired to have no congress with us, we have had equally as much antipathy for them. As is always the case when a people draw inward, we have examined ourselves spiritually, as well as politically. We have sought answers, tried to determine just how and why such an unfortunate and vile fate as being bombed to the edge of oblivion had been visited upon us. There were some who said rather loudly, and quite frequently, that our willingness to consort with "lesser" races had brought the wrath of the Great Maker upon us. We had allowed ourselves to become weak, our purpose to become diluted. The fact that no one could quite agree on just what that purpose might be did not seem to deter the philosophy. The Alliance had assaulted us because it was the Great Maker's will. What an odd combination of paranoia and spiritual resignation that was.

But there was another side to that reasoning. A side that said that, if we were willing to rededicate ourselves to the worship of the Great Maker, the rebuilding of Centauri Prime, and an understanding that the only friend of Centauri could be other Centauri, why . . . then it was possible that the Great Maker might smile upon us once more. In doing so, he might very well lead us to renewed greatness. Most importantly, he would smite our enemies with his wrath and with his mighty hand.

It was partly to that end that Minister Durla installed his former teacher of religion, one Vallko by name, into the newly created position of minister of spirituality. It was a ludicrous concept for a post, I thought, and I was quite sure that there would be an outcry.

I was correct. I am always correct. It is a curse I live under. Well . . . one of many.

Unfortunately, the outcry was one of uniform approval, and many were certain that a new and definitively positive step had been taken toward improving the lot of the poor, beleaguered residents of Centauri Prime. Minister Durla was perfectly willing to support Vallko's tenure by making attendance at spiritual meetings mandatory for the citizenry. But it was not necessary. Vallko's services are invariably packed, the temples creaking at the doors, or at least I am told that it is so. I have not attended any.

Minister Durla scolds me for this. Let him. My response to him is that, if the Great Maker is everywhere, why is he any more at Minister Vallko's temple than in the throne room? Indeed, he has more reason to be in the throne room, for that is where the true power of Centauri Prime resides, and it is there that the Great Maker can and should have the most influence.

It may be, however, that I say this with less forcefulness than I would like, probably because we both know it to be nonsense. The power lies elsewhere.

Durla, of course, thinks that it lies with him, and I'm certain he thinks I am foolish enough to believe that it resides in my hands. It is, in fact, Durla who is the fool, but I am disinclined to inform him of his . . . misapprehension.

Still, Durla does what Durla will. He never misses one of Vallko's services, of course. He likely reasons that it is wise to be seen there, and in that he is quite possibly correct. By being perceived as a regular constituent of Vallko's, he allies himself—by extension—with the Supreme Being. It is a very crafty, very wise maneuver, and one that I can appreciate since it was the sort of thing I would once have done.

After all, it was hardly long ago that I endeavored to make it appear as if I was receiving a blessing from the techno-mages. I did so to boost myself up the ladder of power. It is difficult for me to believe that I now look back upon those occasions as times of innocence.

The news of the misfortune that befell Earth came during one of Vallko's spiritual gatherings. By all accounts, the place went mad with joy. It took long moments for Vallko to calm the assemblage, and his next words were extremely canny and well chosen. What he said was this:

"It is not fit, or meet, or responsible for Centauri to rejoice in the misfortunes of others. Throughout our history, we have dealt with other races with compassion, always with compassion. Granted, there have been races that did not see that compassion for what it was, and rebelled. The Narn, naturally, come to mind. In dealing with them, however—in dealing with any who operated in a manner contrary to the interests of the great Centauri Republic—we did exactly what we had to do. No more and no less.

"And we never, under any circumstances, took joy in the destruction of lives or the annihilation of others. Pride, yes, we took pride, and that is natural and to be expected, for the Great Maker wishes us to take pride in our accomplishments. When we perform an act of greatness, we are doing so in his name and are honoring him.

"But simply taking pleasure in the pain and suffering of others . . . that, my good friends, is not appropriate.

"Instead . . . we shall pray. And the prayer should continue for days, as many days as we of Centauri Prime wish to pursue it. For you see, when they assaulted us, the Alliance transgressed against the chosen people of the Great Maker. They angered the Great Maker. Now they have paid the price. We cannot and must not, of course, ask the Great Maker to relent in his anger against them, for who are we to question his will? He does what he must, as do we all. So instead, my good, dear friends . . . we will pray that the Great Maker gives guidance to the poor souls of Earth. That he makes them, and their allies, realize the error of their ways. For if they do, then the Great Maker will spare them the suffering that they will otherwise have to endure. In fact, he will be happy to spare them, for ultimately the Great Maker is a being of kindness . . . as are we, for were we not made in his image?

"Pray then, my friends. Pray in a loud and sustained manner. Raise your voices and make a joyful noise unto the Great Maker so that he will hear you and know that you are sincere."

It was brilliant, the way he handled it, truly. As repulsive as I find those who manipulate the words and spirit of the Great Maker for their own ends, I must admit that people like Vallko have a style and ingenuity that I can only envy.

Centauri Prime wanted to rejoice over the misfortune of the Humans. But the Humans still have many friends and staunch allies, none of whom would take kindly to the good people of Centauri Prime throwing a very loud, very raucous, and very premature celebration over the demise of everyone who had the misfortune to be stuck on the planet Earth when the Drakh virus was unleashed.

So instead Vallko found a way for the Centauri to vent their sentiments without bringing the ill feelings—and possibly the wrath—of other races down upon us. The celebration would commence at Vallko's direction, and it would be as boisterous as could be. However, for all intents and purposes it was being done, not out of a sense of celebration, but instead in the hopes that the Great Maker would provide succor to our former tormentors.

Very crafty. Very devious. Very, very effective.

There is, after all, a fine line that separates tragedy from debauchery. I should know. I have certainly crossed, and even erased, that line any number of times.

Even now, I hear the "mourning" going on outside. The entire city is lit up and has been that way for days on end. I have no idea where the energy that my people display is coming from.

Part of me wishes to wade into the revelry and tell them the truth.

Oh, yes. Yes, I know the truth, for Shiv'kala has told me. That it was our workers, our excavators, who uncovered the gate that, in turn, led the Drakh to the planet destroyer. Without that weapon at their disposal, they never would have made their attack upon the Earth. We, the proud Centauri, are responsible for the attempted destruction of the Humans. It was a retaliation, commenced because of the Drakh need for revenge—the Drakh wished to strike back at the Humans because of the outcome of the Shadow War. Yet the Shadows brought the darkness to Centauri Prime, a darkness that continues to this day, long after the last of the Shadows has gone. If anything, we should be kissing the Humans' feet and striving to find a way to help them in their search for a cure.

Instead we hypocritically rejoice while pretending to be praying for their betterment and survival.

Why Shiv'kala speaks to me of such things, I do not know. Perhaps he revels in my helplessness, wishing to drive home to me just how ineffective I am at such times. Perhaps he is simply a sadist. Perhaps it is another test.

I tire of the tests.

I tire of a great many things. Yet my fate, if I am to believe the dream that has me dying at the hands of G'Kar, is at least another ten years away. I cannot go through that much time fatigued. I must find something to do.

Senna still represents an interesting project. And Vir . . .

Vir . . . I must find a way to bring him back. Of that, I am quite certain. Granted, his last time here was a disaster, but I think he knows enough to keep his mouth shut and make no mention of Shiv'kala again. But how would I convince my captors that Vir should be allowed to return?

And Timov. What of her?

I have wondered from time to time in the past weeks whether I would hear from her again. A part of me hoped that she would somehow see through the charade. That she would realize the trumped-up charges were for her own good, and that I was desperate to get her off this world for her own safety.

How foolish that sounds, as I write it here. How infinite is one's capacity for self-delusion. Timov has no reason to assume that my little endeavor was anything other than what it appeared on the surface. I am never going to see her again.

Well . . . it is probably for the best.

Yes. Yes, it is.

Two of my wives, if I never see them again, that will be more than satisfactory. But Timov, I will miss. She, I should think, will likely not miss me, and for this I will not blame her.

The celebrations—my pardon, the "prayers"—continue loudly and raucously outside. There appears to be no end to them. I shall not participate. I must remain aloof, above it all. I suppose, of course, that I could go to some insulated room, shut myself off from the boisterous sounds. But I cannot bring myself to do that. You see . . . I still like the Human race, despite all that has happened. I believe that they will rise above this. In fact, I think they will surpass us. I see where the Centauri Republic is, and where the Humans are, and I see them as a star that is only just now beginning to truly burn. Our star, on the other hand . . . is fading. Not that any of my people believe it, of course. Why should they? I do not want to believe it myself. I have a sense of it, though, perhaps because I see myself as the incarnation of the Centauri spirit . . . and I can feel my own star, deep within me, beginning its own steady burnout.

And still the celebration continues.

Would that I could walk among them and tell them that they are very likely extinct, that they simply do not yet know it. I cannot say this to them, however, for they will not wish to hear it and, truth to tell, *I* do not wish to believe it. I hold out hope for my people, all the same, although I hold out even more hope for the Humans.

# — chapter 5 —

Londo had discovered, over the years, that one gets into certain habits, particularly when one is emperor. So it came as something of a shock to him when his habitual pattern was rudely disrupted one morning when he discovered the abrupt absence of Dunseny.

Dunseny had had the great honor of being Londo's personal servant, valet, and majordomo. He had been a retainer at the house of Mollari since the days of old, and had been with the family for as long as Londo could remember. He had first joined House Mollari when, of all things, Londo's father had won him in a rather fortunate hand of cards. They had not expected much of Dunseny, arriving in their service in such an odd and backhanded manner, but Londo's father had been pleasantly surprised. Dunseny, in fairly short order, had proven himself to be efficient, attentive, and completely trustworthy.

Londo had been quite young when Dunseny first came aboard, and at the time Dunseny had seemed quite ancient to him. He was tall, soft-spoken, with piercing eyes that seemed to take in everything so that he could attend to whatever was needed as quickly and efficiently as possible. His hair, cut to a respectable medium height, had been grayish white for as long as Londo could remember. He always wore a suit of black, buttoned all the way to the collar, with no other adornment. The emperor suspected that, were he able to step back in time, he would see that the Dunseny of those bygone years had actually been considerably younger than he recalled. Nevertheless, the illusion to Londo was that Dunseny had never aged. That, indeed, he bordered on the immortal. He had come into this world old, and would remain that way . . . well . . . forever.

For the first years of his reign, Londo had been content to let Dunseny remain at House Mollari, but every so often he had found himself requiring Dunseny's services as valet. He had come to realize that he trusted no one but the faithful retainer to attend to such things. Londo's requests, and thereafter demands, became so regular that Dunseny began—politely, but firmly—to complain. He pointed out that, despite appearances to the contrary, he was not getting any younger, and the running about between House Mollari and the royal palace was wearing on him somewhat.

"Finally! A problem presented to me that is easily solved!" Londo slapped his hands together briskly as if he were about to deal out a deck of cards. Then he declared, "I shall bring you on as my full-time personal valet. You and your family will be given superb quarters here in the palace, and no strenuous commute will ever bother you again, yes? This is satisfactory? Or do you need to discuss it with your wife and children?"

"My wife passed away of the Lung Blight that swept our city three years ago, Highness," said Dunseny calmly. "And my only son was killed during the assault on Centauri Prime by the Alliance."

"Oh," Londo said faintly. He felt terrible, although for the life of him he couldn't quite figure out why. Perhaps it was because, in all this time, he had never even thought to ask Dunseny something as simple and polite as "How is your family?" Certainly, he had assumed, Dunseny would have told him. Instead he had carried on in his duties at the family house, and for Londo as needed.

Londo cleared his throat and straightened his coat, although it hardly needed straightening. "That is . . . a pity. You certainly have my regrets, Dunseny."

"That means a good deal, Highness," Dunseny said with a carefully detached expression. It was impossible for Londo to tell whether Dunseny was being sarcastic. He decided to give the old man the benefit of the doubt.

"So it is settled, then?" asked Londo.

Dunseny bowed slightly. "How can I refuse he who wears the white?"

And so Dunseny had come into Londo's full-time service, while Londo hired certain others, hand-picked by the reliable Dunseny himself, to run the family estate. When Londo awoke each morning, Dunseny was there to awaken him. He was there to lay out Londo's clothes, to prepare his bath, to handle his manicure, to oversee the tasting of the royal food—not that Dunseny handled *that* himself; that questionable honor went to another, a perpetually nervous individual named Frit.

As time passed, Dunseny's responsibilities expanded until he was keeping the royal calendar and attending to the comings and goings of those who wished to see Londo at any given time of the day. Soon it became well known that, in order to see Londo, one had to go through Dunseny first. It wasn't as if Dunseny endeavored to limit access to Londo. Far from it. He simply organized the time of all petitioners, deciding who would take priority and determining what it was that Londo would find most important and worthy of being dealt with first. Invariably, Dunseny's judgment was right on target.

It even caused a miniscandal when, on one or two occasions, Londo had actually turned to the old valet and asked him what he thought of a particular situation that had come before the throne. It would likely have engendered an even greater reaction had Dunseny not offered advice or observations that were accurate, just, and proper. It was difficult for anyone to become upset with him, and indeed Dunseny's popularity within some circles only served to benefit the emperor.

So it was little wonder that Londo let out a most unemperor-like scream one morning when he was awakened by a gentle touch on his shoulder, but opened his eyes to see someone other than his faithful retainer.

It was a young man, around seventeen or eighteen years of age. He wore black clothing, broken by a red sash, and his eyes glittered, unblinking, like some animal peering out appraisingly at him from the jungle.

"Who are you!" Londo shouted. He half sat up in bed, a bit chagrined at the yelp he had emitted, but still determined to muster some of the dignity his high office afforded him. "What are you doing here?"

"I am Throk," said the teen. "I serve Minister Lione as one of—"

"Of the Prime Candidates, yes, yes." Londo gave an impatient wave. He was more than aware of who and what the Prime Candidates were. They were a youth group, in operation for five years now, answering to Chancellor Castig Lione and serving Centauri Prime in a variety of ways, a number of which served to make Londo quite a bit nervous.

Then he rewound something through his head. His eyebrows knit in puzzlement. "Minister Lione? I thought he was Chancellor Lione. This is the same Lione, yes? Chancellor of development?"

"The same," said Throk.

"Since when did he become a minister?"

"Minister Durla oversaw his appointment. Were you not consulted, Your Highness?"

"No, Your Highness was not consulted."

"Is there a problem with the appointment, Your Highness?"

The question immediately set off an alarm in Londo's head.

He did not know what Throk was doing there. He did not know where Dunseny was. He felt as if he was being pelted with information and being challenged to keep up. But the one thing he *did* know for certain was that he most definitely did not want to say precisely what was on his mind in the presence of this individual. This "Throk," this Prime Candidate, might as well have had Durla's head on his left shoulder and Lione's head on the right.

"The only problem I have with it is one of protocol," Londo said coolly. "At the very least, I should be informed of such matters in an orderly fashion, so I am not left open to the possibility of committing some minor gaffe. How would it be

if I addressed Minister Lione as Chancellor? Certainly that
could make for a potentially embarrassing situation, yes?"

"Yes. Absolutely, Your Highness." Throk's face remained
utterly inscrutable. Londo reminded himself never to play
cards with this young man. Then he further reminded himself
that he had absolutely no idea what the young man was doing
in his private chambers.

"Where is Dunseny?" Londo asked.

The slightest flickering of puzzlement danced across
Throk's face. Londo couldn't tell whether what he saw, however briefly, in the teen's expression was a momentary loss of
control, or else a carefully permitted "slip" so as to somehow
ingratiate himself with the emperor. "I thought you knew,
Your Highness."

"Of course I know," Londo said. "I simply have this odd
quirk. I enjoy having people tell me about matters with which
I am already familiar. Again: Where is Dunseny?"

"Dunseny informed Minister Durla that he wished to re-
tire. That he was feeling his age and desired to slow down.
Minister Durla consulted with Minister Lione and it was
felt that—from a security point of view, if nothing else—
appointing a Prime Candidate as your new valet would be the
best fit. I had the honor of being selected. Shall I draw your
bath for you, Your Highness?"

"I do not care," Londo said, "whether you draw a bath or
draw a breath. Dunseny said nothing to me of retiring."

Throk shrugged slightly. "Perhaps he was concerned that
he would be letting you down, and could not bring himself to
face you, Your Highness."

"Perhaps." Londo, however, did not bother to speculate out
loud on the other, more likely, "perhaps." Specifically, that
"perhaps" Dunseny had been forced out for some reason. If
that were the case, then Londo had every intention of doing
something about it.

He rose from the bed and said in a firm, commanding
voice, "You may leave me, Throk."

"Sir, if I have failed to satisfy you in some way as your
valet . . ."

"You have neither failed nor succeeded, for you have not been given the opportunity. There will be no decision in the matter until I have spoken with Dunseny."

"But, Highness, Minister Lione was quite specific in his orders that—"

"Ahhhh," said Londo as he belted his robe tightly around him. "What a fast-rising individual Lione is. Who would have thought that, in such a brief time, he would have ascended from chancellor to the ministry . . . and now, who would have thought it possible! Castig Lione is now the emperor!"

Throk looked puzzled once more, and this time it was clearly genuine. "No, Highness, you are the emperor," he said slowly, as if worried that Londo might have forgotten that.

"You don't say!" said Londo, voice dripping with sarcasm. "For a moment I thought there was some confusion on the matter, what with your giving his orders priority over mine. Or perhaps *you* were simply confused over the matter, Throk? Could that be it?"

Throk opened his mouth a moment, and then closed it. He nodded.

"I thought it was. Now you will leave, unless you feel that further challenging of my wishes would be of benefit to your long-term health. For I assure you, Throk, I have executed men younger, handsomer, and far better connected than you. Admittedly, I have not killed a teenager in some time. But one teenager more or less . . ." and he shrugged his shoulders to indicate just how unimportant such a demise would be in the grand scheme of things.

Throk needed no further hints. He departed the room.

Londo, dressed in a hood and cloak that concealed his familiar visage, rapped firmly on the door of Dunseny's home. It was a small, unassuming domicile, which had been deeded over to Dunseny many years earlier by Londo's father, out of recognition for his faithful service. There was a pause, and Londo knocked again. This time he heard the shuffling of feet, the slow approach by a measured tread that he recognized with as much confidence as he would recognize his own voice.

The door opened and Dunseny peered out. He looked slightly bewildered at first, but then his face cleared as recognition dawned. He bowed slightly. "Highness," he said. "In what capacity might I serve you this—"

Londo made an impatient wave. "Do not stand on ceremony with me, Dunseny. We have known each other too long. To you, I am simply Londo, as will always be the case."

"Very well, Londo."

There was a pause, while the two men stood staring at each other, and then Londo said, "So? You leave me standing on the doorstep without being invited in? Is this how you treat your emperor?"

His gaze flickered over Londo. "Not wearing the white. Incognito?"

"In a manner of speaking. I will not ask again to be allowed into your home . . . a home my family has provided you with."

"Yes, I know. Your generosity has always been unstinting." Still he did not move aside.

"Dunseny," Londo said in a level tone, "what is transpiring here? I learn, thirdhand, that you desire to leave my service? Why? And why do we stand in this manner, as if I am an unwanted salesman?"

"Because," Dunseny replied, "I have nothing to hide."

Londo blinked in confusion. He had no idea what in the world Dunseny could possibly be talking about.

And then, suddenly, like a lightning flash, it came to him.

Someone, somewhere, was watching. Or else Dunseny had reason to believe that might be the case. By remaining outside, keeping themselves in plain view—with, perhaps, portable listening devices or even a passable lip reader in the vicinity—no one could possibly accuse Dunseny of anything.

Dunseny clearly saw the understanding that flashed across Londo's face, for he nodded ever so subtly. Londo tried to glance around without turning his head, but he didn't spot anyone immediately. There were passersby in the street, none of whom seemed to be paying particular attention, unaware that the emperor—the personification of Centauri Prime—was standing among them. Yet spies might be anywhere around them. For that matter, there were other residences nearby, a number of them several stories high. Someone could be watching from any of those.

Londo was certainly accustomed to the sensation of not being alone. With the keeper, the foul, one-eyed creature, forever bonded to him, Londo would never know solitude again. Still, this sensation of paranoia was an uncomfortable one.

"It is my desire," Londo said slowly, "that you return to my employ as my valet."

Dunseny spoke slowly and deliberately, as if the words had been meticulously rehearsed. He was an old man, yes, but he had never seemed old until that moment. "As I told Minister Durla . . . I have served for many, many years, and I feel I need rest."

"Are you ill? Is there some infirmity?"

"As I told Minister Durla . . . I have served for many, many years, and I feel I need rest."

He had repeated it with such word-for-word precision that no doubt was left in Londo's mind as to the truth of things. Whether it had been done to rob him of Dunseny's advice, or simply to further isolate him, or to bring in one of the Prime Candidates to monitor his actions . . . none of the reasons mattered. His voice low and tight, he said, "Were you threatened? Did he threaten you?"

"As I told—"

"Minister Durla, yes, yes, I know! You have made that abundantly clear!"

"Londo . . ." And for the first time, there was a true hint of tragedy in his voice, "I am an old man. I have done my service. Do not ask of me more than I can give."

"If you were threatened, I can . . ."

"Protect me? If I were threatened . . . and I do not claim that I was, I speak merely hypothetically . . . are you saying that you could protect me, Londo, if I had been threatened?"

His eyes seemed to drill deep into Londo's soul, and they

both knew the answer even though Londo did not dare say it.
Dunseny smiled sadly, and spoke words that shredded Londo
with their simple truth: "I am not convinced you can even
protect yourself."

There it was. And the hell of it was, he was right.

"I wish you all the luck in the world with your reign,
Londo Mollari. You will have no stauncher supporter than I.
But if it is all the same to you, I think it would be best if I sup-
ported you . . . from a distance."

The response was little more than a husky whisper. "Of
course. It will be as you desire."

Dunseny nodded in what was clearly gratitude. Londo
stepped back and allowed the door to quietly shut.

In the final analysis, he had indeed been little more than a
salesman, trying to sell one old man on the notion that he was
someone upon whom the old man could depend. As it turned
out, he was not a particularly effective salesman at that.


When the door to the emperor's inner chamber slid open,
Senna was naturally expecting to see the emperor within. So
she blinked in surprise when she saw one of those disturbing
members of the Prime Candidates standing in front of her.
For his part, he studied her as if she were some sort of micro-
scopic bacterium.

No. No, there was more to it than that. He seemed to be appraising her, and even more than that—he appeared to like
what he was seeing. Not surprising: her blue gown was richly
embroidered with gold brocade, and displayed her shapely
figure quite well. Her high cheekbones and level gaze gave
her an almost regal bearing. She found that she wanted to
leap out of her skin, considering it so unclean that she had
no desire to sport it any longer, and run shrieking down the
corridor.

Fighting to retain what protocol would consider the correct
and proper approach, Senna asked, "What are you doing
here? This is the emperor's private residence."

"I am Throk, his new valet."

"Where is Dunseny?" she demanded.

"Elsewhere."

She arched a most unamused eyebrow. "I can see that you are going to be a fountain of information."

"You are Senna, are you not?" he said after a moment. "Daughter of Lord Refa. The emperor plucked you off the streets and gave you a home here in the palace four or five years ago. Educated you, clothed you, fed you. He refers to you as 'young lady' as if it were a title. You are, for all intents and purposes, the daughter he never had."

Sarcastically, Senna patted her hands together in appreciation. "Quite a litany, Throk. And most unfair. You know much of me; I know nothing of you."

"I am Throk, of the Prime Candidates. Beyond that, there is nothing of much relevance."

Senna did not seem particularly inclined to accept that, however. "Oh, I don't know about that," she said, stepping closer to him. "How you came to be the emperor's personal valet, after Dunseny tended to him so well for so long, is certainly relevant."

"You have a very regal bearing," he told her.

It was not a comment that she expected. It flustered her momentarily, and that angered her in turn, because the last thing she wanted was to be at a loss for words in his presence. "Thank you," she said with clear resentment.

"You are welcome."

She turned, yet felt as if his stare was boring straight into the back of her head. There was something truly frightening in that gaze, she decided, something that threatened to draw her in. There was—and she thought she might have been imagining it—an incredible determination to serve his masters. And she sensed that he would be perfectly willing to go over, or through, anyone who stood in the way of his accomplishing that task.

Something told her that the best way to handle Throk was to go on the offensive. Turning back, she looked straight into his eyes. Rather than stand there and be overwhelmed by that steady, unwavering gaze, she took the initiative. "How many of are you there?" she asked.

"Just me," he said.

"I mean, how many of the Prime Candidates are there?"

"Ah. I am sorry. That information is restricted."

"Why?"

"Because Minister Lione has restricted it."

"And why," she inquired, pushing steadily onward, "has Minister Lione restricted it?"

"Because he has," came Throk's answer. Disturbingly, it seemed a perfectly lucid answer to him, even though Senna recognized it for the simplistic circular logic that it was. It was because it was because it was because it was. Such a maddening mind-set could leave them there all day, going in circles.

"I do not understand," she said, making one last effort, "the need for restriction. Has he given you any reason, beyond that he simply desires to?"

"There is strength in numbers and strength in the element of surprise," he replied, startling her slightly that he was saying anything more on the subject. "To conceal the number of your troops gains you an advantage over those who would oppose you."

"But Throk," she pointed out, sounding almost hurt that such a notion would be entertained, "do you consider me an enemy?"

The fact that no answer was immediately forthcoming chilled her. For an instant he seemed like a beast of prey trying to decide whether to devour her.

"I consider you Senna. That is all."

"The lady Senna," she corrected him.

At this, Throk looked only momentarily surprised. "I was unaware that the emperor had conferred a formal title upon you."

"Neither the emperor nor I feel compelled to discuss all matters with everyone."

"The emperor should not keep such secrets."

"I do not consider it appropriate for you, Throk, to decide what counsel the emperor should and should not keep.

Furthermore," and her eyes narrowed, "considering that I cannot even get a straight answer out of you regarding the population of your little club, I do not see that you have much right to complain about such matters as secrecy."

He inclined his head slightly, and there was a mirthless smile there. "The lady Senna is quite correct."

It was then that a familiar voice came from behind. "Well, well . . . getting acquainted, are we?"

Senna stiffened when she heard the tone in Londo's voice. There was a hint of joviality, but she instantly knew it to be false. She had been residing for too long in the palace to think otherwise. She turned to find the emperor walking toward them, and his stride was very slow and very measured. There was none of the bounce in his step that she saw when he was in a good mood. "Yes, Highness. Apparently we are," she said. "Throk here says that he is your new valet."

There was a long pause from Londo and then, his voice sounding measurably forced, he said, "That is certainly my understanding, yes."

"And Dunseny is . . . ?"

Londo permitted the question to hang there for a long moment, and then all he said was, "Not."

Senna thought she caught, from the corner of her eye, a brief smile of satisfaction from Throk.

"I have been taking a bit of a stroll around the palace, Throk," Londo said. He walked up to the young man, arms folded, and continued, "I have not done so in quite a while, you know. I have tended to stick to several small areas in which I feel . . . more comfortable. But now I am taking a good look around, and you know what I am seeing? A goodly number of Prime Candidate uniforms with—and this is the most startling part—Prime Candidates inside them. Some of them even assuming positions of moderate authority, yes." He nodded to Senna. "You have noticed this too, have you, Senna?"

Truthfully, Senna had not. Lately she had not been paying all that much attention to what went on around her. Senna was old enough that she had outgrown teachers. But the participation that women had in Centauri society was sufficiently limited that she hadn't really been allowed that much else to occupy her time. A girl her age was usually primarily interested in finding a husband and seeking social status, but such things were of no interest to Senna.

So she had busied herself in continuing her studies, even though various scholars no longer sought to fill her head with knowledge. Instead she filled it herself, devouring every written word that she could get her hands on. Senna knew, in her hearts, that she was residing in a time of living history, so she felt compelled to familiarize herself as much as possible with all history that had gone before. She sought to delve into schools of thought, philosophies, all manner of things.

Now she realized that this had occupied so much of her time that, over the past months, she had barely been aware of the world around her.

She was also quickly realizing how unaccountably stupid such an attitude was. What good did it do her to learn of things past if she was remiss in applying her knowledge to things present. Still, one of the first rules of surviving in the present was never to let on what you did and didn't know, if you could help it. If knowledge was power, concealment of knowledge—or of the lack thereof—was more power.

"Yes, Highness. I did notice the . . . proliferation of the Prime Candidates," she lied boldly.

"And what do you make of that, eh?"

"That it remains difficult to find good help."

She wasn't quite certain what prompted such a snide retort, but it appeared to delight the emperor, who laughed raucously and declared, "Well said, Senna! Well said!" It did not, unsurprisingly, seem to amuse Throk in the slightest. Still, he was quite adept at keeping his feelings hidden. The only indication he gave that he had heard the comment at all was a slight thinning of his lips.

"She is quite the wit, our young lady, is she not, Throk?"

"If you say so, Your Highness," Throk said delicately.

"How nice." Just as quickly as it had appeared, the humor

vanished from Londo's tone, and he said with a dour harshness, "It is comforting to know that, in some instances, that which I say still carries weight. You may wait for me inside, Throk. I have some private business I wish to discuss with the lady Senna."

"Highness, I . . ." Throk reflexively began to protest.

But Londo did not tolerate it for so much as a microsecond. "It would seem to me, Throk," he said curtly, "that you do not have much future as an aide or valet if you cannot obey as simple an order as waiting in another room. Is it too taxing an ordeal for your Prime Candidate mind?"

Throk opened his mouth to reply, and then clearly decided that not only was a reply unnecessary, but it also bordered on the unwise. So he simply turned and entered the chambers.

The moment the doors slid shut, Senna turned to Londo and demanded, "Highness, are you actually going to let them get away with this?"

"Get away with what?" inquired Londo with a surprisingly placid look. "People come and go. Dunseny chose to leave."

"I don't believe that. Neither do you."

He laughed softly. "Did you know that, not all that long ago in the grand scheme of things, the people of Centauri Prime did not believe that our world was round?"

"Yes. I knew that."

"Did not believing that make the world flat?"

"No," she admitted, "but that is not the point . . ."

"Actually, Senna . . . it is." He placed a hand on her shoulder. "There are battles that can and should be fought, and there are battles that should not be. In the case of the former, let nothing stop you. In the case of the latter, let nothing start you."

"Are you saying—"

"I am saying that the world can be a greater classroom than anything in all the schooling you have received over the past few years. However, you have to pick and choose where the classrooms are, who the teachers are, and what lessons are worth learning. You understand, yes?"

"I . . . think so. You're saying . . ."

But he raised a finger and put it to her lips. "Ah ah ah," he remonstrated her. "In the classroom of life, this is a silent quiz, not an oral examination. Any thoughts you might have, keep them to yourself. Learn by doing, not by speaking." Apparently having said everything he wanted to say, Londo nodded in satisfaction, seemingly to himself, then turned to head into his private chambers.

And when the words came to her, they came out all in a rush. Though she would have done anything she could to stop them, she blurted out, "What are you afraid of?" She swore she could actually see the words departing her lips. She snatched for them, trying to retrieve them, but naturally that did no good. Londo turned again and fixed her with that steady, occasionally unblinking stare he often displayed.

To her astonishment, he replied, "The dark."

The simplicity of the answer caught her off guard, and then she said, "Well, Highness . . . that's not all that surprising. To some degree, everyone is afraid of the dark."

"True. Very true." He waggled a finger at her and told her, "But I am one of the few . . . who knows exactly *why* everyone is afraid of the dark. The others do not. If they claim they do, they are either remarkable fools . . . or remarkably knowledgeable. It will be for you to distinguish between the two."

"Me?" She was obviously confused. "What about you?"

"I?" He snorted. "I can barely distinguish between my various imperial vestments. How fortunate I am . . . to have Throk here to make certain I do not commit some sort of social faux pas."

"Yes. You have Throk," she said, unable to keep the bitterness out of her voice.

"He is an available young man, Senna, with interesting prospects. You could do worse, you know."

She couldn't quite believe what she was hearing. "Throk? You cannot be serious, Highness."

"Have you given thought to it, Senna? It is through a husband, after all, that women gain power in our society . . . attaching themselves to a powerful mate. It would be expected of you by this age. It would not be thought of as at all odd, were you to begin walking the corridors of power while appearing eager and interested in all that goes on around you."

"I'm not interested in gaining power, Your Highness."

"How intriguing," he said slowly, with a smile. "Aside from the kitchen staff, you may be the only person in this entire palace who is not interested in that." He gave it a moment's more consideration. "And I would not wager against the kitchen staff, now that I think about it."

"I wish Timov was still here," Senna said.

"As do I."

She looked at him askance. "They say that she was plotting against you. Was it true?"

"I do not know," he said, although she suspected from the quick flicker of regret in his eyes that he was not being entirely candid. "It is something of a shame, I suppose. To not be able to know who around you can be trusted."

"You can trust me, Highness."

"Yes," he said, but he sounded noncommittal. "There are many others, though. Throk, Durla, the other ministers. All with their own agendas, whispering among themselves, planning, discussing. Conversations to which I am not privy. It would be of great use . . . to know what they were saying. A pity such things are not possible. Well, good evening to you then, young lady."

"Good evening to you, Highness."

She watched him enter his private chambers, the door sliding noiselessly shut behind him . . . and she couldn't help but think that, somehow, he seemed a bit . . . smaller . . . somehow.

It was not until later that evening, when Senna had gone to bed, that Londo's words came back to her and the true meaning became clear. She sat up abruptly and was about to run directly to the emperor, despite the lateness of the hour, to see whether she had properly understood his meaning. Then she realized that to do so would be to undercut what it was he was asking, presuming she fully understood what it was he was asking. So instead she contented herself to lie back down, knowing that it would be a sleepless night as her hearts pounded anxiously in her chest.

Londo lay upon his bed, staring up at the ceiling into the darkness. As always, the darkness looked back at him. "You are there," he said abruptly.

There was a stirring from the wall nearby, and one of the shadows separated from the rest. The Drakh called Shiv'kala slowly approached, and then stopped several feet away. "We are always here," he said.

"I suspected as much. So . . . how much influence did you have in this, eh?"

"Influence?"

Londo propped himself on one elbow. "If Dunseny had not gone quietly, would you have seen to it that he met with an accident? Is that it?"

Shiv'kala laughed. It was the single most chilling sound that he was capable of making. When Londo heard it, part of him wanted to crawl all the way back to infancy and hide in his mother's womb, and even there he would likely find no shelter.

"The Drakh," Shiv'kala said, when his mirth had sufficiently passed, "care nothing about your hired help, Londo."

"You did not position Throk to be your spy, then."

"Do not be foolish. A keeper resides upon you. What further need have we for a spy?"

"I do not know," Londo admitted. "I do not know why you do much of what you do. And if I try to shine light upon you, in my search for answers, your very nature absorbs it."

"Your paranoia is flattering, but unnecessary . . ."

"In this instance," Londo added.

Shiv'kala paused only a moment, and then said, "Yes. In this instance. Minister Durla does not need our urging to keep an ever-closer eye on you."

"Durla. Your favorite. Your cat's-paw. If he knew . . ."

"If he knew . . . it would be no different."

"Then why not tell him?" asked Londo, with a hint of challenge in his voice.

"If you wish."

Londo was startled at that. "You will tell him? Tell him of the darkness that covers this world? Tell him that he is minister only because you put him into place? That he does not truly serve Centauri Prime, but rather the whims of the Drakh—servants for the most dangerous and evil beings the galaxy had ever known? That you even invade his dreams, sending him your bidding and allowing him to think that they are his notions?"

"Absolutely," Shiv'kala confirmed. Then his voice dropped from its normal, gravelly tone to just above a whisper. "And then . . . I will tell him of you. Of all that you have done . . . and will do. Of how he, Durla, has at least some semblance of free will . . . whereas you, monitored by the keeper, have none. That you are both the most powerful and the most impotent man on all of Centauri Prime. All this will I tell him. And every time he looks at you, you will know . . . that he knows. He will know you for the wretched thing that you are. Is that . . . what you desire?"

Londo said nothing. Indeed, what was there to say?

"Do you see," Shiv'kala told him, "how I protect you from yourself, Londo? Someday . . . you will thank me."

"Someday . . . I will kill you," replied Londo.

"It is good to want things," Shiv'kala said.

The door hissed open and Londo sat up, blinking in the light that was flooding in from the hallway. Throk was standing there, silhouetted in the brightness. "I thought I heard you talking, Highness. Is there an intruder?"

Londo half twisted to look behind himself. The area where Shiv'kala had been standing was completely illuminated by the corridor lighting, and there was no sign that the Drakh had ever been there at all.

"I am . . . simply talking to myself," said Londo.

"It sounded as if you were having an argument, Highness."

"I was. I suppose"—he sighed—"that is because I do not like myself all that much." He hesitated, and then said, "Were you standing outside that door this entire time, Throk?"

"Yes, Highness."

"And you did that . . . why?"

"In case I was needed, Highness."

And after he dismissed the Prime Candidate for the remainder of the night, he tried to determine who filled him with a greater sense of foreboding. Shiv'kala . . . or Throk.

## EXCERPTED FROM
### *THE CHRONICLES OF LONDO MOLLARI.*
### Excerpt dated (approximate Earth date) June 17, 2268.

Would that I could keep this journal on a regular basis. But I only feel safe making notations such as this one when my "associate" has lapsed into an alcoholic haze. Since I must consume the alcohol needed to accomplish this, it becomes that much more difficult for me to focus on what I am writing. I hope that future generations will be able to translate my handwriting. And I hope the reader will understand, sometimes I have to cover several months at a sitting, to the best that my occasionally strained memory will allow.

Senna.

I am so proud of her. It did not take her long at all to understand that which I could only hint at. Nor did she ever come back to me, after that veiled conversation, and outright say "You want me to spy on them! You want me to garner information where I can, through whatever means are necessary, and convey it to you! After all, I am 'only' a young girl, presumably looking for a man to whom I could attach myself. And men tend to speak liberally to those females whom they would like to impress."

No, she never questioned, but I knew. The way she looked at me at breakfast the next morning, there actually was a glimmer of excitement in her eyes. An excitement that bespoke an almost conspiratorial air, as if there was some great secret the two of us shared that neither of us dared speak. I could not guide her, of course. Clever girl, though . . . she figured it out all by herself.

Even more clever, she waited—took no immediate action. After all, it would have seemed curious if, after treating Throk so coldly, she had abruptly changed her attitude toward him. Throk may have been many things, but foolish he most definitely was not.

Instead she began slowly. It wasn't difficult; Senna and I habitually dined to-gether several times in the course of any week, and naturally Throk was always there. One evening, when Throk deftly refilled a glass of wine for me, Senna said—as if Throk was not there—"He's very attentive, isn't he."

The remark came out of nowhere. I had a spoonful of food lifted to my lips, but did not consume it. " 'He?' " I said. Then I saw her gaze flicker significantly to Throk, and naturally I understood. "Ah. You mean Throk."

Throk visibly perked up at that. He quickly covered it—I will credit him that. He was really somewhat masterful at internalizing anything that might betray his thoughts to an observer.

"Yet you would think," Senna continued smoothly, "that he would notice I, myself, have no wine at all."

"You do not customarily ask for it, Lady Senna," Throk said.

"A lady need not ask," she told him primly. "A lady is asked by others."

He nodded in acknowledgment of the point and held up the bottle. "Lady, would you care for—"

"I thought you would never ask," she said, and laughed very liltingly.

And I thought to myself, Great Maker, she was born for this. Then I remem-bered who her father was—the late Lord Refa—and I realized that, yes indeed, she truly was born for it. Considering her family tree, it was impressive that I had not yet wound up with a dagger between my ribs.

Then again, the day was young.

Having received her wine, wise girl, brilliant girl . . . she paid Throk no more mind. This no doubt convinced the young man that her comment had merely been a passing observation, a slight jest at his expense.

The next time we ate together, she actually engaged him in conversation. I was surprised—or perhaps not all that surprised, I suppose—that Throk was a bit more outspoken with Senna than he was with me. After all, any inquiry I made as to his background simply got me a respectfully terse reply. But for Senna, he proceeded to put forward what seemed to be his entire lineage. He boasted of his parents, both of them names that I instantly recognized.

Throk was of the House Milifa. Milifa was a member of Durla's circle of ac-quaintances, a group who had come to refer to themselves as the New Guard. I knew them, and their type, all too well. They had opposed Emperor Cartagia . . . but always from hiding. Whenever anyone had spoken of actually overthrowing Cartagia, or trying to do something about his insane rule that was destroying all of Centauri Prime, the House Milifa—along with any number of others—were the first to be the last. They were eager for a change, but even more eager to allow someone else to do what was needed to implement it.

Yes, I knew the type all too well. They only acted when they felt there was no risk of harm to themselves. Which meant that if Throk of the House Milifa was being put into position, and others of his ilk were coming in, then they considered the path to be a fairly obstacle-free one.

Since I was on that path, I was obviously not considered much of an obstacle.

Great Maker help me, they may very well be right.

I could, of course, endeavor to change their thinking, make them work harder to achieve their goals. But for the moment, I am content to let matters unfold as I watch. Let them bluster about, those who speak of how Centauri Prime must return to its destiny of greatness. In their hearts, they are bullies, who will only strike against their enemies once they are convinced that they can crush them completely, without any fear of retaliation.

Now that I think of it, this might be considered a fairly accurate description of me. Perhaps there is less difference between the new guard and the old guard than any of us would care to admit.

So Senna began paying more attention to Throk, and Throk was clearly rather pleased. Not only was Senna an attractive and vivacious individual, but Throk attained a bit more status with his fellow Prime Candidates when he appeared with the "young lady" on his arm. Senna was masterful, managing to keep him at arm's length while all the time making him think that he was worming his way into her affections.

And then periodically she would find ways to convey to me whatever it was she had learned. She would do it in the most casual of ways, saying, "Oh, you will never guess the latest gossip," and tell me in a lighthearted manner all sorts of information that was of varying degrees of use to me. Most of it was of little utility of course. Senna, being young and inexperienced, wasn't really capable of distinguishing what might be truly important. She could not cull the most pertinent information; it simply spilled out, and was left to me to sort it out.

This kept up for several months, and I took it all in. I began to feel like a spider in the middle of a web, watching insects flutter about and trying to determine what might be the tastiest morsel.

Recently, for example, she told me something that may be of tremendous use. Something that might very well enable me to manipulate Durla without his realizing it, and might actually enable me to bring Vir back here with a degree of impunity.

I have come to realize just how important Vir is to all of this. I remain surrounded, watched from all sides. With the addition of Throk to my retinue, and Shiv'kala hovering in the shadows, and the keeper attached to me at all times, I am the single most watched individual on all Centauri Prime . . . possibly in all the universe. Even for dear Senna, there is only so much that she can do. I need someone from outside, someone who can move about, someone who can provide a lifeline to the outside world.

A lifeline.

Interesting choice of words, since oftentimes I feel as if I am drowning in silence.

No matter. Vir shall come back, be free to come and go as need be . . . with Durla's blessing, more's the irony, if I manage this correctly.

In a way . . . a very small way . . . I regret pulling Senna into this morass of subtle espionage. For all her lineage and her teaching, she is still young and naive. But these are fearsome times in which we live, and perhaps I am doing her a favor after all. The sooner she learns to manipulate and deceive, the better chance she'll have of surviving. In fact, if she becomes truly skilled at such things, I might marry her myself. Marry her and then, of course, divorce her. That way she will fit in nicely with my other ex-wives.

# — chapter 6 —

Vir customarily came to the Zen garden on Babylon 5 for thoughtful contemplation. He did not normally stop by for the purpose of having a coronary. Yet, as it so happened, that was nearly what occurred.

It used to be that various individuals gave him a wide berth whenever they saw him. He was, after all, Centauri, and that was not a race that had a particularly positive profile with most others. It was, Vir supposed, understandable. After all, when one bombards another race's world into rubble, there's bound to be some fallout.

But Galen had been right; Centauri Prime had not replaced him as ambassador. Whether they were throwing him a bone or further punishing him, he could not say. The thing was, Vir had almost become accustomed to his status as an outcast. He had grown used to the fact that, although he was supposed to be the Centauri ambassador, he was in fact unwelcome at almost any diplomatic gathering. But then Mariel had entered his life, and things had turned around. Charming, vivacious, Mariel had gathered men to her with greater ease than a sun draws space debris into its orbit. And for a time, Vir had basked in her reflected light. Suddenly it had seemed to him that people looked at him differently, with a new sort of respect. When he passed people in the hall, they smiled, waved, clapped him on the back, and chuckled. Yes, they always chuckled, or laughed, and Vir took this as a sign of pleasure and happiness to see him.

They still chuckled and laughed. But now it galled him, for now he knew the truth. Now he knew that Mariel had been making a laughingstock of him, behind his back. When people looked at him, they saw only a fool.

Mariel had been around a good deal less lately, which suited Vir just fine. He knew that simply throwing her out, severing the relationship, would attract not only her attention but the attention of whomever it was she was reporting to . . . an unknown "chancellor," he had learned, although he didn't know which one.

The thing was, he had been so besotted with her that if he suddenly dispensed with the relationship, she would know something was up. He didn't want to take any chances, so he had settled for arranging to be elsewhere whenever she was around. Naturally, since she simply regarded him as a means to an end, she didn't really care that they kept missing each other. She did keep leaving video messages, clucking about how much she hated that lately they were little more than two ships passing in the night. *She's quite the little actress,* thought Vir.

Still, after months of playing the dodging game, Vir had tired of it. On this particular day, she was scheduled to return from wherever it was she had gone off to, and Vir had no desire to depart Babylon 5, to find somewhere where he could kill time. He was sick of killing time.

It was more than that, though. A cold, burning anger was being fueled within him every time another person on Babylon 5 smiled at him and asked how Mariel was. Even people back on Centauri Prime were interested in her. Senna, of all people, had sent him a message just the other day. It had been a chatty, gossipy message, which was odd considering that he couldn't remember the last time she had contacted him. It hadn't even been sent from within the palace; he could tell by the return frequency. It was from some independent, public communications outfit that anyone could walk in and use.

"I heard from a friend of a friend that you and Mariel are together," she had said. "How interesting. This friend of a friend told me that Minister Durla rather fancies Mariel himself. So you are quite the lucky fellow, actually getting the better of Minister Durla, because you know, no one ever does."

So even on Centauri Prime, where he was persona non grata, they knew of the damnable association. Little did they suspect that Vir's supposed romantic coup had actually cost him terribly. Whatever small bit of standing he might have had remaining to him had been damaged, probably beyond repair.

This knowledge made him want to get back at Mariel somehow. His upbringing told him that, given the circumstances, disposing of her wouldn't be out of line. Any number of dandy little poisons would suit the occasion perfectly. But he couldn't bring himself to pursue that avenue. It simply wasn't his style.

Then again, risking life and limb to destroy a mysterious Shadow base wasn't exactly his style either. Nor was assassinating an emperor, as he had inadvertently done with Cartagia. His style was changing so rapidly that he was having trouble keeping up with it. It was as if another Vir were running on ahead, leaving the original one to gesture helplessly and beg not to be left behind.

He wondered what he was becoming, and further wondered if it was anyone, or anything, he was going to like.

The Vir Cotto who had first come to Babylon 5 had been, in so many ways, a child.

"And all children grow up," he said tonelessly as he sat in the Zen garden, staring down at the sand beneath his feet.

"All children save one," came a voice, so close at his shoulder that he yelped. He jumped from the bench and turned to see who had entered so silently that Vir hadn't even heard him.

"Galen!"

The techno-mage inclined his head slightly in acknowledgment. "The same."

"What are you doing here?"

"Speaking to you. Your time is drawing near, Vir Cotto. And when it comes, you must be prepared for it."

"Prepared for it? Prepared for *what*?" Vir shook his head

with obvious incredulity. "Since techno-mages started advising me, I've had a woman come into my life, embolden me, love me—or pretend she loves me—just to put herself into a position to spy on others. What could I possibly do to prepare myself for that?"

"She used you. Everyone uses everyone, Vir Cotto. When you grow up, you will understand that, and be the greatest user of all."

"*There's* something to look forward to," Vir said dourly. Then he frowned. "Who doesn't grow up? You said—"

"Peter Pan. A Human boy who refused to grow up, and resided instead in a place called Never-never land . . . which you got to by going to the second star on the right, and straight on until morning."

"I don't have time for stories," Vir said impatiently. "You must want something. What is it?"

Galen rose and began to walk. Automatically, Vir got up and fell into step beside him. "You must return," Galen told him.

Vir didn't even have to guess at what he was referring to. "To Centauri Prime."

"Yes. There are forces bringing the world forward to a destiny it truly desires. For every action, however, there is an equal and opposite reaction. That is an immutable rule of the universe. You are to be the opposite reaction."

"Well, here's another immutable rule: I can't return there," Vir said flatly. "I have contacts there, yes, and I've been getting messages to them, and they to me. But you need someone who can walk about freely, who can move in high circles. I'm not that person."

"Yes. You are," said Galen. His eyes sparked with a flint-like precision. "You need to figure out how you can be."

"You figure it out. You have all the answers, after all."

"No," Galen said softly. "No techno-mage has all the answers."

"Really."

"Really." Then his lips thinned in what might have been a smile, although Vir couldn't be sure. "We do, however, have all the questions."

Vir rolled his eyes and shook his head. "I don't know what you expect of me," he said finally. "You're acting as if I have some real influence. At this point, the only influence I have is through Mariel."

"Is she not enamored of you? Would she not aid you?"

Vir laughed bitterly at that. "Mariel aids herself. She wouldn't . . . she . . . sh . . ."

His voice trailed off. An idea was beginning to trickle through him.

"Vir Cotto . . . ?" inquired Galen.

*"Quiet!"* If anyone had told Vir some years back that he would be telling a techno-mage to silence himself, Vir would have thought they were out of their mind. What was even more astounding was that the techno-mage did, in fact, shut up. He cocked his head with slight curiosity, but otherwise seemed more than content to let Vir's train of thought head down the track.

Vir was walking slowly, but his mind was leaps and bounds away. A flood of notions rolled over him. He turned quickly, half expecting to find that Galen had disappeared in the same way that his associates did. But Galen was still standing there, cradling his staff, watching Vir with what seemed to be cold amusement.

"Can you make her love me?"

Galen blinked in a vaguely owlish fashion. "Love."

"Yes."

"You."

"Yes."

The techno-mage said nothing at first. He didn't even move. He was so immobile that he might have had some sort of paralysis spell cast upon him, for all Vir knew.

"You want to control her," he said at last.

Vir nodded.

"You want me . . . to make her so enamored of you that she will do whatever you ask, whenever and wherever you ask, rather than take the slightest risk of upsetting you."

"Exactly," said Vir with grim eagerness.

"And you desire this . . . why?"

"You want me to be able to return to Centauri Prime. I've come to realize that she's the key to it. Londo knew it . . . Londo always knows," Vir said, shaking his head in grudging admiration. "And he got Senna to get word to me, probably because everything he says and does is carefully monitored. That's why she sent it from outside the palace. You would think that that alone would have tipped me off."

"You are a fool, Vir Cotto," Galen said softly.

"Maybe. But I'm a fool that you need." Vir was not about to let himself be intimidated, even by a techno-mage.

"You ask me to make this woman love you. I can do this thing. It is within my power. I can make her love you with such intensity that she will shatter every bone in her body rather than fail you."

"I think we can, you know . . . avoid anything that will call for self-mutilation."

"Indeed." Galen was thoughtful for a moment. "And will you admit to yourself why you have asked me to do this?"

"I already told you."

"No. No." Galen shook his head. He walked toward Vir then, and Vir was sure it was his imagination, but it seemed to him as if Galen was getting taller, wider, more impressive with every step. "That is what you have told me. The truth of it is, though, that you wish to punish her, and you see me as the instrument of that punishment. You do not wish simply to use her. You wish to humiliate her for your own personal satisfaction. It is unworthy of you, Vir Cotto."

"You're wrong," Vir said tightly. "And I don't understand you. You people, you techno-mages . . . you always talk in vague, prophetic, mystical, oblique ways. You don't stand there and psychoanalyze people right down to exactly why you think they do things."

"I save obliqueness for matters of galactic import," retorted Galen. "When I speak of foolish actions and foolish individuals, I tend not to talk in subtext. What is the matter, Vir Cotto? Was I too on-point for you?"

"You were wrong, that's all."

"So you say. And so you will keep saying, probably to your

grave." Galen sighed softly. "Very well, since it is the end we desire, I shall provide you with the means that you desire. But when you do return to Centauri Prime . . . it will be with this."

He held out his hand barely an inch from Vir's face, and there was a flash of light that made Vir jump back. At that, he saw Galen's face register grim satisfaction. Then Vir frowned as he saw a triangular, black device in Galen's palm. He couldn't be sure, but the way the light played across it, it seemed to be shimmering. "What is that?" he asked.

"Shadow technology," Galen told him. "Defies detection by any and all sensory devices you would care to name. Once you have returned to Centauri Prime, as you walk around the palace, or anywhere on the planet, this will supply readings that will inform me of Shadow technology on your Homeworld. The detection range is, unfortunately, limited—Shadows hide themselves quite well. So you will have to be on top of the Shadow tech for this device to work."

"And how will I tell you what I find?"

"You will not. The device will. Wear it anywhere on your person, and it will do the rest. And this," his hand flashed again, this time revealing a cylinder inside a small case no larger than Vir's thumbnail, "will enable me to contact you during the hunt. Insert it into your ear before you arrive on Centauri Prime. It will be undetectable. You won't be able to communicate with me, but I will be able to tell you where to explore if there are any readings that elicit further inspection."

Vir took the cylinder, tucked it into his pocket, then turned the triangle over in his hands. "You're looking for hard evidence that there are Drakh on Centauri Prime."

"We know they are there, Vir Cotto. What we do not know is how pervasive their presence is."

"Why can't you look for yourselves?"

"We have our reasons."

"How did I know you were going to say that," Vir said sourly. "So tell me . . . if there are Drakh . . . and they find me with this thing on me . . . what will they do?"

"Almost certainly, they will kill you."

Vir sighed heavily. "How did I know you were going to say that, too?"

"If they do kill you, Vir Cotto . . . you can take solace in one thing."

"Oh, really? What would that be?"

Galen smiled mirthlessly. "Mariel will mourn for you quite spectacularly."

And with that, he turned and left, his long coat sweeping across the floor and yet, oddly, stirring up none of the gravel that lay about.

Vir had consumed half a bottle of liquor when she arrived.

The damning thing about looking at Mariel was that, every time he did so, he desperately wanted to put aside all that he knew about her. He wanted to believe once again that, when she looked at him, he was all that mattered in her mind and hearts. That he wasn't simply some tool, a buffoon she was manipulating as adroitly as she manipulated everyone. He couldn't do so, however, and he fancied that—despite all her skill in covering what was going through that scheming mind of hers—he could now see the duplicity in her eyes.

"Vir!" she said quite cheerily as she placed her bags in the quarters that they had been sharing for nearly a year. "Vir, you're here!"

"Vir, Vir, Vir is here," he echoed, sounding more drunk than he had realized. Some of the words were slurred.

"It has been ages, darling," she said, and she reached down, took his chin in her hands and kissed him lightly.

Vir wondered when Galen was going to put the spell on her.

Then he looked into her eyes, really looked . . . and she was looking back at him in a most curious manner. It seemed to him, as paradoxical as it sounded, that her eyes were misting over and clearing at the same time. As if . . . as if she was seeing him for the first time . . . but seeing him only under very specific circumstances.

*Great Maker,* Vir thought, *he already got to her—*

And then she lay down on the bed beside him, began to do

things to him. Extraordinary things, and he felt as if he was having an out-of-body experience. Sensations pounded through him that he had only experienced in the vaguest of ways, in the most nebulous of dreams, and never did he think that there was anything like that in real life. Mariel was everywhere, and he twisted and turned, actually trying to get away from her, but it was impossible. There was no holding her back, no holding himself back. His entire body pounded as if there were too much blood in his limbs.

"I love you," she whispered in his ear, over and over again. "My dear, my sweet . . ."

He tried to push her away, but he couldn't muster any strength. He felt as if his mind was overloading, and finally desperation gave him power. He shoved Mariel off before it could go any further, and rolled off the bed. Scrambling backward to the nearest chair, he hauled himself onto it and looked at her, still curled up on the bed, now half naked. Her luminous eyes were full of love, and she started to move toward him once more.

"That's enough," he said. "Just . . . stay right there. Okay?"

She looked up at him, stricken. "Are you sure?"

"Yes. I'm sure." He stood and tried to pull his disheveled clothes together into some semblance of orderliness. It was everything he could do to focus on what was right and proper, given the situation. And part of his mind sneered at him and said, *Right and proper? You asked a techno-mage to brainwash the woman into loving you, justifying a petty revenge by claiming that it will end up benefiting Centauri Prime. You might as well take advantage of what she's offering you. You deserve it, and she'll delight in it.* But as quickly as that suggestion echoed through his mind, he blocked it out.

Was she truly brainwashed? She didn't have a vacant, thought-expunged expression. That had been a concern . . . that she would become vapid, mindless. He could see, though, that it wasn't the case. All the canniness, all the intelligence, all the craftiness that he had come to see and understand was still part of her—all of that was still intact. That came as

something of a relief, because otherwise she would be useless
to him . . .

. . . useless . . . to him . . .

He pushed that thought from his mind, as well, for he
didn't like what it said about him.

Yes, the intelligence was there, but the overwhelming emotion that radiated from her was pure adoration. He hadn't
planned for what had happened earlier. Some part of him had
found it hard to believe that the techno-mage could actually
do as he said he would. When Mariel first went for him, a part
of him still thought it might be some sort of prank. But the intensity of her fervor had swiftly disabused him of that notion.

He felt dirty.

He kept telling himself that he shouldn't. That, of the two
of them, Mariel was by far the one with far filthier hands.
This was a woman who had used sex and raw emotion as
weapons, mere tools in her arsenal. She wasn't deserving of
the slightest dreg of pity for having those tools turned back
against her. Indeed, she had gotten off lightly, for she didn't
know that that was what had happened to her.

Then again, it might be that it was her very lack of understanding that made the whole business so repellant to Vir.

He had had no intention of bedding her, no matter how
tempting the prospect seemed. He had instead planned to
keep her at arm's length, make her feel some of the agony, the
unrequited emotion he had experienced. Certainly the notion
had seemed most attractive when he'd first conceived it. Yet
now he was repulsed by its very essence. He had to seek out
Galen, get him to remove the spell. Restore her to normal so
that she could . . .

So that she could tear him down again. Lampoon him,
spread rumors about him, and make him even more ineffective than he already was.

He stared at her. It was exactly as Galen had said; clearly
the woman was ready to destroy herself lest she disappoint
him. A far cry, certainly, from what the conniving bitch had
been mere hours before. His hearts hardened against her, and
if he didn't like the way he felt at the moment . . .

Well . . . he would feel differently tomorrow.

"Do you not want to enjoy me, Vir, my love?" she whispered. "Shall I not show you how much I love you?"

The answer to both questions was yes, but with a determination and strength of will he did not even know he possessed, he managed not to answer truthfully. Instead he said, "I'm sure it would be a really okay experience . . ."

"Just okay?" Her disappointment was palpable. "Let me show you. Let me erase whatever doubts you might have and provide you with boundless—"

"What I want you to do . . . is not touch me for a while."

"Not . . . touch you?"

"That's right."

She looked stricken. "Not caress you? Not feel your firm flesh beneath my fingers? Not take your wiggling—"

"None of that," Vir told her. "There's, uhm . . . there's a lot of things I have to take care of for a while. I need to focus, and I can't be distracted by, uhm . . . romantic liaisons. So I need you to keep your distance."

"My distance? My . . ."

He shot her a look and she seemed to wilt. Very quietly, she said, "All right, Vir. If that is what will make you happy, then it will make me happy. I live for your happiness." She paused, and then said, "Shall I stay away from you at the party tomorrow?"

"Party?"

"The reception. For the Delgashi ambassador . . ."

"Ohhhh, right. Right." He hadn't paid attention to the social calendar, since he had been planning, until fairly recently, to be gone from Babylon 5 for a while. "No, you should not stay away from me at the party. In fact . . ." He started warming to the topic. This was the reason, he remembered, that he had Galen perform his little miracle. ". . . in fact, you'll show up on my arm . . . and be openly adoring . . . and when you work the room and talk to other ambassadors, you're going to tell them how great I am. How intelligent, how . . . how . . ." His mind raced, and then he said, ". . . how . . . everything I am. All my positive attributes."

"All of them? That could take a very long time, my love. We might be at the party much later than you had previously anticipated."

"That'll be fine," Vir replied, settling into the chair. "With any luck, we'll have all night and into the next morning. I can trust you to do this, Mariel? Because it's very important."

Mariel looked as if the breath had been knocked out of her. Her reaction was so extreme that Vir wondered for a moment if she were being seized by some sort of fit. When she managed to pull some air back into her lungs, she said, "I will be worthy of it, Vir. Worthy of it . . . and you."

"That would be fine."

"Would you like me to . . . ?" She raised herself from the bed and motioned significantly for him.

"No. No, that's quite all right," he said quickly, backing up and nearly toppling the chair as a result. "Just stay right where you are."

"Very well, my love." She arranged the blanket delicately around herself and sat there, perfectly still. Her eyes still large, she regarded him with open curiosity. "Would you not be more comfortable over here, my love?" She patted the bed next to her.

"No. Nooooo, no. No, I'm fine right here," Vir replied. "Comfy cozy."

"All right, Vir." She lay back down, but that adoring stare remained fixed upon him, and he watched until the lateness of the hour got the better of her. Her eyes closed slowly, but inexorably, in slumber. Vir was left alone in the room, and told himself that he had achieved some measure of revenge this night. That he had managed to take back some of that which had been taken from him.

By morning, the pain in his lower back also had something to say about it from a night spent upright in the chair. Mariel, however, was still asleep, and he watched the steady rising and falling of her breasts with a sense of wonder.

"What have I done?" he whispered, and for a moment he half hoped that Galen would magically appear, to answer the question. But instead there was simply her slow inhaling and exhaling, and the sound of his hearts pounding against his rib cage.

The reception could not have gone better, even in Vir's wildest dreams.

Mariel was her usual, animated self. No living soul could have detected any change in her demeanor and deportment . . . right up until she slapped the Drazi ambassador's aide.

Vir didn't see it happen, because his back was to the incident. He was standing at the bar, pouring another healthy draught. He was amazed, not for the first time, at how his alcoholic intake had jumped ever since he had taken over Londo's position as ambassador. Only a few years ago one drink alone would have been enough to reduce Vir to near incoherence. Two would have knocked him cold and left him with a roaring hangover the next morning. Now it seemed he had to drink several times his old levels just to feel any sort of pleasant numbness.

Behind him, he heard a fairly constant stream of chatter, which was customary for such gatherings. And then, with the suddenness of a blast from a PPG, he heard the unmistakable sound of palm across flesh. He turned, partly out of sheer curiosity and partly out of boredom, for no one had been going out of his way to strike up a conversation with him. He'd even been considering just calling it an early evening. He almost dropped his glass when he realized that the origin of the strike had been none other than Mariel. She was facing the aide to the Drazi ambassador, and her cheeks were brightly flushed with anger. The aide was gaping at her with undisguised astonishment.

"How dare you!" Mariel said, and she was making no effort to keep her voice down. There wouldn't have been much point, really. The sound of the slap had been more than enough to capture the immediate attention of everyone in the room. "How dare you speak so insultingly!"

"But you . . . he . . . Drazi not understand!" babbled the hapless aide, and Vir immediately knew what the problem was. This was unquestionably one of the many individuals to whom Mariel had spoken so disparagingly of Vir in times very recently past. Yet now she must have been singing his praises, as ordered, and the sudden change in her attitude had caught the Drazi—and no doubt whoever else was nearby him—completely off guard.

Immediately, trying to head off any kind of major confrontation, Captain Elizabeth Lochley stepped subtly but firmly between Mariel and the Drazi. "Is there a problem here?" the B5 station commander asked. Then, without waiting for an answer, she turned to Mariel, and added, "I don't take kindly to physical assaults upon diplomats. Well, on anyone, actually, but diplomats in particular," she amended. "Diplomatic incidents and little things like wars tend to develop from such unfortunate encounters. Care to tell me what provoked this?"

"He did," Mariel said immediately. "With his snide comments about Vir."

"You yourself said—" the confused Drazi started to protest.

"I myself? What does it matter what stupid things I may have said in the past?" she asked rhetorically. "What matters is the here and the now. And the simple fact is that Vir Cotto is the best man . . . the best ambassador . . . the best lover . . ."

Vir colored slightly at that, then noticed the newly respectful stares coming from everyone within earshot—which at that point was pretty much everyone. This eased his discomfort quite quickly. He even squared his shoulders and nodded in acknowledgment of his newly announced status.

". . . the best everything," Mariel continued. "I will not stand by and see him insulted. He is my love, he is my life." She went to him then and ran her fingers under his chin in a teasing, loving fashion. Vir smiled and bobbed his head affectionately while, at the same time, trying not to feel chilled to the bone. *She deserved it, she had it coming, just keep telling yourself that.* He couldn't tell whether his conscience was buying it or not.

Lochley led the Drazi away, and for the rest of the evening the various diplomats and ambassadors seemed to be reevaluating Vir. It was a delicate game. After all, they didn't know that *he* knew the damage Mariel had done to him. So naturally they tried not to let on, endeavoring to get a feel for Vir without letting him realize that they were doing so. Vir, of course, could tell immediately, and was doing all that he could not to let on that he knew. It was a bizarre sort of shadow dance, and Vir couldn't help but wonder how in the world he had been led onto the dance floor.

It finally reached a point where Vir couldn't stand it anymore. Rather than listen to Mariel extol his many virtues one more time, Vir excused himself and bolted into the corridor. He simply needed some distance, some time . . . and some firm conviction that what he had done was going to pay off in the long run.

His theory was quite simple: if Mariel could be so convincing with the members of assorted races, how much more likely would she be in handling members of her own species? Which meant that if he could get Mariel to start talking to the right people on Centauri Prime, he would be making his triumphant return in no time. The problem was still that he was going to have to figure out who the "right people" were. Londo was definitely not among them. He had, after all, been married to her. She'd been responsible for nearly killing him . . . "accidentally" utilizing a booby trap that she had purchased on Babylon 5. He had divorced her, for heaven's sake. So Vir was quite sure that Londo would be immune to her charms. And Londo had spent a good deal of his life—usually when he was fairly inebriated—regaling people with horror stories of what his wives had been like.

The thing was, Vir was quite certain that the great court . . . even the Centaurum itself . . . was being taken over by new, young, aggressive individuals. They brought with them a large degree of arrogance and self-certainty. Women were not held in tremendous regard within the Centauri power structure, and there was only a handful of exceptions. So no one was likely to consider Mariel a threat. It was that very lack of consideration that Vir could turn into an advantage.

Still . . . when he considered what she had become . . . what he had turned her into . . .

"Second thoughts?"

The question originated right at Vir's elbow, and he was so startled that he was positive his primary heart had stopped.

Galen was standing there, looking at him grimly . . . and even a bit sadly.

Vir automatically looked right and left, as if he were in the midst of a clandestine meeting. No one appeared to be coming, and Vir had a nasty suspicion that Galen had only shown up because there was no one around to see them together. At that moment, however, he didn't much care.

"How did you do it?" Vir asked immediately, without preamble.

"Do it?" Galen raised a mocking, nearly invisible eyebrow. "You mean stir her dedication?"

"Yes."

"I spoke to her."

"You spoke to her." Vir wasn't following. "What did you say?"

"Fourteen words. It takes fourteen words to cause someone to fall in love."

Vir wasn't quite sure he was hearing properly. "That's . . . that's it? Fourteen words? I thought . . . I figured there was some sort of device or something . . . gimmicks . . . technomageish things that reordered her mind or . . . fourteen words? Only fourteen?"

"As with all things in life," Galen told him, "it is quality, not quantity, that matters."

"If you . . . that is to say, if I . . ." Vir wasn't quite sure how to say it, and Galen didn't seem inclined to make it easier for him. "If at some point in the future, I change my mind . . . that is to say, she's not needed to be this way anymore . . ."

"Your resolve weakening already?"

"No," Vir said immediately. "No problems with that. Still sure, thanks."

"I am so pleased." He didn't sound it. "The answer is no. What's done cannot be undone. People say things, words they regret, and then announce, 'I take it back.' Words cannot be taken back, ever. Ever. That is why they should be carefully considered. Children have a rhyme: 'Sticks and stones shatter bones, but names can never hurt you.' They are children. What know they of the truth of things?

"You will always be her greatest priority, Vir. She will be able to function perfectly well in all capacities . . . but your well-being and interests will remain her paramount importance."

There was something in his voice, a tone, which was unmistakable. "You disapprove," Vir said after a moment. "You did what I asked you to . . . but you disapprove."

"I think . . . I liked you better when you stammered more. You had more charm." Galen gave that same chilling smile. "What you have done . . . what I did . . . was nothing less than robbing the woman of free will."

"And what she did to me? What was that?" demanded Vir.

"Ahhhh . . ." The exhale came from him in a manner that sounded almost like relief. "And there it is, finally as I said. You operate out of your injured vanity. That was your motivator."

"You didn't answer my question," said Vir, raising his voice slightly, but still keeping it at a respectful level. The last thing he wanted to do was get Galen angry with him, and speaking in a disrespectful tone might do exactly that. "When she had her free will, she used it to injure me, manipulate me. Is what I did to her . . . what I had you do to her . . . as bad as that?"

"No."

"You see? That's exactly the poin—"

"It's worse," he said, as if Vir hadn't spoken.

Vir had no answer to that, but merely scowled.

"Would you like to know the single greatest tragedy here?"

"Could I stop you from telling me if I wanted to?" Vir replied.

As if Vir hadn't spoken, Galen said, "Even I cannot create love from nothing. There had to be feelings, emotions already present. An ember that I could fan to full flame. Despite what you may have thought, Vir Cotto . . . the woman did feel something for you. Something deep and true. Given time, the feeling might actually have been genuine. But you will never know."

"I don't want to know. Love isn't high on my priority list right now," Vir told him with a bit more harshness than he would have liked . . . and more fervency than he truly believed. "In fact, considering the road ahead of me, I doubt I'd want it, or know what to do with it if I had it."

"Then perhaps I was wrong. Perhaps there are twin tragedies this day."

Once again, Vir said nothing.

"Good luck, Vir Cotto. You will need it," Galen said. He turned and walked off, rounding the corner of the hallway.

"Wait!" said Vir, heading after him. "I still want to know what—"

But when he followed Galen around the corridor edge, he discovered—to his utter lack of shock—that Galen was gone. By that point, he was becoming quite accustomed to the abrupt comings and goings of techno-mages . . . which wasn't to say that he was especially thrilled by them.

# — chapter 7 —

"Come meet us in the Zocalo." That had been the entirety of Mariel's message.

Vir wondered just who the "us" might be, even as he hurried to the Zocalo in response to Mariel's summons.

It had been a very strange month for Vir. Mariel had ceased her sojourns from Babylon 5. Instead she had remained primarily on the station, continuing to be her entertaining self. And all during that time, she had continued to talk up the virtues of Vir Cotto to whomever would listen. Fortunately she was able to do so in such a charming manner that she didn't make a nuisance of herself. Vir had total strangers winking at him, nudging him in the ribs. Zack Allan was back to telling him how Mariel was "all that and a bag of chips," an expression that continued to make no sense to Vir, no matter how many times he heard it.

Even Captain Lochley seemed to be regarding him differently. She said nothing to him at first, merely appeared to be evaluating him whenever he happened to be passing by. Finally Vir had gone up to her and said, "Is there a problem, Captain?"

"Problem? No."

"Then why do you keep acting as if you're . . . I don't know . . . sizing me up or something?" he had asked.

She had smiled slightly. "I apologize. I wasn't aware I was being that obvious."

"Obvious about what?"

"About wondering how such a mild, unassuming individual can . . . how did she put it . . ." In a fair approximation

113

of Mariel's voice, she intoned, " '. . . can reduce a grown woman to tears of ecstasy with one well-placed, gentle caress.' " Then she batted her eyelashes at him.

That was more than enough incentive for Vir to stay away from Captain Lochley.

It was an exercise in the surreal for Vir, considering that, although they continued to share quarters in order to keep up the appearance of the relationship, Vir never touched her. Mariel had seemed hurt at first, but finally she had complacently settled into the life, satisfied that the distance was what Vir truly wanted. And if it was what Vir wanted, that was more than enough for her.

In the night, as he lay upon the spare mattress he had obtained and tossed on the floor, he would hear her whispering to him, calling to him, like a siren of old, trying to tempt him. Galen's words kept coming back to him, and Vir felt as if he was doing penance for his deeds by depriving himself, while his body was screaming to him to indulge himself. *No one would ever know. She says you do it anyway. She wants it. You want it. What matter how it came to this pass. Seize the day, spineless one!* His inner dark side was quite vocal on the subject, while his conscience seemed disgustingly mute. This provided no end of irritation to Vir, who couldn't remember the last time he had had a solid night's sleep.

It had been a very long month.

"Come meet us in the Zocalo." Who could it be?

He hurried into the Zocalo, Babylon 5's most popular gathering place, and glanced around. A number of aliens waved at him and he waved back in an unenthusiastic but determined fashion, even as he continued to scan the room. He spotted Mariel in short order, and there was a Centauri seated across from her at a table. Vir couldn't see who it was, because he was facing away from Vir. But then Mariel pointed and the man at the table turned.

Vir's breath caught in his throat.

"Minister Durla," he said, trying to sound casual but unable to mask his complete surprise. "What an honor. I was unaware that such an . . . an esteemed person was coming to Babylon 5."

"These are dangerous times, Cotto," Durla told him. "I find it best if I do not advertise my comings and goings. The Centauri have too many enemies. We are hated by all."

As if on cue, a half dozen individuals, of varying races, walked past Vir and every single one of them greeted him warmly, or winked at him, and one of them playfully nudged him in the shoulder. There was something about the appearance of boundless virility that simply commanded respect. Vir wondered why that was, and realized he couldn't even begin to hazard a guess. It may have been the single most depressing realization he'd had all year.

"Vir is beloved by all," Mariel said promptly, apparently feeling the need to underscore that which assorted passersby had already made quite obvious.

"Yes. So it appears," Durla said, and although there was a smile etched on his face, there was no warmth in his smile, and a positive chill emanated from his eyes. "I was speaking to Mariel of this, and other matters. The lady Mariel used to be quite the social creature. However, apparently that is no longer the case. She says she is more than content these days to remain full-time on Babylon 5 . . . because of you, it seems, Cotto."

"The minister apparently came all this way to discuss my social calendar, Vir. Isn't that amusing?"

"I have pressing business not far from here," Durla corrected her archly. "I simply thought I would stop by and visit with our ambassador. And what better way to begin that visit than to discuss how our ambassador is doing in his post with the woman he calls . . . lover."

That was all Vir needed. Those few comments told Vir everything that he needed to know.

Once upon a time, Vir had been one of the most "obvious" of individuals, seeing nothing beneath the surface, accepting everything that was said to him. But during his time with Londo, and then on his own, he had learned that people rarely said what was on their mind. Indeed, oftentimes they said

anything but. Unlike Galen the techno-mage, the rest of the
world tended to converse almost solely in subtext, and Vir
had become quite fluent in the language.

He immediately assembled a series of inferences, all of
which seemed quite solid. He knew that Mariel had worked
in some sort of spy or information-gathering capacity. To
accomplish that end, she had made a habit of traveling to
assorted points of interest, and had culled assorted useful
tidbits from those with whom she flirted . . . or whatever it
was she was doing with them. But since Vir had become
the focus of her life, she had been relatively station-bound.
Since she reported to someone on Centauri Prime, that someone must have wondered why her patterns had altered so
drastically.

Vir was quite certain Mariel would have taken no time to
inform her contact of just exactly why she was staying put.
She would, naturally, be waxing eloquent about the wondrous
creature of light that was Vir Cotto. This would inspire an
even greater degree of curiosity.

Had she been reporting directly to Durla? Vir didn't think
so; in the recording Kane had provided him, as evidence of
her duplicity, she had been addressing someone as "chancellor." Durla was a minister at the time of that message, so
she had been speaking to an underling. Why, then, had Durla
come, instead of the underling?

Coincidence? Never ascribe to coincidence that which
could be attributed to a plan.

Besides, Vir already knew the answer. Senna had told him.
Durla had an interest in Mariel, and that was an interest Vir
could readily exploit for all that it was worth.

The man was taken with her. The minister Durla had some
sort of preoccupation with Mariel.

That was all Vir needed to know.

"Yes, yes, that's right," Vir said quickly. He slid into
the seat next to Mariel and draped an arm around her. She
seemed thrilled by the contact. She started to put her hands in
places she shouldn't, and Vir discreetly but firmly placed

them somewhere less inflammatory. "Lovers. My lover. Her and me. What can I say?"

"What indeed," Durla said coldly. In an obvious, and somewhat failed, attempt to lighten the moment, Durla continued, "I was just telling the lady Mariel that she is sorely missed back on Centauri Prime. For far too long has the court been deprived of her sparkling presence . . ."

"Tragic. Absolutely tragic," said Vir. He turned to Mariel and, taking a leap of faith, said, "Mariel, perhaps you should return to Centauri Prime. I know you've been out of the social whirl back home for quite some time." That was, in fact, an understatement. Mariel had been something of an outcast ever since Londo had divorced her. Although her presence on Babylon 5 had naturally precluded her being back on Centauri Prime, certainly she had been considered a pariah.

Fortunately for Vir, Mariel responded exactly as he expected. "What need have I for Centauri Prime when I have you."

"Nevertheless," Vir said, "Centauri Prime is home. To feel its soil beneath your feet, to breathe the good air of the Homeworld . . ."

"I couldn't *think* of going without you."

Perfect. It couldn't have been any more perfect if he had scripted it himself. He turned to Durla and said, with an air of tribulation in his voice, "What can I say? She wouldn't think of going without me. But I fear I'm somewhat . . . how shall I put it . . . I'm less than desirable to certain individuals on Centauri Prime, including—tragically—the emperor. So I reside here, in exile." He sighed so heavily he thought his lungs would implode.

"A true tragedy," Durla agreed. Vir waited. He knew the rest of the sentiment would be forthcoming, and he was absolutely right. "We should do something about that."

"But what can we do?" Vir said with total resignation.

"Yes, what can we do?" Mariel echoed.

"I am . . . not without influence," Durla said slowly. "It may well be that the ambassador's abrupt departure from our Homeworld may actually turn out to be nothing more than a tragic misunderstanding. Allow me to have a talk with the emperor. You are, after all, still our ambassador. You should be representing the greatness of our republic to others. But if you are kept in ignorance of that republic . . . if you can only come so close and no closer . . . your effectiveness is tremendously limited."

"That's exactly what I was thinking!" Vir said with a tone of wonderment. "You and I, we're thinking on the same level, Minister! Who would have thought?"

"Who indeed," Durla responded dourly, but he quickly brightened. "And of course, the lady Mariel would accompany you, I assume."

"Oh, naturally. Naturally," Vir said quickly. "That goes without saying . . . although, you know, it never actually hurts to say it."

"Yes. There are things that should always be said. For example . . ."

There was a long pause on Durla's part, and the break in the conversation caught Vir's attention. "For example?" he prompted.

"Well . . . we should always discuss our successes. And our failures as well. That way we can be candid with each other. We can all know where we stand."

"Candor is a good thing," Vir agreed. "I mean, after all, we're all on the same side, right? We all want what's best for Centauri Prime."

"Absolutely," said Durla. "For example, I had an archaeological dig that I was overseeing. Something that was providing jobs for many grateful Centauri. But the project seems to have fallen apart. It is, in short, a failure. Even a tragic failure, it seems." He lowered his voice and shook his head. "Lives were lost. A sad, sad thing. You . . . wouldn't know anything about that, would you . . . Ambassador?"

Immediately, Vir's mind was screaming. What did Durla know about Vir's presence on K0643? Had Renegar or Rem Lanas told Durla that Vir had been there? Did he associate Vir with the destruction of the Shadow base? Did he even know about the base?

Vir's impulse was to start talking, and keep on talking. That was what he had a tendency to do whenever he was nervous. But it had never been clearer to him than it was at that moment that he was going to have to change his method of operation. Clamping his teeth shut with a visible effort, Vir considered the situation, and decided that the absolute last thing he could do was give in to his primary impulse.

"What is there to know, Minister?" he asked.

"Perhaps nothing. Perhaps a great deal."

"Well," said Vir, steepling his fingers and fixing a calm, level gaze on Durla. "At such time when you have decided which it is, you can let me know and we can talk further on the matter. Isn't that right, Mariel?" he inquired.

He got the exact answer he expected. "Whatever you say, Vir," she said, smiling that high voltage smile at him. She turned back to Durla. "Is he not brilliant?" she asked.

"Brilliant," Durla agreed flatly. He rose from the table. "It has been a pleasure speaking with you, Ambassador. And I look forward to seeing you on Homeworld again as soon as possible."

"And I you, Minister." Feeling uncustomarily bold, Vir inquired, "That project of yours . . . I would hope that there are others to replace it, considering that apparently it has fallen through?"

"Oh, yes. Yes, there are always other options," Durla said. "I am always coming up with new concepts, new ideas."

"How fascinating." Vir leaned forward, all ears. "I've always wondered . . . where do great thinkers such as you get your ideas?"

Durla actually laughed softly at that, as if the question—or perhaps the answer—was very amusing. He leaned forward, resting his knuckles on the table, and said, "Dreams, Ambassador. I get them from my dreams."

"What a productive use of your slumber. Here, all I ever get is a good night's sleep," said Vir.

Durla's already thin smile became even more so. It was as if his lips were vanishing from his face entirely. "How very fortunate for you. Good day to you, Ambassador . . . my lady

Mariel." He took her hand and kissed her knuckles suavely, then turned and walked away.

Vir watched him go, never taking his eyes from him. Mariel, for her part, seemed to have forgotten the minister immediately. Instead, she was taken with the notion of returning to Centauri Prime. "Will it not be wonderful, Vir? You and I, in the thick of society. There I will be, with you on my arm, so proud. The proudest woman there. Everyone will look at us, and I can only imagine what they will say."

As it happened, Vir could imagine, as well. Londo would be chuckling over Vir's foolishness, just as Timov had displayed astonishment that Vir would take up with the potentially lethal woman. Durla would be watching for some crack in the relationship that would allow him to move in. Perhaps he wouldn't even wait. Obviously he had had designs upon Mariel for some time, and was only now feeling confident enough in his position of power to make a move. That very confidence might prove to be extremely problematic for Vir. And then there would be everyone else, who would likely wonder what the slightly buffoonish Vir Cotto was doing arm in arm with the emperor's cast-off wife. They might not necessarily hold Mariel in the same esteem that the diplomats on Babylon 5 did. Once they returned to Centauri, any number of possibilities presented themselves . . . none of them particularly pleasant.

She took his hand, then, and whispered, "Did I please you, Vir? Did I handle him in a way that satisfied you?"

He felt a twinge of guilt, and he thought of the things Galen had said to him. It made him feel small. Once again, he felt as if, after everything he had been through, he was little more than a plaything of the techno-mages. Only months before, he had felt like a galactic hero, fearlessly battling Drakhs . . . well, battling Drakhs, at least . . . and single-handedly destroying secret bases . . . well, single-handedly with help. Yet now he looked into Mariel's eyes, and felt smaller than the smallest of Centauri.

\* \* \*

That night, after settling into bed, he dreamed. It was a very short, but very stark dream. Mariel was simply standing there, looking at him, making no motion toward him. The top of her head was gone. From the headband up, there was nothing, as if a huge section of her brain had simply been removed. And there were tears rolling down her face. No audible sobs accompanied; there was just the wetness. He reached toward her to wipe away the tears, but he could get no closer to her. A distance behind her, Galen was there, shaking his head, but otherwise mute.

Vir startled himself awake. Across the room from him, Mariel was sleeping soundly. But something prompted him to draw close to her, and when he did so he could see that there were dried tears upon her face.

He sat back and pondered the notion that it took only fourteen words to get someone to fall in love with you.

Only fourteen words. It seemed like so few.

He leaned forward and whispered to Mariel, "I'm sorry."

Only two words. It seemed like more than enough.

But it was not. And he knew it. And there wasn't a damned thing that he could do about it except fall back into a fitful sleep, while trying to convince himself that what he had done was right. Unfortunately, there were not enough words in all the Centauri language to do that.

# EXCERPTED FROM
## *THE CHRONICLES OF LONDO MOLLARI.*
### Excerpt dated (approximate Earth date) August 1, 2268.

It was so simple.

Durla puts forward an air of utter confidence, but it is only an air. He has come too far, too quickly, you see. His position as minister was a gift to him from the Drakh, who perceived him as a useful tool for their assorted plans. As a result, he was thrust into his position with no experience in the ins and outs of court intrigue. He has learned quickly and well . . . but he is still learning.

I, on the other hand, could teach seminars.

Getting him to visit Babylon 5 was simplicity itself.

Secrets are the currency in which we all trade. Senna's little investigations, her chats and probes, had told me what I needed. The New Guard, namely Durla and his ilk, still had not quite grasped the notion that keeping certain things to themselves could only benefit them. But they were still relatively young and foolish, and so when they learned things about each other, they had a habit of speaking of it to one another. The more one speaks of things, the more likely those things are to reach certain ears.

Ears such as mine.

It had been during one of my routine meetings with Durla, to discuss upcoming public projects. He was, at that point, seeking approval for a new structure that was to be overseen by newly minted Minister of Development Lione, in conjunction with Kuto, the minister of information. The design for the structure was simple and elegant. It would be the tallest building in the area. It would loom like a great tower over the city, gleaming pure and white, and it would have no windows. To me, it sounded most claustrophobic, but Durla insisted that it was for the security and protection of those who worked within. "Spies are everywhere," he said to me with great significance.

This building was intended to house assorted offices and bureaus dedicated to the rebuilding of Centauri Prime, and to the service of the public. It was felt that, by making it so plainly visible, it would be a source of inspiration to all of Centauri Prime. It even had a name, a name which the perpetually avuncular Kuto had come up with during one of their brainstorming sessions. He dubbed it the Tower of Power, and it was a name that—Great Maker preserve them—stuck. Ghastly name, that, but they seemed pleased with it, and it was their eyesore, after all, so I suppose they were entitled to call the beastly structure anything they wished.

So there was Durla, in the throne room, and he was pointing out to me the beginning of the Tower of Power's construction. "It will point the way, Highness," he told me with confidence.

"To where?"

"To the stars. To our destiny. To the legacies that we will leave."

"I see. Of course," and I sighed heavily, "what good are the stars when one has no one to share them with, eh?"

It was a comment calculatedly conceived to snag Durla's attention, and it succeeded perfectly. He looked at me with curiosity. Normally I contributed very little to our "conferences." He spoke. I listened, and nodded, and gave approval to whatever it was he wished to do. We didn't chat or make small talk. So for me to say something vaguely approaching normal discourse was most unusual.

"How do you mean, Highness?" he responded curiously.

I sighed even more heavily. "We speak of legacies, Durla, but what do we mean, really? Is our legacy the achievements we strive for? The changes we make on Centauri Prime?"

"Absolutely," he nodded.

But I shook my head. "What you and I do here, someone else can undo when we are gone. We delude ourselves into thinking that we do something of permanence, but there is no certainty in that. No," and I waggled a finger, "the only true legacy for which we can strive is family. Loved ones. People to whom we will mean more than programs or building plans or imperial mandates."

"I . . . never thought of it quite that way, Highness," said Durla, but he didn't appear quite certain of what it was I was saying.

"I have no loved ones, Durla. My one wife will forever hate me . . ."

"But Highness, you asked me . . ."

"I know, Durla, I know. Do not be concerned; I am not attempting to blame you for the end of that relationship." I shook my head. "There were good reasons for doing what I did, and having you do what you did. I do not regret them. But she is gone now. I have no children. Daggair, one of my former wives, is skulking about, who knows where. And as for Mariel . . ."

He looked at me askance. I could see that I had finally caught his attention. Thank you, Senna. "What of her, Highness?"

"I understand she resides with my former aide. Amazing, is it not?" I shook my head. "He does not understand her as I do."

"What is there to understand, Highness?"

I waved dismissively. "Oh, you do not care about these things . . ."

"The female mind is always of interest to me, Highness," he said with as close to a smile as that wretched man was capable of achieving.

"Well," I said, rubbing my palms as if I was warming to a topic of great interest, "Mariel adores men of power. She is drawn to them. She sees Vir as such, I suppose, perhaps because of his connection to me. I am something of her nemesis, you see, and she will do anything to try to get back at me. That is the way such women are; they are obsessed with indulging their petty vengeance. Why," and I laughed at what I was about to say as if the very notion were absurd, "I would wager that if she could find a means of coming here to the court, to achieve some sort of success, then flaunt that success in front of me, why . . . she would be in heaven. Her heart would be filled to overflowing with joy . . . to say nothing of devotion to whatever man could put her into that position. Ach! But we speak of foolishness! I waste your time, Durla, when I am sure you have far more important matters of state to attend to."

"I . . . always have time to discuss whatever you deem worthy of discussing, Highness." He sounded properly obsequious in tone. Once upon a time, he had always had that tone. Of late, he had spoken with arrogance far more in keeping with his elevated level of self-importance. But in this particular instance, some of the old Durla was peeking through.

From that point, I gave it no more than ten days before he would travel to Babylon 5, to meet with Mariel. The thing was, I had no real idea of what would happen from that point on. The truth was, Durla was not Mariel's type. I knew that for a certainty. Powerful he may be, and Mariel is indeed drawn to powerful men, that much was true. But Durla was a puppet. He did not know it, of course.

But Mariel would have known. She had an infallible sense of what true power was, and her instincts would inform her that Durla was but a surrogate for some other person, or persons, who wielded the true power. Consequently, she would not be interested in Durla, possibly without even fully realizing just why she had no inclination toward him.

I knew that I was leaving a good deal up to Vir. I was giving him an opportunity, but that was all that I could give him. I was unsure of just what sort of true attachment Mariel might have to Vir, but I could only assume that it was artificial. Nor did I think that Mariel was likely to transfer her "affections" to Durla, unless she was absolutely positive that somehow it would bring her power.

So it would be up to Vir to realize that this was his means of returning to Centauri Prime. Durla would show up with a mission to find the means of bringing Mariel back, and Vir would have to find a means of not only causing that to happen, but of making certain he was part of the equation.

In a way, I suppose it was something of a test. Truthfully, I had no idea if he was up to it or not. But I had begun to believe, to some degree, in fate. If he were destined to return to Centauri Prime, then he would find a way. If it was not meant to be, why then, he would not.

So Durla went to Babylon 5, and Durla returned . . .

And today, Vir is returning to Centauri Prime, with Mariel on his elbow. They have already arrived at the palace and, by all accounts, she is utterly devoted to him. I have to admit: I am impressed. It appears Vir has outdone himself. It could be, of course, that Mariel is simply pretending, although why she would engage in such shenanigans is a matter of curiosity.

I could, I suppose, take some pride in his actions. Oddly, I am not sure whether I should or not. Any man who can wind up with Mariel professing undying devotion is a man that, perhaps, should be feared. I hope I have not done myself a disservice. It would be somewhat ironic if I wound up going to extra effort, just to bring a nemesis into my very backyard. After all, I had always thought that nemesis to be G'Kar. I wouldn't be expecting my greatest enemy to be wearing the face of a friend.

Then again, fate has a habit of making its own choices.

# — chapter 8 —

At first Gwynn couldn't be quite sure that she had come to the right place.

She made her way through the streets of Ghehana, one of the seamiest sections in all of Centauri Prime, and certainly the worst part of the capital city. She did so adroitly, masking her presence with practiced ease. It wasn't that she was invisible, but anyone who happened to glance in her direction simply didn't notice her; their gaze would have slid off her without registering any sort of actual presence.

It would not, however, serve in all circumstances. As confident as she was in her ability, the shadows stretched all around her in this particular section of town, and she found herself checking to see whether the shadows moved. This was not paranoia on her part. The Drakh seemed to move in and out of darkness with as much facility as their departed masters. She had the very disturbing feeling that the Drakh would have no problems discerning her being there at all.

She paused outside one building that had the correct address—she was supposed to find Galen here. She placed her hands against the front door and closed her eyes, reaching out. Yes. Yes, Galen was definitely within. She sensed mage energy that could only be originating with him.

The door, however, was locked. This provided an impediment for her for as long as it took her to say, "Open." The door immediately attended to her and opened. What was interesting to note was that the door was not an automatic one, and only three people present on Centauri Prime would have been capable of getting it open simply by telling it to do so. Gwynn was one, the other was inside, and for all she knew, the third might be, as well.

As it turned out, he was. Finian was standing right there when the door opened up, and he bowed to her with a sweep of his cloak. As annoying as his attitude could be sometimes, she had to admit that she was pleased to see him. The months after the passing of Kane had been hard on Finian, for they had been friends for many years, and Finian had not taken Kane's death well at all. He had been so despondent over it, in fact, that there had been some talk about his place within their society. Finally, it had been Galen who had spoken on his behalf, which struck Gwynn as curious. Galen had spent almost no time with Finian, had barely said ten words to him, as far as Gwynn knew. Yet he had spoken so passionately on Finian's behalf that the others had given the young mage adequate time to come around.

Apparently he had, although Gwynn thought she could still see traces of mourning in his eyes.

"Where is he?"

"No patience for niceties, Gwynn?"

"Good evening, Finian. Where is he?"

"Upstairs."

Gwynn followed Finian up a narrow flight of stairs, which creaked under her feet. A smell of moisture wafted through the air; something was leaking somewhere. She could also hear vermin scuttling around within the walls. This wasn't exactly where she would want to establish her summer home.

At the top of the stairs, she had to duck slightly under a low overhang and step over a puddle, and then they emerged into a small room where Galen was seated. Hovering in front of him was a holographic display that was constantly shifting, and it only took Gwynn a moment to realize that it was some sort of point-of-view device. In Galen's hand there was a small, black object, which was glowing softly in the dimness. She recognized it immediately as a recorder. It was taking in all the images from the display.

"Is he in?" she asked.

Galen nodded. "Nothing untoward so far, however. Still, the evening is young."

"Unless he's caught. Then the day is over," Finian pointed out.

"He knew the risks," Gwynn said.

Finian's eyes narrowed. "And if he does, what of that? Are we then not to be concerned? Tell me, Gwynn, just how cold are you, anyway?"

Gwynn's temper flared and she did her best to pull it under control. "Now listen to me, Finian . . ."

"A better idea," Galen's sharp voice cut in, "is if you both be quiet." He was studying the holograph. "Vir . . . nothing so far. Keep as you are, though. If I see something that requires further investigation, I will instruct you. Do you understand?"

The holographic image moved up and down once. Vir must have nodded.

There was silence for a moment, and then Gwynn said softly, "He's quite brave, actually."

"He does what needs to be done," said Galen. "No more, no less."

"As do we all. Which reminds me, Galen . . . how transpire things with the *Excalibur*? Does the captain there . . . what is his name again?"

"Gideon."

"Does he know that you are here when you are not there?"

"No. Nor, I should think, would he care. Given the situation on Earth, he has more pressing matters to concern himself over than my whereabouts."

There was silence for a time, as the holographic view continued to change. Then it stopped. Vir had come to a halt. Galen leaned forward and said intently, "Vir Cotto. Can you hear me? Is everything all right?"

No response.

"Vir," Galen prompted again, this time with just a touch more urgency. "Vir, are you . . ."

Suddenly the image moved again, swiftly side to side. It was as if Vir had jerked his entire body. Then the image started moving again, indicating that Vir was once more underway.

It was the first time that Galen had allowed any of the tension he must have been feeling to show. He sat back and let out an unsteady sigh, then pulled himself together and went back to watching the holographic representation with all the emotion of a statue.

Then, so softly that she could barely hear herself, Gwynn said, "Do you think anyone suspects what Vir is doing? What he is up to?"

"If they do," Galen replied slowly, "then he is very likely dead."

"Does he know that?" asked Finian.

Galen looked at him levelly. "Let us hope not."

And suddenly, Galen sat upright, as if galvanized into action.

"Vir!" he said sharply. "Don't go in that room! There's something there . . . some terrible danger!"

But the holographic image started to shift again. Vir wasn't doing as Galen instructed; instead he was heading into the very room Galen had just told him not to enter.

"He can't hear me," Galen said.

"They know. They must know," said Finian. "And there's nothing we can do to save him."

Even before Gwynn arrived at her destination, Vir found himself back at court. It was bustling and active, exactly as he remembered it. There was a gathering being held in the Great Hall, and it seemed to Vir that Durla and his associates certainly enjoyed partying.

It was somewhat disconcerting for Vir to realize that virtually every familiar face was missing. Lords Teela and Surkel, Minister Dachow, High Minister Sulassa . . . even old Morkel was gone, and Morkel had been there forever. Morkel had managed to survive even Cartagia, and that was a formidable challenge in and of itself. Now they were gone, every one of them, replaced by individuals who obviously knew one another, and all of whom were quite friendly with Durla.

Durla, for his part, seemed extremely interested in determining that Vir and Mariel were having a good time. He

brought person after person, minister, chancellor, assorted
Prime Candidates, all before Vir and Mariel in a steady pa-
rade of faces and names so dizzying that Vir knew he'd never
be able to keep them all straight.

Mariel, for her part, remained her charming self. Whatever
stigma had been attached to her being a cast-off of the emperor seemed to have dissolved, mostly because it was clear
that Durla was making every effort to make certain that
Mariel and Vir were part of the in crowd. It seemed to Vir that
Durla was determined to let Mariel see just how respected
and powerful he, Durla, was.

Vir was finding it hard to quibble with the treatment they
had received thus far. When they had received the summons
from Centauri Prime, stating that the emperor was willing to
set aside his "differences" and welcome Vir back with open
arms, Vir had been of two minds. He had been pleased, since
it meant being able to return to the planet that had given him
birth, and there was certainly that sentimental attraction for
him. It also meant that he would be able to accomplish that
which he had promised Galen he would accomplish. He
would be able to see for himself just how pervasive, if at all,
the Shadow influence was on Centauri Prime. He knew there
was *something* present, certainly. After all, Londo's disagreement with him had come from his mention of a name, a single
name—Shiv'kala. Obviously that was a name associated
with something dark and fearsome that Londo did not wish to
have spread about. That alone was enough to support the notion that something frightening stalked Centauri Prime.

Londo had still not made an appearance, and Vir was beginning to wonder if he was going to do so at all. After all,
despite Vir's suspicion that Londo was the guiding hand or-
chestrating his return, he had no real proof. If there was one
thing Vir had learned, it was that he could not possibly know
Londo's mind for sure. In many ways, Londo had long ago
become a stranger to him. Every so often Vir saw flashes of
the man he had once known, but only flashes. It was as if that
man was a beacon of light, enveloped by darkness and only

able to peer out for the briefest of moments before being enveloped by the shroud once again.

"You are Vir Cotto?"

He turned and saw an individual whom he had witnessed in action on vid, but not seen in person. "Minister Vallko. Yes, I'm . . . that is to say, right. I'm Vir Cotto."

The minister of spirituality looked him up and down for a long moment. He was a head shorter than Vir, and yet Vir couldn't help but feel as if the minister towered over him. "A pleasure," he said at last.

"To meet you, too. I've seen some of your meetings. Your prayer meetings, I mean. You're very persuasive. Very powerful speaker."

Vallko bowed slightly, but he did so without breaking gaze with Vir. "I am but the instrument of the Great Maker. What humble gifts I possess come from him."

Something that Galen had said to him months before returned to him. He had liked Vir better when Vir stammered. Since that time, Vir had come to a realization: others would very probably like him better that way, as well. In recent years, Vir had found that his thought patterns had become clearer, more laser-sharp. If he so desired, he could put forward a very polished and confident face. But that might very well put people on their guard, and it was probably going to be better for Vir if people thought that he was a bit of a bumbler. Better to be underestimated than overestimated.

So when he addressed Vallko, he played up the hesitancy in his speech. "That's very, uh . . . humble," Vir said. "Self-effacing and, well . . . everything else."

"Thank you," Vallko said again, and Vir could see assessment filtering through Vallko's eyes, which were cold and appraising. "It helps that we are all of one mind. We all care about what is best for Centauri Prime."

"Absolutely," Vir said, his head bobbing furiously.

"What do you think is best?"

Vir's head stopped bobbing. He noticed that one or two other ministers appeared to have slowed in their glide around the party and were giving an ear toward the conversation. "Me?"

"Yes. You."

Vir sensed the trap being laid for him. He laughed, and then smiled wanly. "What I think is best is whatever the Great Maker thinks is, you know, best. And me, I don't . . . you know, I think that there are others much more, you know . . . that is to say, qualified . . . to decide such things. So I'm more than happy to listen to their advice. Like you. People like you. What is in the interests of the Great Maker, do you think? Does he, you know . . . talk to you directly, by the way? Like, a huge voice from all over . . . or does he, I don't know . . . write to you. Drop you a line. How does that work, I'd really like to know." He stared at Vallko with open curiosity, obviously anticipating some deeply intriguing response.

Vallko laughed softly as if he'd just been told something quite amusing. "I am not blessed enough to converse directly with the Great Maker. I divine my knowledge from those to whom he has spoken. The greatest, wisest of us. And there are . . . feelings," he admitted, apparently grudgingly. "I have feelings of what the Great Maker would like for his people, feelings that I convey to the followers."

"And you have a lot of followers," Vir said admiringly.

"They are the followers of the Great Maker. I am merely his vessel."

"Well, that's . . . that's nice," said Vir, apparently at a loss for words. He just stood there, seeming to have nothing more to offer to the conversation.

Vallko looked him up and down once more, and then made a small *hmmf* noise that certainly sounded to Vir as if he was being dismissed. Then Vallko inclined his head slightly and walked off, the other assorted courtiers following suit, leaving Vir to his own devices.

He saw Senna over in a corner, surrounded by assorted Prime Candidates. He remembered Throk from one of his previous trips to Centauri Prime. The lad had grown by at least half a foot, and he seemed even more forbidding than when Vir had first met him. He also seemed to be paying a good deal of attention to Senna, who was playing and being charming to several of the Candidates. She cast a very quick glance in Vir's direction, and he had a feeling that she would have given anything to break away, but that didn't seem possible. She gave an almost imperceptible shrug and then looked back to Throk, who was babbling on about something that Vir couldn't begin to discern. Throk's attention was taken from Senna at only one point: when Mariel walked by. She didn't appear to notice him, but he reacted to her passing with a sort of goggle-eyed stare before pulling himself back into the moment and returning his attentions to Senna.

"You will never have a better time."

The voice was in his head and Vir jumped slightly. He had forgotten that he had inserted the listening device into his ear, but there came Galen's voice, loud and clear. Galen, of course, was correct. No sign of the emperor, none of the guests was paying him any particular mind. If he felt like strolling around the palace, now was when he should do so.

"Okay," murmured Vir, before remembering that it wasn't a two-way audio link. He checked to make sure that the small triangular recording device was still in place, just under his coat, and then—trying to look as casual as possible—strolled out of the great hall.

He strode up and down the palace corridors in a rather aimless fashion, trying his best to look as casual as possible. He hummed a tune to the best of his recollection, although he suspected that he was botching most of the notes. He walked into this room and that room, as if he were giving himself an extended guided tour. He heard Galen's voice in his head from time to time.

"Vir . . . nothing so far. Keep as you are, though. If I see something that requires further investigation, I will instruct you. Do you understand?"

Vir, to indicate compliance, bowed at the hip, to mimic the shaking of a head. Then he kept moving.

He had gotten to sections of the palace that he had never before been in. At one point he heard footsteps, moving with swift, sure strides. Guards. No one had specifically told him that he wasn't supposed to be there . . . but then again, no one had specifically told him it would be okay.

He glanced around nervously, then saw a large statue to his right. It was Cartagia, of all people. The sight of the emperor whom he had assassinated caused his hearts to skip a beat. The statue was a remarkably powerful, lifelike rendition, superbly carved. The demented smirk was so perfectly rendered that he was certain it had been carved in life. But it had been defaced, someone having scribbled words across the chest. At least, Vir thought it was words, but he didn't recognize them. It said "Sic Semper Tyrannis."

The footsteps were drawing closer. Vir backpedaled and took refuge behind the statue, trying to will himself to be even thinner than he already was. His mind was already racing, trying to determine a cover story. If he was found, he could always say that he had been inspecting the back of the statue for any further damage.

Around the corner they came: two members of the Prime Candidates. Vir could see them clearly from where he was positioned.

Their faces were remarkably slack. The look on them was almost supernatural, as if their minds were elsewhere. Then, right as Vir watched . . . a change passed over their expressions. Their tread slowed, and they looked at one another as if seeing each other for the first time. They glanced around, apparently a little puzzled as to why they were where they were. One shrugged, as did the other, and they continued on their way. They were so caught in their personal moment of befuddlement that neither of them afforded the slightest glance in Vir's direction. He had no idea what to make of what he had just seen.

He started down the corridor once again. He wasn't sure why it should be so, but he felt himself feeling colder. It was purely in his imagination, though—he was sure of that. But he wasn't entirely certain why . . .

Certain why . . .

Why . . .

The next thing he knew, there was a voice in his ear saying, "Vir Cotto. Can you hear me? Is everything all right?"

At first, Vir said nothing. It was as if he had to remind his body to respond to the commands from his brain. Something had completely blanked him out.

"Vir," and Galen's voice was sounding more concerned than before. *It's nice to know he cares,* Vir thought mirthlessly. "Vir, are you . . ."

He still wasn't moving, however, and it was with tremendous effort that he pushed himself forward. His feet felt tremendously heavy, but each step took him farther and farther, and soon he was walking with—if not confidence—at least some degree of surety.

He wasn't sure if it was his imagination again, but it seemed to him as if there was less and less light. What in the world was going on, anyway? It was as if he'd entered a floating black hole.

There was a room off to the left. He glanced in. Nothing. Another room to the right, and still nothing. Every step, though, it was becoming harder and harder to focus. He realized belatedly that the two young Prime Candidates had come from a cross-corridor, and had not actually been in this particular section of the palace at all.

Every nerve in Vir's mind was telling him that he would be well advised to get out of there. But he was concerned that he might not have such an ideal opportunity again. He had to keep moving, had to hope that he was going to be able to pull this together—whatever "this" turned out to be. He suddenly wished that he had a weapon on him, which would have been an interesting experience for him considering that he'd never used one before.

He suddenly realized that he wasn't hearing Galen in his ear anymore. Perhaps the techno-mage simply had nothing to say.

Then he saw the door.

His eye had almost gone right past it, which was curious in and of itself. Given that this was the palace there was nothing extraordinary about it. It was a large double door, decorated with elaborate carvings around the edges. It seemed to have a slight reddish tint to it, although Vir couldn't be certain whether that came from the door itself or was just some sort of trick of the light.

He studied it for a long moment, waiting to see if there was any response from Galen.

Nothing.

The chances were, then, that it was perfectly safe. Either that or Galen wanted him to go in and see what was what.

Once upon a time, Vir would have hesitated. Indeed, he might very well have headed in the opposite direction entirely. But he had been through too much at this point in his life to be afraid of something as benign as a door. Besides . . . he was invincible.

Still . . . even invincibility didn't mean that one couldn't exercise a reasonable amount of caution.

He placed one ear against the door to see if he could hear anything.

It felt like ice.

He pulled his head away, momentarily concerned that the door was so cold that his ear was going to stick to it. It pulled away from the door easily enough, but the sensation had been extremely disconcerting.

"What's going on here?" he wondered out loud. The door was antique, with an elaborate handle on it. It didn't slide open and close automatically like most of the doors in the newer sections of the palace. In a way, Vir felt as if he was stepping back into another time.

He gripped the handle firmly.

In his entire life, Vir had never been as close to death as he was at that moment.

Galen did not panic. Never came close. But he immediately turned to Gwynn and Finian, and said, "We have to get word to him. Have to stop him."

"If we go in, the Drakh will know we're there," Gwynn said flatly. "They were able to detect us within the Shadow base, and that was in unfamiliar territory. They've had several years to lace the palace with detection devices. They'll know the moment we're there."

"We have to do something! Look!" Finian said, pointing at the holographic representation still floating before them.

There was the shimmering outline of the door. And on the other side of it was a distinctive outline—that of a Drakh. There was something else beyond the Drakh, something else in the room that was great and dark and pulsing, and Gwynn couldn't make out at all what it was. But she knew one thing for sure: within seconds, Vir was going to see it, and it would be the last thing he ever saw. For the Drakh, from his body posture, was clearly poised and ready to leap upon Vir the moment the doomed Centauri set foot within. It figured that the Drakh wouldn't simply lock the door in order to prevent intruders from entering. Anyone who was curious enough to intrude into that area was someone the Drakh wanted disposed of.

"There's no time. They have wards against us," Galen said.

"What?" Galen's words were stunning to Gwynn. "They've actually erected wards?"

But Galen wasn't talking to her. Instead he was leaning forward intensely, as if trying to get through to Vir with sheer force of will. He saw Vir's hand entering the holo image, reaching for the handle to open the door. "Vir!" he shouted. "Vir . . . back away from it! Do not go in there! Hear me, Vir! *Vir!*"

*"Vir!"*

Vir froze in place at the unexpected voice that seemed to explode within his head. He turned and blinked in surprise, like an owl in the full glare of daylight. "Londo?"

The emperor of the great Centauri Republic stood at the far end of the corridor, and it was impossible for Vir to tell what was going through his mind. Was he about to erupt in fury over Vir's presence in this part of the palace? Would he lecture him over his involvement with Mariel? Would he demand to know why Vir had dared set foot back on Centauri

Prime when it had been made quite clear to him that the best thing for him to do was stay off the Homeworld for good?

Londo approached him slowly, swaying slightly. Vir tried to determine whether he was drunk, but he didn't think so. Then he realized what it was: Londo was out of breath. It was as if he'd been running from some other point in the palace to get to Vir before . . .

. . . before what?

Vir wanted to glance back at the door, but something stopped him from doing so. He wasn't quite sure why, but he didn't want Londo to realize that he had almost entered there. Or perhaps . . . perhaps Londo already did know. It was so hard to say for sure. Nothing seemed certain anymore.

Londo slowly strode toward him, and Vir braced himself, uncertain of what was about to happen. And then Londo covered the remaining distance between them with quick, urgent steps, and he threw his arms around Vir in a hug so forceful that Vir thought it was going to break his ribs. "It is good to see you," he whispered. "It is very, very good." He separated from him then and gripped Vir firmly by the shoulders. "You," he said decisively, "should always be at my side. That is the way it was meant to be with us, yes?"

"Well, now, I don't know anymore, Londo," Vir said slowly.

"You do not know? Why?"

Londo had a firm arm around Vir's shoulder, and he was starting down the hallway, away from the door. Vir had absolutely no choice but to fall into step next to him. "Well," Vir said reasonably, "the last time we saw each other, you told me that we had separate paths to walk, and we should walk them from a distance. And right before that you knocked me cold because I said . . ." He felt Londo's fingers suddenly clamp onto his shoulders with such force that, with a bit more strength, his arm might find itself dangling from the socket. ". . . because I said something you said I should never say again."

The grip eased, ever so slightly, on his shoulder. "That is

correct," said Londo. "But that was last year, Vir. Things change."

"What things have changed, Londo?"

"Have you not noticed? You've had time to mingle here, I take it. Meet and greet all of the various ministers and political heads of Centauri Prime. Certainly you must have some observations to make regarding them, yes?"

"Well . . ." Vir paused. "Putting aside the fact that I don't know any of them . . ."

"Ah . . . that is not a fact that I would put aside so quickly, Vir. There are no familiar faces anymore, Vir. And those faces that are there . . . they seem to look right through me, as if I were not there. Do you know what, Vir? When enough people look at you as if you are not there . . . do you know what happens next?"

"You . . . stop being there?"

"That," sighed Londo, "is unfortunately absolutely correct. I am not looking to you to be here all the time, Vir." He stopped walking and turned to face Vir, and this time when he took him by the shoulders, it was almost in an avuncular manner. "But your last visit was so unfortunate, so tempestuous . . . I just want you to feel that you can come and go here as you please. That you will not be a stranger here."

"If that's the case, why didn't you simply invite me back here? Why all the subterfuge?"

"Subterfuge?" Londo raised an eyebrow. "I'm not certain exactly what you mean."

There was a hint of warning in his voice, and Vir immediately realized that he had erred. He wasn't sure why or how. It was just the two of them. There was no one else around, as near as Vir could see. Londo didn't even have a retinue of guards following him. So it wasn't as if they had to watch everything they said. Then again . . . how could Vir know for sure? There might be spy devices planted anywhere and everywhere. Why not? After all, he was carrying a device on him that—at that moment—was feeding information directly to Galen.

So if he went into detail as to the little bits of information that Londo had been feeding him, he might very well betray all Londo's efforts, to someone who was listening in on their every word.

The slightest flicker from Vir's gaze to Londo was enough to let the emperor know that he understood. Out loud, however, Vir said mildly, "I suppose 'subterfuge' isn't the right word. I suppose what I'm asking is, why didn't you just come right out and say so."

Londo nodded ever so slightly in mute approval. Without saying a word, they had said everything. The rest was simply for the benefit of whomever else might be listening.

"It is not simply for me to say," Londo answered him. "There are many considerations that must be made these days. For all the power that I wield, there are others whose feelings must be considered."

"Others such as Durla," Vir said hollowly.

Londo inclined his head slightly. "Durla is minister of security. You, Vir, seemed on quite friendly terms with Timov. We know what happened with her."

"But that's—"

Londo didn't let him finish. "And let us not forget that you are stationed on Babylon 5."

Vir wasn't following. "So?"

"So you spend a good deal of time associating with members of the Alliance. They are rather pervasive on Babylon 5, after all. I think—and this is purely my speculation, mind you—I think Durla does not entirely know where your loyalties lie."

"My loyalties?" Vir actually laughed bitterly at that. "Londo, the people on Babylon 5 regard me with suspicion because I'm Centauri. If it weren't for Mariel charming all of them, none of them would even be speaking to me. As it is, even with their speaking to me, I know they still don't trust me. Perhaps I should tell Durla that . . ."

"Oh yesss. Yes, you do that," Londo said with heavy sarcasm in his voice. "You go right to Durla and tell him that the Centauri ambassador to Babylon 5 garners no respect and is not trusted. That is certain to elevate your stature here at court."

He knew Londo was right about that, but wasn't entirely sure where to take it from there. "So . . . so what do you suggest?"

"You are here, Vir. For now . . . that is enough. Durla seems inclined to tolerate your presence here, and that should be enough to keep the situation stable for the time being. From what I understand, Mariel is working the same magic here that she was able to perform on Babylon 5. We have a new court, you see. The stigma attached to her, as a discard of the great Londo Mollari, seems far less problematic for all the new faces presently inhabiting the court. We should not be surprised over that, Vir."

"We shouldn't."

"No. Because, you see, the Centauri have no sense of history. There was a Human who once said 'Those who do not listen to history are doomed to repeat it.' You know," and he chuckled softly, "for a backward race, those Humans certainly know what they're about."

"Did a Human say those words scribbled on Cartagia's statue?"

They had passed the statue only moments before, and Londo cast a glance behind him, even though the statue was out of sight. His eyebrows knit a moment in confusion, and then he remembered and smiled, showing his pointed canines. "Ahhhh yes. Yes, they did. I wrote them."

"You?" Vir couldn't help letting his surprise be in evidence. "You did?"

"Yes. I wrote them in honor of you . . . our answer to Earth's Abraham Lincoln. Oh, wipe off that innocent look upon you, Vir. Did you think I wouldn't find out? Helping to save the Narns. Do you think me entirely without my own resources, Vir?" He made a scolding, clucking noise with his tongue. "You must think me the greatest fool on Centauri Prime."

"Oh, no, Londo!" Vir protested. "I don't!"

"It's all right, it's all right," Londo told him. "In all likelihood, it's an accurate enough assessment. The point is, Cartagia died at your hand. And part of you . . ." His voice softened. "Part of you died that day, too. Yes?"

"Yes," Vir said softly.

"Well . . . when Abraham Lincoln died, his assassin called out, 'Sic semper tyrannis.' It is an old Earth tongue called Latin. It means 'So is it always with tyrants.' Anyone who is a tyrant can look forward to similar unhappy endings. Words for us both to live by. For me . . . and for you . . . when you are, eventually, emperor."

"The prophecy," Vir sighed. "Sometimes I wonder whether to believe it. Sometimes I wonder whether to believe in anything."

"I stopped wondering about that a long time ago."

"And what was the answer you came up with?"

"Believe in nothing," Londo told him. "But accept everything."

Vir laughed bitterly at that. "And if you do that . . . what? You'll live longer?"

"Oh, Great Maker, I hope not," sighed Londo. "But it will make the time you are here that much more tolerable."

Minister Castig Lione threaded his way through the courtiers and got to Mariel's side. She was deep in pleasant conversation with several others when he placed a hand on her arm and said, "Lady Mariel . . . if I might have a minute of your time?"

"For you, Minister?" She smiled that dazzling smile that could bring most mere mortals to their knees. "Two minutes."

She draped an arm through his elbow and together they moved off from the crowd. Castig Lione guided her, gently but firmly, to his office in another wing. Because of his great height he had to bend somewhat to do so, but he managed to accomplish the task and still look less than foolish. The moment his office door was sealed behind them, he turned to face her with a grim expression on his face. "Would you mind telling me," he said briskly, "what you are playing at, milady?"

"Playing at?" She looked genuinely puzzled. "I do not understand, Minister."

"You, Lady Mariel," and he stabbed a finger at her, "are supposed to be working for this office. You are supposed to be reporting to me. Instead," he said with arch sarcasm, "you appear to be spending most of your time under Ambassador Cotto."

She didn't come close to losing her composure. "Are you implying I am not doing my job, Minister?"

"No, I am not implying it. I am coming right out and saying it. The amount of valuable information you have been turning in regarding the Alliance has dwindled. Need I remind you, milady, that this office is serving to keep your account at a healthy level. You would do well to remember that, unless you believe that Ambassador Cotto's personal fortune will be enough to sustain you."

"Vir is not a rich man, Minister, and furthermore I resent—"

"I resent this game you are playing, Lady Mariel," Lione told her flatly. "Cotto was simply supposed to be a cover, a means to an end. Yet you seem to have lost sight of that and become genuinely enamored of him. That is not tolerable."

"A woman's heart cannot be regulated by memos and mandates, Minister. It's high time you remembered that."

"And it is high time you remembered, milady, that Vir Cotto is—"

"Is not up for discussion, Minister. That aspect of my life is personal."

"A personal life is a luxury you cannot afford to have, milady," Lione shot back.

"As long as I am associated with you."

"Correct."

"Very well," she said with a small shrug. "Then I will resign, effective immediately."

"It is not that simple, milady," Lione said.

"It is for me."

"No. Not for anyone." His voice became low and—most frighteningly—friendly. "You are a spy, Lady Mariel. There are those who would not be pleased to know that their confidences have been leaked to this office. I assure you that I can make certain, with no hint of connection to this office, that some of those individuals find out just what you have been up to."

Mariel glared at him, her jaw steely and twitching. "You would not dare."

"Yes. I would. Tell me, milady . . . how long do you think you would survive then, eh? You and your beloved Vir Cotto. I would not care to take those odds."

She was silent for a long moment. "What do you want?" she finally asked.

"What you do in your own time is of little interest to me, milady. But I want more of your time devoted to me. I want it to be as it was. If it is not," and he smiled, "then it will not be anything. And neither will you. Is that clear . . . Lady Mariel?"

"Perfectly." Her grimness of expression was a marked contrast to Lione's.

"Good. Enjoy the rest of the party, then. And I shall look forward to hearing from you . . . on other matters."

It was the laughter that followed her out that most angered Mariel, and she resolved to make certain that Lione paid for his arrogance at the earliest opportunity.

# — *chapter 9* —

It was early the following morning, and few were stirring within the palace, when Vir quietly made his way out. The one thing that had made the evening slightly bearable was the fact that, when Vir had gotten to the quarters assigned to Mariel and him, Mariel was already asleep.

There was something different about her, he noticed. Usually she appeared utterly relaxed, sleeping the slumber of those who are content with their lives and all the decisions therein. But there was something about her this night that seemed . . . taut. Something was on her mind, and Vir wished that there were a way of climbing into her head and seeing what was in there.

Perhaps Galen could—

No. He pushed that notion straight out of his head, even as he worked his way down to Ghehana.

Despite the ungodliness of the hour, the streets and sidewalks of the seamier side of Centauri Prime were bustling with a variety of individuals with whom Vir would be very happy to have no association whatsoever. Some of them glanced his way, but Vir took care not to make eye contact with anyone. It was a childish notion, he knew, the thought that as long as he didn't actually look at someone, they couldn't harm him. The very idea was enough to make him laugh over the absurdity of it. Except he didn't feel like laughing.

He knew exactly where he was supposed to go, the address having been whispered in his ear. Shortly after Londo had walked with him back to another section of the palace, Galen's whispering had started up within his ear once more.

He thought it might be his imagination, but Galen sounded ever so slightly rattled, and even a bit relieved. This actually wasn't a pleasant impression to have. If something had occurred that was enough to disconcert a techno-mage, Vir was rather daunted to think that he might very well have been in the middle of it.

He tried to ignore the steady smell of the area around him. There had been rain earlier, and there were still thick globs of dirt and mud on the streets, which Vir had to do his best to step around. He realized that, if he was going to make any sort of habit of coming down to Ghehana, he was going to need special shoes . . . or, at the very least, shoes he didn't particularly care about.

Someone broke off from the darkness as Vir approached his goal, and for a moment he assumed it to be one of the techno-mages. But instead, it was a surly individual, who eyed Vir balefully. He said in a low, wine-soaked voice, "Give me money."

Vir stopped in his path. "I . . . don't have any money," he said cautiously.

The next thing he knew, there was an object in the man's hand, and he was advancing on Vir. "Find some," he rasped.

Vir's instinct was to run. And then, for no reason that he could readily discern, he suddenly realized that he wasn't afraid. All he felt at that moment was annoyed. The thought of everything that he had been through, all the emotional turmoil that he'd sustained, steeled him. He stopped backing up and instead stood his ground. "Get out of here," he said sharply.

The somewhat drunk and belligerent Centauri who had been advancing on Vir paused, looking confused. Vir realized that he must have looked like fairly easy pickings, and the would-be assailant couldn't understand the abrupt change in Vir's attitude. "What?" he said, sounding rather stupid.

"I said get out of here. I have better things to do than waste time with you."

There was the unmistakable sound of metal sliding from a

container, and a sharp blade emerged from the handle in the man's hand. He said nothing more, but came straight at Vir.

Vir backpedaled, but not from fear. Instead, he crouched and scooped up a large handful of dirt and mud. He threw it with a strong sidearm toss, and the thick sludge landed in his attacker's face. The man coughed, blinded, and waved his hands around as if he were capable of gripping handholds floating in the air. Vir, meantime, did not hesitate. He stepped quickly forward and swung his right fist as hard as he could. His knuckles collided with the man's chin and Vir immediately realized that bone striking bone was an extraordinarily stupid idea. His fist seized up and convulsed in pain, and he let out an agonized yelp. His attacker, however, wasn't in a position to hear it, for he went down, apparently unconscious before he even hit the ground. The knife that he had been wielding clattered to the cracked pavement.

A full thirty seconds passed, Vir rooted to the spot. Then he began to tremble as he just stared at the man lying senseless a few feet away. The anxiety of the moment caught up with him, and it was frightening, but it was also exhilarating.

"Nothing like fighting for your life to make you appreciative of it, eh?"

He turned and found Finian standing nearby. The knife was in Finian's hand. He was looking at it, apparently studying his reflection in the blade, which was long and straight. "Nice weapon. Do you want it?"

Vir automatically started to say no . . . except he heard the word "Yes" come out of his mouth.

"Ah. Vir Cotto, hero. Play the role . . . to the hilt," he said dramatically, and he handed the weapon over to Vir, handle first. Vir moaned softly at the pun, but nevertheless retracted the blade and slipped the knife into the inside pocket of his coat. "Come," Finian continued. "This way." With a small smile, he added, "I am pleased that you are here. I feel so much safer now."

Vir let the remark pass. Instead, he followed Finian toward a building, briefly affording a glance at his erstwhile attacker.

Odd. His assailant had seemed so big before, somehow. Now he appeared pathetic. And Vir . . . Vir felt tall.

He followed Finian into the nearby structure, and up the narrow steps to a landing where Galen was waiting for him. Galen was simply standing there, holding securely onto his staff and watching Vir with glittering eyes. Gwynn was nearby, her gaze flickering from Vir to Galen and back again.

"You are alive," Galen said. He seemed mildly surprised. For obvious reasons, this did not elevate Vir's spirits. He turned and entered a room.

"Shouldn't I be?" asked Vir, following. He wasn't entirely sure he wanted the answer.

"It was a near thing," Galen told him. "Look."

The holographic image that had been generated via Vir's recording device hung in the air in front of them. His eyes went wide when he saw the creature skulking on the other side of the door that he had been about to open, and another shadowy shape beyond. He could feel all of the resolve and confidence that he had accrued from his encounter outside, and all of it was leaking away from him as he stared, transfixed, at that . . . that . . .

"Shiv'kala." The name suddenly came to him. He looked to Galen for confirmation.

But it was Gwynn who answered. "Quite possible," she said, "although we cannot know for sure. That, however, is not the most disturbing image you will see."

"That isn't?" The notion that there could be worse than that was almost too much for Vir to take. When he thought of how close he had been to mindlessly wandering into the middle of that . . . that Drakh nest . . .

He felt anger bubbling within him, but he wasn't entirely sure where to aim that anger. At first he wanted to direct it at the techno-mages for thrusting him into the midst of the danger. Then he wanted to unleash it instead at Londo, who had helped to foster an atmosphere in which these . . . these creatures could skulk about. "What could be more disturbing than that?" Vir demanded.

"Do not ask questions, Vir . . . to which you do not really

want the answer," Galen replied, but his hand was already moving. It passed through the holographic image, which now was replaced by another, more familiar image than the creature lurking behind the door. There was Londo, bright, smiling, or at least forcing himself to smile. Coming toward him with arms outstretched and cheer etched on his face and . . .

And something else.

Vir leaned forward, not quite sure what it was that he was looking at. "What . . . *is* that?" he whispered.

There was some sort of fleshlike curve on Londo's shoulder. The view of it, however, wasn't as clear as the rest of Londo's image in the picture. Londo drew closer, and now it came into clearer relief. It was like some sort of . . . tumor or . . . something. Vir shook his head in confusion.

"That . . . lump? Is it . . . is it some sort of illness? Why didn't I notice that before?"

"It is a kind of illness, yes. A sickness of the soul, implanted by the Drakh," said Gwynn, speaking with an intense grimness.

"It is called a keeper," Galen told him.

"A keeper? It's . . . *called* something? What do you mean? That thing's not alive, is—"

And then the keeper was looking at him. Its fleshy exterior stirred, as if from a sleep, and its single, malevolent eye opened and looked straight at him.

Vir let out a shriek of terror. To his own ear it was a pathetic sound, weak and womanish, but he couldn't help it. It was reflex. He backpedaled, his legs going weak, and Finian caught him before he fell. A few minutes earlier, he had brazenly faced off against an armed opponent, and patted himself on the back for his stalwart action. Yet now he was screeching and running from something that wasn't even there.

Except it wasn't simply the image of what he was seeing. It was seeing it perched on the shoulder of someone whom he had once trusted.

And two words went through his head: *Poor Londo.*

"Wh-what does it do? Does it control his actions? Read his mind?"

"In a manner of speaking. It does not superimpose its will upon him . . . but punishes him in a way that can make refusal to cooperate very . . . uncomfortable," Gwynn told him. Her voice seemed to be dripping with disgust; the creature clearly appalled her no less than it did Vir, though she was handling it with a bit more equanimity. But only a bit, which Vir derived some cold comfort from. "Nor does it read his mind . . . but it reports his actions to the Drakh. It is merged with Londo, bonded. It will be with him until he dies."

It happened so quickly that it took Vir completely with-out warning. Staring into the single eye of that monstrosity, think-ing about what it must be like for Londo to have that thing permanently attached to his body—never being alone, never a moment's peace—a wave of nausea swept over him that would not be denied. He felt his gorge rising and stumbled over to a corner of the room. There he heaved until no contents remained within his stomach . . . including, he sus-pected, a few pieces of the lining. He gasped, revolted at the smell on the floor near his shoes, and then he stepped back. He couldn't bring himself to look directly into the eyes of the techno-mages, so ashamed did he feel. When he did glance up, Gwynn was looking away; Finian appeared sympathetic, and Galen's face was a mask of unreadability.

It was as if clearing the food from his stomach helped him to focus his thoughts, oddly—and disgustingly—enough. He took a slow, shaky breath and didn't even bother to apologize for his loss of control. After all, what was there to say about that? Instead he said, "That . . . thing . . . the keeper . . . can it be affected by alcohol?"

"Affected?" said Gwynn, looking slightly confused. Vir had a feeling she hadn't expected anything approaching a co-herent sentence out of him at that moment, much less a fully formed thought.

"Affected. Impeded. If Londo drinks enough . . ."

"Yesss . . ." It was Galen who spoke. "Yes. The keeper would be susceptible to it. The emperor would be able to operate with a relative amount of privacy."

"And it would probably take less to get the creature drunk than it would Londo," Vir mused thoughtfully.

It was all becoming clear to Vir. With the mental picture of that frightening, single eye seared into his brain, it was as if he was suddenly seeing the past with true clarity. Things Londo had said, attitudes, passing comments . . . they all made sense now. And . . .

And Timov . . . well, that was obvious, too, now, wasn't it. She *had* to be gotten rid of, forced to leave. Vir's belief that they were becoming closer hadn't been his imagination after all. That had been what prompted her precipitous departure. Londo must have engineered it, doing so not because he truly wanted her to depart, but because he was concerned over her getting too close. What sort of true intimacy could anyone develop with a sentient pustule seated upon one's shoulder, observing every moment of intimacy?

All of Londo's actions were comprehensible . . . and pitiable . . . and . . .

Great Maker, what had Londo gotten himself into?

"Could they have implanted the creature against his will?" Vir asked hollowly.

Galen shook his head. "No. He may have had trepidation about it . . . but ultimately, the bonding can only occur when the recipient is willing to allow it to happen."

What hold could they possibly have had upon him? How could they have forced him to endure such an invasion of his body, of his mind? Could it be that he actually welcomed it? Vir found that inconceivable. Londo had too much pride. To permit a creature whose perpetual presence would remind him that he was nothing but a puppet of shadow-dwelling monsters—there was no way that Londo would have welcomed such a thing.

And if they did force it upon him in some way, how horrific must that have been for him? To stand there, helplessly, while that . . . that thing was bonded to him, for life . . .

Vir had no idea what to feel. Suspicion, fear, horror, pity, all warred for dominance in him.

"I have to talk to him," Vir said. "I have to let him know that I know. I have to—"

"Are you that eager to be a dead man?" Galen asked bluntly.

"No, of course not, but—"

"Acknowledge the keeper, you doom yourself. It is your choice."

"Galen is correct," Finian said. He did not look unsympathetic to Vir's plight, but it was clear that he was firmly in Galen's court on this. "Look what happened to you with the passing mention of Shiv'kala, one of the Drakh. If you let Londo know that you are aware of the keeper's presence, the Drakh will likely not let you draw your next breath."

"It was one of your kind who told me to mention Shiv'kala in the first place. And you almost sent me wandering straight into a death trap in the palace," Vir said hotly. "How nice to know that you've suddenly started worrying about my welfare. Why? Because you think you're going to need me for something else, as well?"

"We did not intend for you to wander into a death trap," Galen said. "We lost contact with you. Undoubtedly due to interference by the Shadow tech. I regret the inconvenience."

"Inconvenience! If I'd walked into that room, I would have been dead!"

"And we would have been inconvenienced," Galen replied levelly.

"Ha. Ha. Ha," Vir said, making no effort to hide his lack of amusement at Galen's retort. Then he turned back to the holograph which had shifted angle. Londo had draped an arm around Vir's shoulder as they walked. And there, from this new perspective, Vir saw the keeper even closer than before. There it had been, mere inches from his face, peering at him with that unblinking, unnatural eye, and he had not known. He could feel it now, boring into his brain . . .

"Shut it off," Vir said.

"It will be instructive to observe the—"

*"Shut it off!"*

Galen stared mildly at Vir for a moment, then waved his hand slightly and the image disappeared.

No one said anything for quite some time. Finally, it was Gwynn who stepped forward, and said to Vir, "You begin to understand what we are up against."

"What we've seen here," Finian pointed out, "is only that which a cursory examination of the palace was able to uncover. There is likely much, much more. The Drakh infestation goes straight to the heart and soul of Centauri Prime."

"A heart that is clotted. A soul that is blackened," said Vir. He was shaking his head, scarcely able to accept what his own eyes had seen and what he knew now to be absolutely true. "Do I tell Londo? Go on a drinking binge, put the keeper out, find a way to tell him I know?"

"Absolutely not," Gwynn said forcefully, and there was shaking of heads from the other two techno-mages, indicating their agreement. "The situation is not only as bad as we feared, but worse. We had been holding out hope that, with you serving as a positive influence upon him, Londo could be won over to our cause and help to eradicate the Drakh. We know now that cannot possibly be the case."

"Absolutely correct," Finian confirmed. "Londo cannot be trusted. It's that simple."

"It's more complicated than that," Vir shot back. "Despite everything that's gone on—in fact, now that I know the truth, it's more like, *because* of everything that's gone on—Londo is my friend. He—"

"He cannot be trusted," Galen said, indicating that the subject did not warrant discussing.

"It's not just a matter of trust. We need to help him."

"You wish to help him? Kill him."

The cold-bloodedness of Galen's suggestion was horrifying to Vir. "Kill him. Just like that," he echoed with incredulity.

"Just like that, yes."

"I, personally, don't expect you to do that, Vir," Gwynn said with a glance to Galen, "but, in many ways, you would be doing him a great favor."

"Forget it. He's my friend."

"He's their ally. That is all that matters."

"Not to me, Galen. Not to me," he said with fiery strength in his voice and growing contempt for the techno-mages. "You know what? You know what? In a lot of ways, you're no different than the Drakh. Hell, no different than the Shadows. You use people for your own ends, and you don't give a damn who gets hurt as long as your goals are accomplished."

"We are more like our enemies than we care to admit," Galen said, which surprised Vir somewhat. He hadn't expected any sort of confirmation of a sentiment spoken mostly in anger. "Nevertheless, there are . . . differences."

"Such as?"

"We have more charm, and we're better dancers," Finian offered.

Everyone stared at him.

"I thought the moment might benefit from a bit of humor," he said.

"Would that something humorous had actually been said." Gwynn sniffed.

"Fine, then," Finian said, obviously annoyed that his moment of levity had been so soundly rebuffed. "So what do you suggest we do?"

"The information must come from someone trustworthy," Galen said thoughtfully, stroking his chin. "There are those who will not trust anything associated with a techno-mage. There is one reasonable course of action. I shall tell Gideon. He, in turn, will convey what we have learned to the Alliance, where—"

"Where they can bomb us into nonexistence?" said an alarmed Vir. "They'll learn of something Shadow-related existing on Centauri Prime, assume the worst—"

"Probably a safe assumption," Gwynn said.

Vir pointedly ignored the comment, and continued, "—and the bombs will start dropping again. And this time they won't back off until they've flattened us."

"Sheridan, then," suggested Finian. "Gideon trusts Sheridan. If he—"

"Not Sheridan. Not Gideon. Not nobody," Vir said with an

air of finality. "This is an internal problem on Centauri Prime. So we'll handle it internally. That's all."

"There is far more at stake here than that," Gwynn made clear to him. "We're not talking about some low-level politician lining his pockets with graft. We are speaking of an entire race using Centauri Prime as its stronghold, with a biologic weapon perched on the shoulder of your world's emperor . . ."

"That's right. My world. *My* world," Vir said in no uncertain terms. "And I will attend to my problems on my world, and we will keep them that way. I don't want others catching wind of this. If they do, it'll be a bloodbath, and I will not be a part of that."

Gwynn appeared ready to square off and go head to head with him, possibly on matters of priorities, or possibly just to have the opportunity to beat the crap out of him. But the slightest touch of Galen's hand on her shoulder stilled her. Vir wondered whether Galen was simply quite persuasive, or whether there had been some ensorcellment employed. Galen looked him up and down, and finally asked, "What, then, will you be a part of, Vir Cotto?"

"I won't turn against Centauri Prime."

"You have to do something. You cannot simply walk away from what you have seen here."

"I'll keep an eye on things. Keep myself apprised. Learn what there is to learn, make certain that things don't go too far . . . or if they do, then I can . . . I can . . ."

"Then you can what?" said Galen.

"Then I can make them go back to the way they were."

Galen shook his head. He did not look particularly convinced, and Vir couldn't entirely blame him. He didn't sound especially convincing. But he spoke with a conviction that he was not entirely certain he felt. "Look, the fact is, you need me."

"Do we?" There was cold amusement reflected in Galen's eyes.

"You said it yourself. You need me to put something together. I can do that, but it will have to be done slowly. It's obvious now that I can come and go as needed."

"Coming and going may be insufficient."

"Then what would be sufficient, Galen?" demanded Vir in exasperation. Before the techno-mage could say anything, he suddenly put up a hand. "No. Never mind. I know what to do."

"What?"

"It's enough that I know. Let's leave it at that."

"Let's not," Galen said firmly.

Their gazes met, and Vir knew that Galen wasn't about to let this go. It was obvious that the techno-mage was not happy at all with the notion of simply keeping covered up the darkness that had infested Centauri Prime. He was obviously still leaning toward making public the firsthand proof they had acquired. But Galen knew that, in doing so, he was effectively dooming all of Centauri Prime. The Alliance would not see the Drakh influence as a cancer that could be surgically removed; they would simply sweep in and kill the patient, and then pat themselves on the back for a job well done.

It was Gwynn, however, who spoke, as if she had read his mind. "You desire to know how we are different from the Drakh, Vir? The Drakh would put your race on the firing line and care nothing for their actions. The death or survival of the Centauri carries no weight with them, one way or the other, except in terms of how it serves their interests. We do not wish to be the bearers of information that will cause the demise of the Centauri, unless we have to. Provide us with reasons not to, and we will be able to cooperate with you. But you must give us something—or we can give you nothing."

So he told them what he had in mind.

To a great degree, he was making up his strategies as he went. He was fully cognizant of the fact that they would take time, and he made that clear to them, as well. The techno-mages listened patiently, thoughtfully, and when he was done, they looked at one another. To Vir, it seemed as if they were communing. He had no idea whether that was within their power to do, and at that moment he didn't care overmuch. All that mattered was making sure that Centauri Prime survived for as long as possible. Every day that passed meant another day that the Drakh could spread their influence . . . but it also meant another day that his people were alive, and where there was life, there was hope.

"Very well, Vir," Galen said after a time. "I still do not approve—"

"I don't need your approval," Vir interrupted. "Just your silence."

"For now."

Vir inclined his head slightly in acknowledgment. "For now, yes."

"Good luck to you, then," Finian said. "There's a good deal riding on your ability to accomplish these things, Vir."

"Are you vaguely under the impression that I'm unaware of that?" Vir said, sounding more snappish than he would have liked, but understandably so given the circumstances, he thought. "Now if you'll excuse me—"

He turned, and suddenly Galen said, "Oh, and Vir . . . one other thing . . ."

Vir whirled toward him, his patience as frayed as rotting leather. "What, Galen? What 'one other thing' are you going to toss at me now? That I should be careful because I'm risking not only my life, but also those of others? That I shouldn't trust you to keep your silence? That out there, the people of Centauri Prime are blissfully sleeping, unaware of the fact that we are conspiring to try and prevent them from certain annihilation, and that I'm probably never going to sleep again? That my best, and possibly only, friend in the world, has a one-eyed parasite on his shoulder and is suffering every hour of every day, and that the only way he'll ever know peace is in the grave, and I can't do a damned thing about it, so I shouldn't let it worry me? Is that what you are going to say?"

Very mildly, Galen replied, "No, I was going to say you might want to remove the microphone from your ear. It won't stay in there forever, and you shouldn't have to answer questions if it falls out at an inopportune time."

"Oh. Uhm . . ."

But there didn't seem to be a lot he could say in response to that.

He tapped the device out of his ear into his palm, placed it on a table, and walked out without a look back.

"That man," Finian said, "is the last, best hope for peace in the galaxy."

"I think I'm the one who's going to have trouble sleeping tonight," Gwynn said dourly.

I wish there were some way I could have prevented it.

Alas, poor Vir. It was inevitable, I suppose. Here he was, the poor fellow, making another return visit to Centauri Prime, in the company of Mariel. And he leaves without her. In a way, it is the most beneficial thing that could have happened to him. What is most remarkable is the brave face that he is putting on it. But I do not believe it. Vir is the type to give his heart fully, and not wisely, and he could not have committed a more grievous error than giving it to Mariel.

But to lose her to . . . that . . . person? Feh. Whatever difficulties I may have with Mariel, no matter how poisonous I consider her, it grieves me to see Vir hurt . . . even as I am led to believe that this is probably the best thing that might have happened to him.

# — chapter 10 —

Durla leaned forward in his chair, clearly not certain that
he had heard Vir properly. "Do I . . . what?" he asked.

"Want her," Vir said flatly. He was speaking with a remarkable air of boredom and disdain that Durla would never have
thought possible from the ambassador. It was possible that he
had underestimated him. But before he made any adjust-
ments in his view of Vir, he had to fully understand what it
was that Vir was asking. "Do you want Mariel?" Vir repeated.

"Ambassador," Durla said in a slow, measured tone, "putting
aside for a moment my personal wants and desires . . . the
lady Mariel is a free woman. She cannot be bartered."

"Women," Vir said, "do as they're told. Of course," he
added ruefully, "they have an annoying way of letting us
know what they want so we can tell them to do it, eh?"

Minister Durla had trouble believing this was the same
person he had met with on Babylon 5, in the Zocalo, a little
less than a year ago. Vir seemed so . . . so blasé. So world-
weary. Durla had also believed that, when they had first met,
Vir had felt some degree of trepidation toward him. Now,
however, the ambassador was speaking as if they were old
friends. Durla wasn't entirely certain what was prompting
this degree of familiarity, and although he also was not sure
that he appreciated it, he wasn't entirely sure that he disliked
it, either. He had thought he'd had Vir Cotto fairly well
pegged as a harmless buffoon. If he was wrong about that,
then it might be entirely possible that Cotto actually posed a
threat. On the other hand, he might also prove useful. It was
far too soon to make a judgment.

"Certainly," Vir continued, "you must have noticed that the lady Mariel is paying an annoying amount of attention to you."

"She seemed . . . quite friendly, yes," said Durla. "But I wasn't attributing it to anything save general sociality."

The truth, of course, ran far deeper than that.

Durla had known Mariel since they were both young, and he was in love with her, had been for as long as he could remember. She had always aroused a hunger within him as no other woman had, before or since. In order to attract her attention and interest, he had raised her from obscurity—a condition prompted when Londo Mollari had dismissed her—and assigned her to work under Chancellor, and later Minister, Lione. She owed everything about her current return to status to Durla, and he had silently—and foolishly, it seemed— waited for her to notice and appreciate him.

Instead she had hooked up with Vir, so that Durla barely made any impression on her. It had been enough to drive him to paroxysms of fury.

When he had finally managed to calm down—a process that had required several months—he had decided that he had had enough of subterfuge. Under the guise of desiring the return of Vir Cotto and a reinstatement of his relationship with the emperor, all out of his concern for Londo's well-being, of course, Durla had arranged for Vir and Mariel to be his occasional guests. During that time, he had done everything that he could to attract her notice, to impress her with his power and privilege. That was, after all, what she ultimately sought.

However, it had seemed to him that his efforts had remained utterly in vain. Oh, she was polite enough, charming enough . . . but she spoke incessantly of Vir and of how wondrous an individual he was, to the point where Durla was wondering why he had even bothered. He had reached a point where he had resigned himself to never having Mariel, because he couldn't begin to understand how the woman's mind worked.

And now, all of a sudden, Vir had simply wandered into his office, dropped down into a chair opposite Durla's desk, and began chatting. From nowhere, his "offer" in regard to Mariel had been broached. Durla wanted to think it some sort of absurd joke. After everything he had done, after the scheming and involved placement of individuals . . . it couldn't be that simple, could it?

"It's more than being sociable, I assure you," said Vir. For a moment he looked uncomfortable and fidgeted slightly in his chair. He lowered his voice slightly, and asked, "Can I trust your discretion, Minister?"

"Of course! Absolutely," Durla said.

"Because I have my pride, the same as any man. And this, well . . . this situation . . . is not one that I am exceedingly pleased over."

"It never leaves this room," Durla assured him.

Vir leaned forward, his fingers interlaced, and in a low voice—as if concerned that they were being overheard—he said, "The fact is, the woman doesn't stop talking about you. Whenever we are alone, and even in the company of others back on Babylon 5, she speaks of nothing *but* you."

"When she is with me, she speaks only of you."

Vir waved dismissively. "A cover, nothing more. She is a subtle creature, the lady Mariel, and it wouldn't be in character for her to speak so effusively of you when you're near her. But she hasn't been covering as well lately as she had been. You must have noticed."

Durla thought about it, and realized that Vir was right. She had been looking at Durla differently. Her hand, lighting upon his shoulder, had remained a bit longer than would have been normal. She had definitely been more flirtatious.

He had been afraid to hope, though . . . hadn't dared allow himself . . .

"But what she says to me in private, well . . ." Vir shook his head. "She's made her sentiments quite clear. The simple fact is that she wants you, Durla. She's dying to be with you. And, to be blunt, I'm getting tired of listening to it. Listening to her pining away. And as for our sex life, well," and he snorted ruefully. "How do you think I felt when she cried out, 'Oh yes, yes, Durla, yes!' at exactly the time you wouldn't want to hear another man's name mentioned. I mean, honestly!"

"How . . . how embarrassing that must have been for you. And to admit it now . . . But . . ." He shook his head. "I don't understand. If she desires to be with me, why doesn't she just . . . I mean, she is not your chattel, your property . . ."

Vir looked even more uncomfortable than before. "Well, to be honest . . . in a way, she is."

His eyes narrowed. "What do you mean?"

"I mean," Vir said with a great sigh, as if unspooling a deep secret, "that the Lady Mariel is not . . . how shall I put it . . . not with me completely of her own free will."

At first Durla had no idea at all what Vir could possibly mean. But then he did. In a hoarse whisper, he said, "You're . . . blackmailing her?"

Vir looked taken aback. "Blackmail? You accuse me of blackmailing my own paramour for the purpose of getting her to be with me?"

"My apologies, Ambassador, I didn't mean—"

"Don't apologize. That's pretty much it."

Durla had no idea what to say. On the one hand, he found it repulsive. On the other hand, he almost admired Cotto for the sheer audacity—to say nothing of the almost jovial way in which he admitted to it. "What are you, uhm . . . how do . . . that is to say . . ."

"What am I blackmailing her with?" He shrugged. "It really wouldn't be honorable of me to say, now, would it."

"Perhaps. But then again, it isn't exactly honorable of you to have blackmailed her in the first place."

"A good point," admitted Vir. "But then again, a man who lusts after a female will do just about anything. Besides . . . she served a very specific purpose. She made me look good."

"Look good?" Then he understood almost immediately. "To others on Babylon 5."

"Exactly. You know, Durla, you've seen her. A man with a woman like that on his arm, fawning over him . . . it can't help but raise him in the estimation of other men. But let's be honest, okay?" He leaned forward. "Look at me. Seriously,

look at me. Do I look like the kind of man that a woman like
Mariel would be drawn to? I have my moments, certainly, but
let's face it: I'm not her type. You see, though, why I wouldn't
want this information to leave the room."

"Of course, of course. For others to think that she stayed
with you simply out of fear that you would expose her via
some ... extortionist threat. Still ... you are essentially
saying you want to be free of her, for all intents and purposes.
To 'give her' to me, as you put it." He leaned back in his chair,
his fingers interlaced. "Why? If there is one thing that I have
learned, Ambassador, it is that people rarely act out of the
goodness of their hearts. Generally speaking, they want
something. What do you want?"

Vir let out a long, unsteady breath. Some element of his polished demeanor seemed to be slipping, and it might well be that
his genuine emotions were beginning to slip through. Without looking at Durla, he said, "Believe it or not, Minister—I
was once a decent man. A man who never would have dreamt
of forcing a woman to be with him. I . . . used to be someone
else. Someone I liked better." His gaze flickered back to
Durla. "I have been viewing some of Minister Vallko's prayer
meetings lately. Got them via vid delay on Babylon 5. Even
went to one in person this morning. And he was talking
about what Centauri Prime should be, and what we should
be. Of what we should be living up to, and how we should be
aspiring to what we once were."

"The minister is a very inspirational speaker," agreed
Durla. His chest swelled slightly with pride. "I chose him,
you know. As our spiritual minister."

"Did you. I'm not surprised." He let out his breath in a
slow, steady stream. "In any event . . . I was thinking about
what he said . . . about being what we once were. And I found
I was getting . . . nostalgic, I guess is the right word. Nostalgic for the kind of man who would never have done what I
was doing. I suppose that sounds ridiculous."

"No. Not at all."

"Of course, there's the question of whether you are interested in her?" His eyebrows arched in curiosity. "Are you?"

It was everything that Durla could do, all the control he could muster, not to shout *Yes! Yes! For as long as I can remember! For as long as I have felt passion for any woman, I have wanted her!* Instead he was the picture of calm as he said, "She is not . . . unattractive. Indeed, some might even term her vivacious. I admit, I have not been particularly aggressive in the pursuit of women as of late. There have been so many things on my mind. It is difficult to attend to affairs of the heart when one is weighed down by affairs of the state."

"Oh, absolutely . . . absolutely. Still . . . we have a problem here. Perception is everything, as I'm sure you know. I am trying to do the right thing, but I do not need people to believe that I was tossed aside by the lady Mariel in favor of you. I don't have to tell you how that will make me look." Durla nodded, and Vir continued, "Nor do I desire that people know the circumstances under which Mariel stayed with me. You, on the other hand, don't want people thinking that you are getting a woman who was tossed aside by not only the emperor, but by the ambassador of Babylon 5. That, likewise, would not reflect well on you."

"All valid points."

Vir leaned forward intently. "How much do you like her? Really like her, I mean?"

Durla looked at him askance. "What," he said slowly, "are you suggesting?"

Vir smiled. "Are you a gambling man?" he asked.

"Under the right circumstances," said Durla. "Tell me what you have in mind."

Ever since the bombing, there had been a systematic eradication of anything remotely related to Humans, Earth, or the Interstellar Alliance in general. For a while Humans and their assorted absurd influences had been stylistically quite popular on Centauri Prime, but ever since Earth had become the mortal enemy, Vallko had been calling for an aggressive return to the Centauri roots. Naturally, the Centauri had been happy to accommodate him in all things.

Or nearly all things. With one notable exception that proved particularly convenient in Vir's current plan.

Poker.

The insidiously addictive card game had worked its way so thoroughly into Centauri culture that, no matter what Vallko might demand in terms of isolationist activities, no one—especially the upper classes, with whom it was so popular—was inclined to give up what had become a preferred pastime. So a rumor was begun that poker had actually been invented by an early Centauri ambassador, who had in turn introduced it to Humans, and so the game continued in its popularity.

This particular evening, a fairly brisk game was underway. Londo knew that it was happening, and as he sat in the throne room, he thought of how—once upon a time—he would have joined them. Now, of course, he was emperor. It would be considered unseemly, inappropriate. What would people think?

"I am the emperor," he said out loud with a sudden start of realization. "Who cares what people think?"

He rose from his throne and headed for the door. Throk was immediately at his elbow, saying, "Highness, I thought you said you were staying in for the evening . . ."

"As I do every evening. I tire of repetition. Life is too short, Throk. We go."

"Where do we go, Highness?"

Londo turned to him, and said, "In my day, I was quite the poker player. I understand there is a game going on right now. Take me to it."

"Highness, I don't know that—"

"I don't believe I asked for your opinion on the matter, Throk," Londo told him flatly. "Now . . . will you do as I instruct, or must I attend to this on my own . . . and find a way to make my displeasure clear to you at a later date?"

Moments later, an uneasy Throk was leading Londo down a long corridor. From the far end of the hall they actually heard laughter. It seemed to Londo he could not recall the last time he had heard anything approaching genuine merriment in the palace. Instead the place seemed to be suffocating in intrigue, backroom politics, and deals that usually did not bode well for the good people of Centauri Prime.

The laughter approached a truly high-decibel level, and he could make out people speaking in a scoffing tone, apparently not believing something that one of them was saying. Londo could make out a few words here and there: "He's not serious." "A bold move." "You would not dare."

And then there was a sudden silence.

At first Londo thought that the abrupt cessation of noise might be due to his arrival on the scene, but as he entered he saw that all attention was focused away from the door and instead on two players at the table. His blood froze when he saw who they were.

One of them was Vir. The other was Durla. Each was peering at the other over fans of cards that they were clutching in their respective hands. Also seated around the table were Kuto, Castig Lione, and Munphis, the newly appointed minister of education and one of the most singularly stupid men that Londo had ever met. Their cards were down; clearly they were not part of this confrontation.

Londo wasn't sure whether he was happy or distressed that Vir was among them. The more acceptance that Vir had among the ministers, the easier it would be for him to come and go, and therefore the more likely it would be that Londo could have him around to chat with whenever he desired. On the other hand, the last thing he wanted was for Vir to become like those power-grubbing predators.

"Did I come at a bad time?" inquired Londo.

They looked at him then, and started automatically to rise. "No, no, don't get up," he said, gesturing for them to remain where they were. "I was thinking of joining you . . . but matters seem a bit intense at the moment. I assume there are some elevated stakes before us?"

"You could say that," Vir commented.

Kuto stirred his bulk around on his chair to face the emperor, and said, "The ambassador has wagered his paramour."

"What?" The words didn't entirely make sense to Londo at

first, but then he understood. He looked at Vir incredulously. "You are . . . not serious."

Vir nodded.

As much antipathy as Londo felt for Mariel, something about this made his stomach turn.

"Vir, she is a free woman. You cannot 'wager' her . . ."

"Actually, I can. She will respect a debt of honor, should it come to that," Vir told him.

"But how can you use her as you would a . . . a marker!" demanded Londo.

"Because I was out of money," Vir said reasonably. "And besides . . ." Vir gestured for him to come over and, when he did so, held up his cards. Londo looked at them. Four kings.

"Oh. That's how," said Londo.

"The ambassador is seeking to cause me to rethink the wager," Durla said thoughtfully. "And the emperor is aiding him in this. Hmm. Whether to take the bet or not. A considerable amount of money and a woman on the line. The woman has no true monetary value, for her own resources are limited, but there is a certain . . . nostalgia value to her. What to do, what to do." He looked at his own hand, and then said, "Very well. The bet is called."

Vir placed his cards down triumphantly, a smile splitting his face. Durla blinked in obvious surprise. "That," he said, "I was not expecting."

"Thank you," said Vir, reaching for the chips that represented his winnings.

But without taking a breath, Durla continued, "Just as, I am sure, you were not expecting . . . this." And, one by one, he placed four aces upon the table.

There was a stunned hush around the table. Londo looked from one to the other, waiting for some sort of word, some type of reaction. And then Vir laughed. He laughed long and loud, and then reached over and gripped Durla's hand firmly. "Well played!" he said. "Very well played! I will inform Mariel at once."

"You are an honorable man, Vir Cotto," Durla said formally, "and a most formidable opponent. I have nothing but the greatest respect for you."

Vir bowed graciously, and stepped back from the table.

"*Viiir.* A moment of your time," Londo said, falling into step beside him, and they walked out of the room together. Londo opened his mouth to speak, then became aware of the footsteps behind them. Without even looking back, he said, "Throk, some privacy if you would not mind."

Throk, by this point in their relationship, knew better than to argue, and he faded back from the scene.

"Vir," Londo said briskly, "what do you think you have done? Might not Mariel have something to say in this matter?"

"Not really," said Vir coolly. "She won't mind. To be honest, I think she was getting bored with Babylon 5, and nostalgic for the halls of home. What's the matter, Highness? Don't want to have to deal with her hanging about the palace? Worried?"

"No, I am not worried . . ."

"You should be," Vir's voice suddenly grew harsh. "She tried to kill you, Londo. We both know that. Oh, she claimed it was an accident. She said she had no idea that the statue was rigged. But it's not true." All the words came out in a rush. "She knew before she set foot on Babylon 5 that you were planning to divorce two of your wives, and she wasn't going to take any chances. She'd had past dealings with Stoner, and arranged with him to bring the artifact to Babylon 5 for 're-sale.' When Stoner sold it to a merchant, he slipped the merchant a note that a certain elegant Centauri woman would come by and express interest in it . . . and that she would simply point rather than pick it up, since the touch of any Centauri would trigger it. So if you have any sympathy for her, Londo, I wouldn't if I were you."

Londo was stunned by the outpouring of information. "How do you know all this?"

"She told me."

"And she told you . . . why?"

"Because I asked her. Recently, in fact. Oh, but don't

worry, Londo . . . she's no threat to you anymore. She has . . . other considerations."

"Vir, putting aside what you have told me—and I admit, it is a good deal to put aside—I was not concerned about Mariel so much as I was about you."

"Me? Why? I would think you'd be happy I'm quit of her."

"Because," Londo gestured helplessly, "she seemed to make you happy. I thought she had, perhaps, changed. Yet now I see," and his gaze searched Vir's face for some sign of the naive young Centauri he had once known, "that she has not changed half as much as you."

"I grew up, Londo. That's all," Vir told him. "It happens to all of us. Well . . . all of us except Peter Pan."

"What?" Londo blinked in confusion. "Who?"

Vir waved him off. "It doesn't matter. Londo, look . . . with all respect to you and your position and everything . . . just stay out of it, okay? This simply isn't your concern."

And with that he picked up the pace and hurried off to his quarters, leaving an extremely perplexed emperor in his wake.

Mariel had almost finished gathering her things when there came a chime at the door. "Yes?" she called as the door slid open, and then she blinked in surprise. "Well. To what do I owe the honor?"

Londo entered, his hands draped behind his back, and he said, "Hello, Mariel. You are looking well."

"Greetings, Highness. Should I bow?" She made a formal curtsy.

"Oh, I think there is little need for such formalities between us, my dear." He approached her slowly and carefully, as if she were an explosive. "So tell me, Mariel . . . what is your game this time, eh?"

"My game?"

"You have switched allegiances, I hear. From Vir to Durla. Decided that he represents your best hope at getting up in the world?"

"In case you had not heard, Londo," she said evenly, "I was

not present at the game where I was bartered away. No one asked me my opinion. But Vir has made it quite clear to me that his honor is on the line. I have been given no choice in the matter. Besides—" she shrugged "—Durla is a pretty enough man. He seems to fancy me. He is well positioned within the government. Vir had charm and humor, but that will only go so far. This is a fairly practical happenstance for me. And I have long ago lost any illusions as to what my purpose in life is."

"And what would that purpose be?"

"Why, Londo . . . to make men happy, of course. Did I not do that for you?" She smiled sweetly and traced the line of his chin with one slim finger. "There are some things in which I have always excelled."

"Including manipulation of events when they suit your fancy. Answer me truthfully, Mariel, if such a concept is not entirely foreign to you: Did you arrange that card game somehow? Did you mastermind this entire business?"

"Why on Earth would I need to 'mastermind' anything, Londo?" she demanded, a bit of the carefully held sweetness slipping away. "If I decided I preferred Durla to Vir, what was to stop me from simply approaching Durla . . . especially if, as you likely suspect, I care nothing for Vir save how he suits my purposes. Why would I feel the need to resort to some sort of convoluted business with a card game?"

"I do not know," Londo said thoughtfully. "But if I find out . . ."

"If you find out, then what, Londo? All parties are satisfied with the outcome of what transpired this evening around that table. The only one who seems to have difficulties with it is you, and you are not involved."

He took a step toward her, and in a flat voice said, "It occurred on Centauri Prime. I, the emperor, *am* Centauri Prime. That makes me involved. Something in this business is not right."

"Something on this planet is not right, Londo. Perhaps you'd better serve the interests of Centauri Prime if you concentrated on that, rather than the outcome of a hand of poker."

The door opened once more and a member of the Prime Candidates was standing there. "Lady Mariel," he said with a sweeping bow, "I was sent by Minister Durla . . ."

"Yes, of course. That bag, and that one there," she pointed to several packed suitcases. "I have arranged for my belongings from Babylon 5 to be sent to me as soon as possible." She turned to Londo and looked at him with wide, innocent eyes. "Is there anything else, Highness? Or am I dismissed?"

His jaw shifted several times as if he were cracking walnuts with his teeth. "Go," he said finally.

"By your leave," she said with another elaborate curtsy, and she headed off down the hall, leaving Londo scowling furiously and wondering what in the world had just happened.

She had haunted his dreams.

The dream image of Mariel had come to him, years ago, and told him to begin the dig upon K0643. And in later months, the dreams of Mariel had made repeat visits, and told him to do other things. She had been his dream guide, the means by which his mind had worked and planned and plotted the destiny that Centauri Prime was to follow. At first when she had come to him in his dreams, he had not remembered it upon waking. But in later weeks and months, the fragments had coalesced. The connection, the bond between them—spiritually, only, of course—had become more firm, more intertwined, with every bit of guidance that his subconscious mind had given him. He had even taken to sleeping with a recording device next to him, so that if he happened to wake up during one of his dream sessions, he would be able to grab the device and make a record of whatever thought had occurred to him. That way nothing would ever be lost.

And in many of those dreams, she had promised that, sooner or later, she would be his. All it would take was patience and dedication, and she would eventually come to him of her own volition.

Now it had happened.

He could scarcely believe it.

She stood there in his room, clad in a gown so sheer that—

at certain angles of light—it was practically invisible. "Hello, Minister," she said.

He entered the room on legs that suddenly felt leaden. "Greetings, Lady," he replied, and he realized that his voice sounded rather hoarse. He cleared it forcefully. "I think you should know that . . . if you desire no part of this . . ."

She came slowly toward him. To Durla, it seemed as if she were gliding across to him on ice, so minimal were her movements, so gracefully did she walk. She faced him and draped her arms around his shoulders. "I am," she said softly, "exactly where I wish to be . . . with exactly who I wish to be."

"This is . . . so abrupt," he said.

But she shook her head. "To you, perhaps. But for me, it has been long in coming. I have admired you from afar, Durla . . . Certainly you must have realized that when you came to Babylon 5."

"You spoke mostly of Vir."

She laughed, her voice chiming like a hundred tiny bells. "That was to make you jealous, my dear Durla. Certainly a man of the world such as yourself must have seen through it. A man who has accomplished all that you have accomplished, done all the things that you have done. Why you," and she began to undo the top of his shirt, "are the single greatest leader on this planet. Everyone knows that."

"Everyone does, eh?" His pride was swelling, and that wasn't the only thing.

"Of course! Who is it who conceives of, and oversees, all the reconstruction projects? Who is the power behind the emperor, developing programs, picking the key people for the right positions? Who has a true vision of what this world should be? Who stirs the people's hearts and souls? Did you not conceive of the Tower of Power? Did you not handpick Vallko to uplift the spirits of all Centauri Prime? And who knows what other grand plans you have!"

"They are grand, yes." He paused. "Do you want me to tell you about them? Are you interested?"

"I am interested only in that they are reflections of your greatness," Mariel said, and her warm breath was in his ear.

He thought his legs were going to give way, and it was all he could do to remain standing. "But we need not hear of such matters now. We have other things to do . . . things of much greater interest," and she took his face in her hands, "and you have been waiting for them . . . for quite some time. Haven't you."

He nodded. His throat was seized up; he couldn't get a word out.

"Well, you don't have to wait any longer," she said, and she kissed him slowly, languorously.

Their lips parted, and he whispered, "You knew . . . somehow you knew, all this time, didn't you."

"Of course I knew."

"About the dreams . . . how you've been in them . . ."

Her gaze flickered for just the briefest of moments, and he took it to be confirmation of all his beliefs. Then he was entirely caught up in the moment, as she said quickly, "Yes, all about the dreams. All about all of it. And this is where we are meant to be now, Durla . . . our time and our place."

She was undoing something at her shoulders, and the gown slid from her. And then he was upon her, like a ravening creature, unleashing something that had been pent up all this time . . .

And as they came together, she took herself out of her mind. Vir's image filled her mind, filled her body, and she thought of how it had all come to this.

*I have been bad,* she thought, *and led a bad life, and have done terrible things and used people, and this is my punishment. Because Vir told me Durla is the key to it all. That Durla will have information that we need. That I must be by Durla's side, always, for that is the only way I can get information to Vir as he needs it. Being with Durla is what will make Vir happy, and I must make Vir happy. If I do not make him happy, I will die.*

*So I must leave him to be with Durla, to be where my beloved Vir most needs me. But whenever Durla's arms are around me, whenever he loves me, it will be my Vir that I am feeling and thinking of. And someday, someday, my Vir will come for me, and we will be together forever and ever, through death and beyond. And this . . . this means nothing in the meantime. Nothing at all. I will smile and gasp and whisper small names and say all the things that are meaningless unless I say them to Vir, but they will keep Durla, and I will be able to learn from him what I need.*

*I will be the spy that Castig Lione calls me, and I will cooperate, and be everything Durla wants me to be so that I can be what Vir needs me to be. Vir, I love you, I love you so much, come for me soon, Vir, I will wait . . . wait forever and ever . . .*

And when Durla saw the tears running down her face, she told him that they were merely tears of joy, and he believed her because it felt so good to believe . . .

Vir stood on the balcony that overlooked the wonders of Centauri Prime. He thought about what was going to be needed to keep the people safe, and the sacrifices that had to be made.

He thought of how Durla adored him now, for he had given Durla that which the minister most desired while, at the same time, maintaining both their dignities. For that, Durla would be eternally grateful.

He knew Durla's type all too well. Creatures who operated with a sense of manifest destiny, and a certainty that fate was going to play things their way and ultimately give them everything that they wanted, if they simply persevered. He might have some initial trepidation, but Vir knew that Durla would not question Mariel's willing defection too much, for the last thing he would want to do under the circumstance is look too closely at what had been handed him.

It all had to be handled internally. All the darkness, all the lies, all of the frightening presence lurking just out of sight— it was up to Vir to have to deal with it. Vir and whomever else he could gain as an ally, willing or otherwise. Because if the Alliance or Sheridan or any of them caught wind of anything that was going on, then Centauri Prime would end in flames. Vir was certain of that much. He could not see that again, could not go through that horror one more time. He would do whatever was necessary to stave off such a horrible happenstance.

Because it was going to get worse.

He had made some initial inquiries. He had gone to men such as Rem Lanas and Renegar, men who had barely survived the horror of K0643. They knew that Vir had tried to warn them, and had come to realize that when Vir Cotto spoke of warnings, then those warnings were ignored at one's extreme peril. And they were hearing things, distant things, stories from friends of friends of friends. Stories of parts of Centauri Prime being harnessed for very, very secretive work, but they weren't bringing in just any Centauri worker, oh no. No, apparently the ministry wasn't happy with the outcome of K0643, and because scapegoats were needed, the workers were targeted. It must have been that the workers, in their ham-handed way, had mismanaged and mishandled that dig.

So now there was new work being done, work of a secret nature, and it appeared that the workforce was being culled entirely from the Prime Candidates. The youth of Centauri Prime, the hope of the future, being employed for some sort of dark and fearsome business that Vir could not even begin to guess at.

He needed to know more, but Lanas and Renegar were nervous, at least to start out. He knew that they would come around, that they could and would provide him with more. They, and others like them who were becoming aware that something was terribly wrong on their beloved Homeworld—although just how wrong, Vir was not prepared to tell them. Not yet. Vir needed someone inside, and quickly.

There had been only one likely person.

He had told himself it was the only thing to do. And when the morality of it got to him, he thought of wicked women and of how the punishments they received were certainly due to their wickedness. And of how those who administered those punishments were pure of motive, without any stain upon their souls.

He thought of all that, and then felt a cold wind cut through him, unseasonably chilly. He drew his robe tight and gazed up into the cloudless night sky, and he clung to that rationalization until he could sustain it no longer. Finally, he spoke the truth that he and only he knew.

"I am damned," he said to the emptiness around him, and there was no one within earshot to tell him otherwise.

**EXCERPTED FROM**
*THE CHRONICLES OF LONDO MOLLARI.*
**Excerpt dated (approximate Earth date) May 5, 2270.**

The idiots. The blind idiots.

Did they truly think that they could continue along this path without someone noticing? Did they believe that Sheridan and his associates would continue to be blissfully unaware of what is happening here?

I knew perfectly well that there were scans being done from orbit, every so often. We have had no privacy here on Centauri Prime. They watch over us as if we are children, making certain we do not scamper about in a woodpile with a lit flame. They worry that we will hurt ourselves . . . hurt ourselves by developing weaponry or militarization that will be used against them, thereby forcing them to try and annihilate us.

Apparently Durla and his brilliant associates had the beginnings of a war machine being created on the continent of Xonos, the former stronghold of the Xon—the other race on Centauri Prime, which we wiped out many years ago. There was machinery being created there, which Durla claimed was to be used for agriculture. Agriculture! As if Sheridan was going to believe that. And the next thing I knew, I was left attempting to smooth over the ruffled feathers of the Alliance, assuring them that no, no, we Centauri are a peaceful people who harbor no hostility toward anyone.

Sheridan did not buy it for an Earth second, I'm sure. He said he wanted the Xonosian buildup dismantled. That there was concern the devices being developed there could be used for war. Durla is having fits. Vallko is getting the people stirred up and angry over this new Alliance oppression. Kuto is endeavoring to put a positive face on all of it, but is not coming close to succeeding—and I suspect that lack of success is by design.

And today . . .

Today I almost killed Throk.

He has shown increased designs upon Senna, and although she has been polite and receptive—even teasingly flirtatious—she has tended to keep him at arm's length. I have noticed that for some months now, and if I had noticed it, then certainly Throk did as well. He was becoming increasingly frustrated that their relationship was going just so far, and no further.

Last week, he approached me about arranging a marriage with her. When he walked into my throne room, I assumed that he was approaching me simply in his capacity as my aide. Imagine my surprise when he said, "Highness . . . I wish to discuss the prospect of marriage."

I stared at him in confusion for a moment, and then said, "Throk, I admit that I have gotten used to you as my valet, but I hardly see the need to formalize our association in that way."

Ah, Throk. No sense of humor. "No, Highness. Between myself and your ward, Senna."

Now I admit my inclination was to think of Senna as little more than a child, and about Throk the same way. I realized, though, upon his inquiry, that not only is she of marriageable age, but that Throk would very likely be only the first of many . . . presuming that I did not agree to the match.

Throk spoke very properly, very formally. "I desire to arrange a match with Senna. I come from the respectable house of Milifa, my father is—"

"I know who your house is, Throk," I said impatiently. "I know your lineage. You wish to be husband to Senna? You are aware of what that entails? You are prepared for the responsibility?"

"Yes, Highness. I think she will make a superb first wife."

"Indeed." Why did I not consider that a ringing endorsement? "And how does Senna feel about the concept?"

He looked extremely puzzled. "Does that matter?"

"Not always," I admitted. "But it does to me, in this case." I turned to one of the guards and requested that he bring Senna to me. Within minutes she entered, quite the grown woman. I felt bad for her; she had spent most of her time in recent months socializing with the Prime Candidates who were inhabiting virtually every corner of the palace these days. There were almost no women in the palace aside from serving women. I could have done better on her behalf, in finding her females to associate with. But I suppose it was a bit late to start worrying about such considerations.

"Senna," I said, "Throk here has asked that I arrange a marriage."

Her eyes sparking with slightly evil amusement, Senna said, "I hope you two will be very happy together, Highness."

I turned to Throk and said, "She has learned her lessons well."

Throk did not seem amused. Then again, he never did, so it wasn't as if that was anything new.

"Senna," I said, feeling that dragging things out would not help matters. "Do you wish to marry Throk?"

Her gaze flickered from him to me, and then, not unkindly but firmly nevertheless, she said, "Since you are asking me, Highness . . . I have nothing but respect and friendly feelings for Throk. But I do not wish to marry him, no. There is no insult intended. I do not wish to marry anyone."

"Well, there it is then, Throk," I said, turning to him.

He looked as if he had been utterly blindsided. "That . . . is it? There is to be no discussion?"

"She has said no. There does not seem to be a good deal of latitude in that decision. No is no, and I suspect—since it is Senna we are discussing here—that no amount of chat will convert no to yes. Senna, however, clearly hopes that you will be able to remain friends. I naturally hope that you will be willing to honor her request."

"But a woman does not have a say in the matter!" Throk insisted, somewhat stridently.

"Under many circumstances, yes," I agreed. "But these are not many circumstances. These are circumstances that I am controlling, and I will value Senna's wishes over yours. That is all."

As it turned out, it was not all. Later that day, when I was passing Senna's room, I heard arguing. I recognized both raised voices; Senna and her frustrated suitor were obviously having a bit of a difference of opinion. My first inclination was to allow Senna to handle the matter. She was, after all, an independent young woman who knew her own mind and was more than capable of handling someone like Throk.

But then there was the angry retort of skin striking skin. Senna's voice cried out, and I heard a body hit the floor. I stepped toward the door, but it did not open. Angrily, I turned to my guards and pointed mutely to the door. Without a moment's hesitation, they stepped forward and forced the door open. I strode in ahead of them, a breech of protocol but I doubt that they could have stopped me.

Senna was on the floor, as I suspected she would be. Throk stood over her, his hands balled into fists, and he was shouting, "You have shamed me in front of the emperor! You have——" That was when he noticed me. Immediately he straightened up and started to say, "Highness, this is not what——"

I did not feel like hearing his explanations, or even the sound of his voice. I did not care how much influence certain "others" had over Throk's service to me. With two quick steps, I was right in front of him. It might not have been fair, but at that moment I saw all the frustration, all the arrogance, all the difficulties and scrabbling for power from all those around me, all personified and condensed into this one individual.

I drew back a fist and swung. It was, I am pleased to say, an impressive blow, particularly considering how out-of-practice I was. Throk's head snapped around and he went down without a sound. It was, I confess, a bit disconcerting, that silence. He glowered up at me, and he did not even put his hand to his chin to rub the area where I had struck him. Apparently he did not want to give me the satisfaction of seeing him in pain.

"I believe," I said tersely, "that your time in my service is ended, Throk."

"Minister Durla assigned me to——"

"Minister Durla works for me," I thundered. "I decide what will be! Not him! Not you! Me! Minister Durla will find something else to assign you to, and I can only suggest, for your continued health, that it be something that will not bring you into contact with Senna. Now get out of my sight!"

He got to his feet, not slowly, but not with any overt hurry either. He looked at me for a time, and I notched up my glower. He looked down at that point, which I took some small measure of pride in noting. And then, without another word, he walked out.

"Are you all right, young lady?" I asked.

"I . . . did not need to be rescued, Highness," she replied. "I could have handled him myself." Then she smiled ruefully and put a hand to the part of her face that was still flared red from the impact. "But I appreciate not having had to."

"Do not think upon it any longer. He is out of your life, for good. I shall see to that."

Tomorrow I will be speaking with Lord Durla, making sure that Throk is given an assignment that will keep him far away from her. I hope she does not end up losing her association with the other Prime Candidates. I could wish for a better set of friends for her, but at least it's people roughly her own age with whom she's having social intercourse. There is something to be said for that.

If only I could handle this business with the Alliance as easily as I dispatched Throk. A quick punch to the face and that was all that was required. The realm of politics is, unfortunately, slightly more complicated.

At least, I think it is.

Perhaps I should try punching Sheridan in the nose someday and see if anything positive comes from it.

# — *chapter 11* —

"Mr. Garibaldi will see you now."

The secretary was so remarkably gorgeous that Lou Welch had a hard time removing his gaze from her. "Breathtaking," he muttered.

"Pardon?"

"This office," Lou said quickly, gesturing around them. "It's really impressive." He rose from his seat and continued, "Me and Michael, we go way back. God, his living quarters were smaller than this outer office. He's come a long way."

"Yes. He has." The face remained lovely, but the smile was thinning in a slightly unattractive fashion. "And if you go on in, I'm sure he'll be happy to tell you just how far."

"Hmm? Oh! Yes, right," Lou said, and he headed into the inner office.

Garibaldi rose from behind his desk, hand extended, a broad smile on his face. Welch couldn't help but admire the trim shape Garibaldi had kept himself in. He'd been concerned that the years spent running the major conglomerate of Edgars/Garibaldi Enterprises might have softened Garibaldi up, but he knew at once that his concerns had been misplaced. Garibaldi looked as whipcord sharp as ever when he stepped forward, and said, "Lou! Lou, it's great to—"

His eyes narrowed. "What's wrong," Lou said, puzzled.

"You have hair," Garibaldi said.

"Oh. That." Slightly self-conscious, but simultaneously preening, Welch ran his fingers through his thick shock of black hair. "I had a thing done."

"A thing. Uh-huh," said Garibaldi.

"Kind of went in the opposite direction from you, huh, Chief? Put the 'baldy' in Garibaldi, did ja?"

"My secret weapon," Garibaldi deadpanned, in reference to his own hairless pate. "I bounce light off it into the eyes of my enemy, blinding them. Plus, if I'm marooned on a desert island, I can reflect the sun off it to summon passing airships. You get stuck on a desert island, Lou, all you get to do is pick sand mites out of your follicles. Sit down, sit down. Can I get you something to drink? Club soda or something?"

"No, no, I'm fine, thanks," Welch said.

Garibaldi walked back around his desk and dropped down into his seat. "So," he said, steepling his fingers, "why don't you tell me what you've been up to."

"Well, now, Chief . . . you're the one who tracked me down, invited me to come here to Mars for a chat," Welch said slowly. "Why don't you tell me what I've been up to?"

"First off, you don't have to call me Chief," Garibaldi said. "We're not on B5 anymore. 'Michael' will be fine. Even 'Mike.' "

"Okay, Chief."

Garibaldi rolled his eyes, and then he refocused himself. "Okay," he said gamely. "Basically, you received a promotion to personal guard for President Clark . . . but then you re-signed from EarthForce back during the . . . unpleasantness. Since then you've been serving as a private security consultant for a number of small firms. In addition, you've gotten yourself quite a reputation as a tracker. People call you 'The Ghost.' You have a knack for not being seen when you don't want to."

"I blend in well," said Welch. "It's the hair."

"I'm sure it is," said Garibaldi. "You don't know it, but you've actually worked for Edgars/Garibaldi a couple of times. Some of our smaller holdings."

"I didn't know that."

"Actually, you probably did."

"Well, yeah, I did," Welch admitted. He leaned forward, curious. "So what's up, Chief? You didn't bring me here just to catch up on what I've been doing."

"Take a look at this," Garibaldi said. He cued up an image on the computer screen behind him, and some aerial views of what appeared to be a construction site of some sort appeared. "What do you see?"

Welch frowned as he studied it. While he did so, Garibaldi's intercom beeped at him. He tapped it, and said, "Yeah?"

His secretary's crisp voice came over. "Your eleven o'clock appointment called. He's running a little late, but he'll be here as soon as he can. He apologizes profusely for any inconvenience."

"Not a problem. Let my wife know that we'll probably have to push lunch back half an hour, will ya?"

"Yes, sir."

"Your wife." Welch shook his head in wonderment. "Still hard to believe those words are coming off your mouth. Funny . . . I thought for a while you had a thing for that Psi Corps woman . . . what was her name?"

"Talia," Garibaldi said, tonelessly.

"Yeah. Do you ever hear from her? Whatever happened with her, anyway?"

Garibaldi appeared to consider for a time before replying. "She had a change of mind. So . . ." and he gestured toward the images on the screen.

Welch immediately knew that he had unwittingly stepped in some sort of delicate territory, and promptly decided that it wouldn't be a good idea to press the matter. Instead he said, "Well . . . seems to be some sort of munitions factory. Where is it?"

"Xonos. A sparsely populated continent on Centauri Prime. Shots were taken by an Alliance probe, about a week ago. Centauri claim that it's actually tools being developed for agriculture. Stuff to clear land."

"You could clear land with it," Welch said slowly. "Of course, if anyone were living on the land, they'd be cleared, too." He drummed his fingers on the table.

"What are you thinking, Lou?" Garibaldi asked.

"I'm thinking that it looks like a munitions factory. That if they wanted it to look like a tool development site, they could have done so. I'm thinking that it looks exactly like what they want it to look like. Did they know that they're being watched?"

"Oh, yeah."

"Okay. So I'm thinking decoy."

Garibaldi nodded. "Exactly. They erect a site that our probes can't help but spot so that we can all argue about it, and distract us from what they're really up to."

"And that would be . . ."

"We don't know," admitted Garibaldi. "And *that* is what President Sheridan would like us to find out."

"Us?"

"He wants this small, Lou, at least for the time being. The Interstellar Alliance is busy haggling with Centauri Prime over this site. Let 'em. If this is all there is to it, then we don't have to get anyone worried. If, on the other hand, there's more to it, then the president wants to be the first to know about it and—with any luck—shut it down before things get out of hand."

"Sounds to me like he's out to treat the Centauri with kid gloves. Any particular reason?"

"I don't know that I'd characterize it as kid gloves. I know he'd like to avoid an all-out war. And I think, in a way—for old time's sake—he'd like to see Londo manage to turn things around for Centauri Prime."

"You mean turn things around so that, instead of feeling beaten and suppressed, they feel ready to launch a war again?"

"Not that much around," Garibaldi said. "At any rate, he wants to dispatch a team to Centauri Prime that would be equal parts diplomatic and equal parts—"

"Snoops."

"Exactly. What the president wants is a small group of people who know Londo from the old days, and hopefully can appeal to sentiment to make sure that this doesn't spiral out of hand. At the same time, he wants some folks who are cynical and suspicious enough to be able to take a hard look at things, find out what's going on, and do what needs to be done. He wants me in on it. And I'm figuring that having you to cover my back and check around wouldn't be a bad thing at all. So . . . are you up for it, Ghost?"

"The job pay or am I doing this out of the goodness of my heart?"

"Goodness of your heart."

"Then I'm in."

Garibaldi laughed. "Lou, I was kidding. Of course the job pays. You're being hired."

"Terrific. Then I'm even more in than I was before. Sounds exciting, Chief. The two of us against Centauri Prime. They don't stand a chance."

"Well, now, I figured maybe we'd even the odds just a bit. It's going to be three of us."

The intercom beeped at them again. "Your eleven o'clock is here, sir."

"Should I wait outside?" asked Welch.

"No, no, not at all. Actually, this is the third member of our little group. Send him in," he said to the intercom.

"This third guy someone who'll fit in on Centauri Prime?"

"Oh, yeah," said Garibaldi. "He'll blend perfectly. Hardly anyone'll even notice him. He can walk around on Centauri Prime and not get a second look.

The door slid open, and Welch turned and rose from his seat. Then he blinked in surprise. The newcomer took several brisk steps, stopped, and then half bowed with his fists to his chest. "Greetings, Mr. Garibaldi. And Mr. Welch, is it not?"

Welch was so surprised that he didn't even bother to hide his incredulity. He turned to Garibaldi, and said, "*He's* going to fit right in on Centauri Prime? *Him?*"

"Trust me," said Citizen G'Kar of Narn, with an amused glimmer in one eye. "You won't even know I'm there."

# — *chapter 12* —

It was rare that Londo actually allowed himself to display genuine emotion in front of Durla, but this was one of those very rare times. He rose from the throne even as he gaped in astonishment. "Are you sure? Positive?"

Durla nodded firmly. "There is no question, Highness. Positive identification was made when they came through customs."

"That he sent Mr. Garibaldi does not surprise me," Londo said slowly, beginning to pace the throne room. "And Welch, I vaguely remember him. He is obviously there as backup for Garibaldi. But G'Kar? *Here?*"

"He was a most impressive individual," Durla said. "I was there when he broke free of his restraints in defiance of Cartagia. It was . . . the most remarkable thing I have ever seen."

"It may well be the most remarkable thing that ever was," replied Londo. "I am not entirely sure whether Sheridan is brilliant, or a fool, or both."

"What shall we do, Highness?"

Londo looked bemused. "You are asking me what to do? Minister, I am stunned. Shocked and appalled. Customarily, you tell me how things will be, and that is that. To what do I owe this honor?"

"You diminish your contribution, Highness," said Durla.

"I know precisely what my contribution is, Durla. Do not seek to fool me. It ill becomes you. Or has Mariel schooled you better in the ways of deceit?"

Durla stiffened when Londo said that. "I do not see the need to insult the lady Mariel, Highness."

"Believe me," Londo said firmly, "no one could insult the lady Mariel." He waved it off dismissively. "Very well. Simply put, they will be extended every courtesy. They are here to speak. Let them speak. Obviously, Sheridan has hand-picked this particular group of individuals because he hopes to play upon old loyalties."

"And . . . has he succeeded?" asked Durla.

Londo snorted derisively. "My loyalty, Durla, first, last, and always, remains to Centauri Prime. As you well know."

Durla bowed and said, "As you say, Highness."

"Yes," Londo said faintly, and with less conviction than he would have liked, "as I say."

As they approached the front steps of the palace, G'Kar slowed a bit. Garibaldi noticed it and hung back, causing the guards who were escorting them to stop. He put a hand on G'Kar's arm, and said, "Is everything all right?"

"Just . . . some unpleasant memories," G'Kar said slowly. "Odd. I had thought that they would not pose a problem. Interesting how there are always new things to learn about oneself, isn't it."

"Very interesting," Garibaldi agreed. But from the look on his face, he wasn't sure what they were talking about. "Do you want to wait out here for—"

But G'Kar shook his head firmly. "I will be fine. Do not worry about it. After all I have been through, I think I can handle a bit of unpleasant nostalgia and a flight of stairs." He took a deep breath and, moments later, they were entering the palace.

Several ministers were waiting there to greet them. None of them were familiar faces to G'Kar . . . save for one. He stared at him for a moment, and then said, "Have we met, sir?"

"Not really, no. I am Minister Durla," answered the Centauri. He introduced the others who were with him, and the one who caught G'Kar's attention the most squarely was the one known as Vallko, minister of spirituality. "The emperor is most anxious to meet with you," Durla told them. "Right this way."

They followed their escort down a long hallway, and G'Kar couldn't help but notice the guards who watched them warily. No . . . him. They were watching him. G'Kar was beginning to wonder if his presence there wasn't meant to serve primarily as decoy. Everyone would be so busy watching him, that they wouldn't pay nearly as much attention to Garibaldi and Welch.

The silence was broken only by the sounds of their footsteps until Vallko finally said, "My understanding is that you are something of a religious figure on your Homeworld."

"So I have been designated," G'Kar admitted. "It is not a status that suits me, truth to tell. Fortunately enough, I have managed to convince my people to accept me in a manner that is more appropriate."

"And that would be?"

"As an advisor. A proponent of restraint and . . . dare I say it . . . wisdom. But I do not wish to be considered a god, or even a leader. I am more than content to let others lead, and I will simply stand on the sidelines and applaud or do what I may to guide their efforts."

"Restraint." It was the minister introduced as Lione who now spoke, as if G'Kar had said nothing beyond that word. "What an odd word to hear from a Narn. You are generally considered a rather warlike race, with restraint being a term that has little-to-no meaning for you."

"Yes, I have heard that, too. Then again, I have also heard that the Centauri are a vomitous pack of lying, rapacious bastards." There were audible gasps of anger from the ministers, and Garibaldi fired G'Kar a look that the Narn ignored. He was speaking so pleasantly that it was hard to believe that he was attempting to give offense. "Now, of course, whenever such calumnies are uttered, I step right in and say 'No, no! One must not believe what one hears!' Oh, certainly, the Centauri imprisoned me several times, and gouged out my eye, and covered my back with so many whip scars that to this day

I still cannot sleep properly. But is that any reason to condemn an entire race? Of course not! Broad and unfair characterizations are anathema to civilized society, don't you agree, Minister?"

The towering Lione looked as if he were ready to assault G'Kar with his bare hands, but Durla merely smiled in what seemed polite amusement. "Wholeheartedly, Mr. Ambassador."

"Please, please . . . ambassador no longer. 'Citizen' G'Kar will suffice."

"Citizen G'Kar it is. This way, please."

They walked down another hallway, and G'Kar noticed that Lou Welch seemed to be frowning at something. He tried to see what had caught Welch's curiosity, and it quickly became evident: it was the black-suited young people who seemed to be all over the palace. Black, with some sort of red sash over them like a badge of honor. "Who are they?" G'Kar abruptly asked, indicating one of the passing young men, who fired him a glance.

"The Prime Candidates. Our youth group," said Minister Lione.

"Ah. Hitler Youth," Lou Welch said.

Lione looked at him in confusion. "What?"

"Nothing," Welch said promptly, apparently happy to let the matter drop. Lione shook his head in a manner that indicated he found all Humans to be extremely puzzling.

They were ushered into the throne room, which was empty. *Londo always did prefer to make an entrance,* thought G'Kar, and his instinct was quite correct. Moments later Londo walked in with such enthusiasm that he seemed like a white-clad tornado. "Mr. Garibaldi!" he called out as if Garibaldi were on the opposite side of the city. "Citizen G'Kar! Mr. Walsh!"

"Welch," Lou corrected him.

"Ach. Who cares? You're here, whatever your name is. Sit, sit." He gestured toward the Centauri who had accompanied them. "You may all leave us."

G'Kar was pleased to see that the ministers looked decidedly

disconcerted. "Highness," Durla said slowly, "if you are going
to discuss matters pertaining to Centauri Prime, should we
not be here to represent the people's interests?"

"I am the people," Londo replied. "One of the many bur-
dens that I happily bear. When old friends chat it is merely a
get-together, Durla. Bring in ministers, and suddenly it becomes a council. There is no need for that at this time. But
rest assured, if I feel that someone is needed to escalate matters to the breaking point and beyond, I will send for all of
you instantly. Now you may go."

"But Highness," Durla began.

Something in Londo's demeanor shifted quite subtly. "Do
not confuse my use of the word 'may' with the notion that you
actually have a choice in the matter."

Durla mustered his dignity, then gestured to the other ministers. They followed him out and the doors shut behind them,
leaving only a handful of security guards behind.

The fact that the guards were there, though, was enough to
convince G'Kar immediately that Londo wasn't going to say
anything that he wasn't comfortable with having repeated to
Durla. It was his suspicion, based not only upon Londo's
passing comments, but also his abundant knowledge of just
how Centauri politics worked, that Londo was under careful
watch at all times.

"So—" Londo rubbed his hands together "—how long
will you be here, eh? If you wish, I can provide a tour of Centauri Prime. You can see all that we have accomplished."

"That . . . is actually what we've come to talk about,"
Garibaldi said, shifting in his chair. He leaned forward, resting
his arms on his knees. "As you know, we were sent by the
president . . ."

"Yes, yes, Sheridan informed us of your visit. I cannot tell
you the rejoicing there was, knowing that the Alliance is so
concerned about our welfare, that they feel the need to check
on us constantly. It is very uplifting to the spirit, yes, to know
that we are so beloved."

Garibaldi ignored the sarcasm. "The factory on Xonos . . ."

G'Kar watched Londo very carefully. Mollari certainly

had the ability to keep his cards close to his vest, but G'Kar fancied that, by this point, he could tell when Londo was out-and-out lying. Londo, however, looked at Garibaldi with what could only be considered wide-eyed innocence. "The agricultural site, you mean. I had this discussion with President Sheridan. We have, as your people say, beaten our swords into plowshares, Mr. Garibaldi. Would you now take issue with how we plow?"

"There's just concern that things may not be the way that they're being presented to us."

"In other words, you think we are lying."

"Not in other words," G'Kar spoke up. "Those are exactly the right words."

Londo, to G'Kar's surprise, laughed slightly at that. "Now I see why he is here," he said, indicating G'Kar. "He says all the things that will anger me, leaving you free to be as charming as possible. Or at least, as charming as is possible for you."

"Look, don't get the wrong idea . . ."

Londo rose from his seat. "I cannot do more than be open with you, Mr. Garibaldi. I can do nothing more than hide nothing. You are free to look wherever you wish upon Centauri Prime, at whatever you wish to examine. Inspect the facility on Xonos . . . I shall arrange transportation for you there tomorrow."

"Why not tonight?" Garibaldi said quickly.

"Tonight if you wish," Londo shrugged. "I had thought you would be tired, and desire some time to recover from your trip. But if tonight is what you desire," and he turned to his guards to arrange it.

"No, no, that's all right," said Garibaldi. "Tomorrow would be fine. No need to put anyone out. You're right, we could use some time to rest up."

"Very well," Londo said, equally agreeably. "Your guest chambers are already arranged, and tomorrow . . . tomorrow we shall take a trip to Xonos. Now, if you'll excuse me . . . affairs of state that must be attended to, and all that."

"Thank you, Your Highness," Garibaldi said formally.

" 'Your Highness?' " Londo looked both surprised and amused. "Please, please, Mr. Garibaldi. We go too far back, you and I. You, and your associates, can feel free to address me as," and he paused dramatically, " 'Your Majesty.' "

"Why are we waiting until tomorrow?" Welch asked.

Garibaldi was busy unpacking the few articles of clothing he had brought with him. Welch, who had brought even less than Garibaldi, already had his gear stowed in the adjacent room. "Because there's not going to be anything there," Garibaldi told him flatly. "Whenever people are eager to have you inspect something—their apartment, their ship, their planet, whatever—doesn't matter. It means they've already got whatever it is you're looking for safely tucked away where they think you'll never find it."

"So you're saying his being willing to be forthcoming is just proof that he's covering something up."

"More or less," said Garibaldi. "There's one of two options here, Lou. Either the Centauri really are up to nothing . . . or they're up to something, but it's not here."

"Which begs the question of, if they are up to something . . . where is it happening."

"Yup. Any thoughts?"

Welch gave the matter some consideration, pacing the room while scratching behind his ear as if trying to tickle his brain into operation. Finally he said, "You believe in gut hunches, Chief?"

"You've known me this long, you have to ask me that?"

Welch chuckled at that and then grew serious again. "Those kids. Those Prime Candidates. They were all over the place, did ja notice?"

"Yeah, I noticed. It was kind of spooky. No matter which corner we turned, there were more of them. It was like running into clones of the same person."

"I think they might be the key to this. Or at least they might be worth exploring."

"What do you have in mind?"

Welch stepped out onto the narrow balcony and gestured

for Garibaldi to join him. He did so, and Welch pointed. "See 'em?"

Garibaldi looked where Welch was indicating. There was a small cluster of the Prime Candidates heading in the direction of the city. They were moving in synchronous step, with such perfect regimentation that they might well have been the same person, simply replicated.

"So I was watching them from my balcony a little bit ago. There were more of them, heading in exactly the same direction, and some coming back, also from the same place."

"You want to follow them."

"Exactly, Chief. See where they lead. See what comes up."

"All right," Garibaldi said. "When did you have in mind?"

Welch abruptly coughed, very loudly and hoarsely. Then, with a greatly exaggerated croaking, he said, "I think I feel a cold coming on. It should be pretty nasty by tomorrow."

"I'll send your regrets along," Garibaldi said.

G'Kar heard the soft footfalls behind him and did not even have to turn to see who it was. "Hello, Your Majesty," he said.

Londo came up behind him, his hands draped behind his back, and he was clearly puzzled. "Londo. You, G'Kar, of all people, know that 'Londo' will more than suffice. I was told you were down here. Is there any particular reason? Were the accommodations I provided for you so wretched that you think a dungeon would be preferable?"

For that was indeed where they were; in the subterranean dungeons far beneath the palace. G'Kar was standing at the doorway of one particularly odious chamber, with a stench so foul that Londo had to fight to repress his gag reflex. He heard the faint scuttling of tiny claws across the floor and wondered what sort of vermin were running about within.

"Oh, no, the room you've arranged for me is more than satisfactory," said G'Kar. "I am simply reminiscing about this . . . my home away from home."

At first Londo had no idea what G'Kar was talking about, then abruptly he understood. "Of course. This was where Cartagia put you. This is the very cell."

G'Kar nodded. He actually patted the door frame as if he was happy to see it. "You would probably say that your Great Maker moves in mysterious ways, Londo. I would tend to agree. Cartagia put me in here with the hope of breaking an enemy of Centauri Prime. Instead he is long gone, and I have survived and have become far more formidable than even Cartagia could have imagined. I learned a great deal while I was down here. It helped to forge me into what I am today."

"And . . . what are you today?"

"Do you mean . . . am I your enemy?" G'Kar said.

"Yes."

"Ah, that is the nice thing about matters being the way they are between us, Londo." He turned to face the emperor. "We do not have to mince words, you and I. No, Londo. No, I am not your enemy."

"If you were, would you tell me?"

"A reasonable question. No. Very likely not."

"I see," sighed Londo. "You are disgustingly candid, G'Kar. It is a trait I once found charming. Now it is merely annoying. And tell me . . . if you were my friend, would you tell me that?"

"Of course I would," said G'Kar.

There was silence.

"You," Londo said, "are the single most irritating individual I have ever met."

"You see?" G'Kar replied. "What could be more proof of friendship than that? Who but a friend could be anywhere near as irritating as I am?"

At that, Londo laughed low in his throat. "Would you care for a drink, G'Kar? For old time's sake? For the memory of whatever it was we once were . . . or might be again?"

"That," G'Kar said briskly, "sounds like an excellent idea."

G'Kar turned away from his one-time prison and followed Londo up to his private quarters. Halfway there, a most surprising face greeted G'Kar. "Lady Mariel!" he said as he saw her approaching from the other end of the hallway. "A pleasure to see you!"

"Likewise, G'Kar," she said softly. "I had heard that you had once again graced us with your presence."

"Are you," and his questing glance went from Londo to Mariel and back, "in favor once more in the court?"

"In a manner of speaking," she said with that customary dazzling smile. "Not in the emperor's favor, particularly . . . but in favor nonetheless."

"Does she not remain as charming as ever?" said Londo jovially. Then he laughed, as if he were about to say something preposterous. "You know, we three should get together more often. We always have so much fun when we do."

"The last time we did, as I recall, you almost died," G'Kar reminded him.

"Yes, yes, I know. That is what provides the fun, yes? That sense that anything can happen. You know," and he lowered his voice conspiratorially, "I actually thought . . . you will laugh . . . I actually thought that you, G'Kar, and you, Mariel . . . were having an affair."

"No!" said Mariel, shocked. "Londo, how could you?" G'Kar's face bore a similar look of incredulity.

"Oh, the imagination plays remarkable tricks, my dear," Londo told her. "At one point during my party, I saw G'Kar toss a grape to you. The passing of fruit is a quaint Narn custom that is part of the Narn courting ritual. The fruit symbolizes sexuality, or some such thing. Yes, G'Kar? Yes? No? Am I recalling correctly?"

"I've heard something about that old tradition, yes," G'Kar said dismissively, "but sometimes, Londo, a grape is just a grape."

"Yes. So I hear," Londo said. "In any event, what is past is past. Mariel . . . would you care to join us?"

"Oh, I don't think so, Highness," Mariel said. "I had best be to bed. There are others who require my attention."

"To bed, then. G'Kar . . ." and he gestured for the Narn to follow him. "I hope you were not offended by my little speculation," he said as they continued down the hall, the Lady Mariel heading off in the opposite direction.

"Not at all, Londo."

And then, in a low voice, Londo said, sounding no less friendly, "I know the two of you were together, G'Kar. Please do not insult my intelligence by implying that I am unaware of that which is so obvious. I would hate to become enemies again, particularly over a woman who means so little to me. We understand each other, yes? Good! So . . . did you know that, as emperor, I have the best wine collection in all of Centauri Prime?"

"Somehow," said G'Kar, "I'm not the least bit surprised."

# — chapter 13 —

Lou knew that the journey to Xonos would guarantee that Garibaldi, G'Kar, and Londo—plus whatever assorted guards and such were going to be accompanying them—would be gone until the late evening. That had been what he was hoping for, because the cloak wasn't at its most effective during broad daylight. Early evening was fine, and nighttime . . . well, nighttime, forget it. There was simply no chance of spotting him, no matter how hard you looked. Somehow the cloak seemed to stretch and shape the shadows to conceal him, so it took minimal effort for him to keep his presence concealed.

"Cloak" was probably a misnomer. He had never really known what he should call it. A "web," perhaps. A "screen" might also be accurate enough. But somehow, "invisibility cloak" gave it a certain panache.

The "Ghost." He'd heard that name mentioned, and it always amused him tremendously. If they only knew. If any of them only knew.

He'd kept to himself during the day, naturally. After all, if he was claiming that he was ill, the last thing he'd want to do is gallivant around the palace in what was obviously the pink of health. So he spent the day reading, keeping the door closed, allowing meals to be brought to him—during which he covered himself up in the bed and made assorted disgusting noises so that the servants would be inclined to leave the food and depart as quickly as they could.

When he saw the sun sinking on the horizon, however, that was when he made his move.

He removed the delicately woven cloak from the hidden bottom of his suitcase and unfolded it carefully on the bed. He'd never forget the day that he had stumbled upon it, exploring that fallen ship on Cygnus 4. He'd been working a security gig at a power plant there, employed by an eccentric owner who was convinced that hordes of crazed Martians—little antennaed green ones, not the real thing—were trying to take over his factory. While he'd been there, planetary sensors had detected a ship entering the atmosphere, a ship that had spiraled down and disappeared from the sensors as quickly as it had appeared. Welch, along with a team, had been dispatched to inspect it and make sure that no crazed Martians with their killer death rays were emerging to conquer the relatively unappealing Cygnus 4.

What Welch had found was a ship unlike any he'd ever seen. It looked slightly like one of those bizarre spiked ships that had shown up on ISN several years before, but it had significant differences, as well. It was as if it shared the same technological base, but had gone off in another direction.

He had discovered a creature therein, a creature unlike any race he'd seen before, even on Babylon 5. Grey-skinned, and chilling to the bone. The thing had been killed upon impact, and Welch couldn't have been happier. He had the feeling this wasn't something he wanted to face while it was breathing.

And upon further inspection—while telling the rest of his people to stay back in case there was some sort of danger—he had discovered the cloak.

He hadn't known what it was at first. He had, however, managed to scare the hell out of himself, for he had seen the fine, silvery, woven fabric and had attempted to pick it up. In doing so, he let out an alarmed yelp as his forearm abruptly vanished. Convinced that he had permanently maimed himself, Welch had fallen back, only to find his arm rematerializing instantly. He stared stupidly at his arm, turning the hand back and forth as if to assure himself that it was, in fact, there. Then he reached for the fabric once again, a bit more confidently this time. He'd wrapped it around his hand, and that disappeared as well, but this time he wasn't the least bit alarmed.

He had never seen anything like it, and he was reasonably certain that it had no parallel in current science. The closest comparison he could make was that it was like a changeling net, except what it did was transform anyone over whom it fell, so that they effectively blended seamlessly into the background. Through experimentation, Welch had discovered its limitations, including the fact that it remained deactivated as long as it was folded in upon itself. Unfolded, however, it began working instantly—a tremendous inconvenience that time he had unthinkingly tossed it into his bedroom and then taken half a day to find the damned thing again.

None of the others in his security team had seen the cloak, and he hadn't been about to volunteer knowledge of its existence. Instead, he had carefully hidden it, and used it judiciously on subsequent jobs. He had, as Garibaldi made note, acquired quite a reputation, although people didn't truly realize just what it was he was getting a reputation for.

So there on Centauri Prime, Welch draped the cloak around himself, head to toe. He looked down and could see the rest of his body perfectly. That was one of the aspects of the cloak that it had taken him a little while to understand: Once he was completely under it, he was visible to himself. But if any part of him was uncovered, then he himself couldn't see the parts that were hidden. It made a strange kind of sense to him. The only thing he could figure out was that the cloak somehow managed to bend light around it, convincing onlookers that they were seeing things around it. But if light was completely bent away from whoever was wearing it, then that meant light wouldn't be reaching the wearer's eyes, and he would be effectively blinded. So obviously the thing was crafted to make sure that didn't happen. How, he couldn't even begin to guess.

He did know that if he brought it to an EarthGov lab or something, they could probably figure it out. But he sure as hell would never see it again, and he wasn't about to let such a valuable acquisition slip through his fingers.

He emerged from his room, glanced right and left, then

started down the corridor. Two guards were approaching. Just to play it safe and make sure that the cloak was functioning, he made a grotesque face and tossed an obscene gesture at them. They didn't acknowledge his presence or give him so much as a glance.

Perfect.

Lou headed toward the main entrance of the palace, and while on his way he heard youthful voices. Unless he very much missed his guess, that was a group of the Prime Candidates, on their way out. He congratulated himself on his timing, which apparently could not have been more perfect.

Sure enough, there was half a dozen of them heading out. Welch couldn't help but notice that they didn't seem to interact like normal teenage boys. There was no banter, no bravado, no strut or cock-of-the-walk attitude. Instead they spoke in straightforward, businesslike terms. They kept their voices low, obviously wanting to keep Prime Candidate business to themselves. This was definitely not a group that Welch would comfortably have fit in with, even when he had been a teenager.

They headed away from the palace, going in the same direction as the other groups that Welch had observed the previous day. Lou fell into step behind them. As always, he kept his strides modest, and was careful not to swing his arms or in some other way move in a remotely jaunty fashion that might possibly dislodge the cloak. The last thing he wanted to do was suddenly materialize. Needless to say, that would likely have attracted attention.

They headed into town, and Welch caught sight of a massive tower that looked to be about in the center of the city. He'd heard someone make passing reference to it when they had first landed on Centauri Prime. The "Tower of Power," they'd called it. It was supposed to be symbolic. As far as Lou was concerned, it was symbolic of how much of an eyesore people could construct in their city if they were really, really dedicated.

They kept on moving, Lou right behind them. The farther they got into the city, the more nervous Lou felt. He was invisible, yes, but he wasn't intangible. There were quite a few folks on the streets, and people could still bump into him if he wasn't careful. Since no one was making any effort to stay out of his way, it was everything that Lou could do to stay one step ahead of Centauri passersby. He also almost managed to get himself killed when he forgot that a passing vehicle couldn't see him and wasn't about to stop for him. Only fast reflexes and a bit of luck enabled him to get out of the way in time.

During that near-accident, Welch momentarily lost sight of the Prime Candidates. For a moment he thought he'd completely blown it, but then he saw them turn a corner, and he sprinted after them. Luck was with him, for that section of the sidewalk happened to be clear of pedestrians for the moment. Otherwise, he would never have managed to keep up with them; either that, or he would have had to act as a sort of invisible football lineman, knocking people out of the way so he could get to where he was going.

One of the things he noticed was how people seemed to look at the Prime Candidates. He considered them to be a fairly creepy bunch of young men, but it seemed to him that Centauri chests swelled with pride when the Candidates walked past. Welch couldn't believe it. The truth was so obvious and clear to him: here were the youth of Centauri Prime, being brainwashed into good little soldiers who did whatever they were told with no thought, no conscience. Welch believed as much in the chain of command as any military man, former or no. But he also knew that swearing to obey orders, at least in EarthForce, didn't mean tossing aside morals and doing whatever was asked of you, no matter how repellant. Although he hadn't seen much of the Prime Candidates in action, he could see it in their eyes, in their demeanor. These kids didn't care about anything except their organization and the people who ran it.

He saw them head into a fairly nondescript building that was set off by itself. There wasn't anything on it to identify it as a gathering place. Yet, not only did the group of Prime Candidates that he had been following enter, but several others came out. It was enough to make Lou very, very curious as to just what might be inside the building. Might be nothing. Might be something useful. No real way to tell unless he went in and looked around . . .

He had no desire to simply walk in, though. An invisible entrance might be noticed. So he took up a post just outside the door and waited. He had all the time in the world. He leaned against the wall, started to whistle softly, and then caught himself and shut up. He did so just in time; a man walking by was looking around in mild confusion. He shrugged it off and continued on his way.

Then the door slid open. Two of the Prime Candidates emerged, deep in conversation about something called Morbis. The name meant nothing to Welch, but he tucked it away into his brain, for subsequent reference. The moment they were clear, the door started to shut again, but Lou bolted for it. The door paused a moment automatically, its detection device registering Lou's presence even though he was invisible. But there wasn't an alarm setup for the door; it simply had a detector to inform it when to open and close. The brief stutter-stop-and-start of the door didn't attract much notice from the Prime Candidates because it was so brief. One of them obviously thought he had noticed something out of the corner of his eye, for he hesitated and glanced back at the door. But it slid closed without any problem, so he chalked it up to a momentary glitch before heading off on his own business.

The place didn't seem particularly imposing or impressive to Lou. Nevertheless, he wasn't about to dismiss it. The furnishings were very stark and utilitarian, but what there was, was meticulously maintained. Everything was scrubbed down and shining. He heard small groups of the Prime Candidates speaking in different rooms, but their conduct within those rooms was no different than outside. It was all very business-like. Obviously the Prime Candidates never felt the need to let down their hair . . . no pun intended.

Welch moved very carefully. He didn't want to bump into

any of them within the narrow confines of the halls. That would be extremely bad. Even so, moving with caution, he was able to get a feel for the downstairs section of the place. Mostly it was a series of small meeting rooms. Several of them were empty, and the rest of them had small groups of Candidates, talking in a way that indicated they were being debriefed, or something else official. He saw their reflections gleaming in the polished surfaces and wondered how many man-hours it had taken them to hone everything to that kind of shine.

There was a flight of stairs to his right. Welch placed a tentative foot on the first step, wanting to make sure it didn't make any noise. It seemed to be sturdy enough, and he put more pressure on it until he was standing on it with his full weight. The step didn't emit so much as a squeak. Slowly he made his way up the stairs, moving with increasing confidence, to say nothing of a sense of urgency. After all, if someone came trotting down the steps, they might bang right into him.

He got to the upper floor, and this one seemed a bit different from the downstairs. Here there appeared to be genuine offices, rather than chat rooms. He could only assume that it was where the "upper management" of the Prime Candidates came to work. That, however, might provide him with more information.

A Prime Candidate walked out of one of the offices. He had a look of concentration on his face, and he seemed to exude authority. As he walked past Welch, another of the Prime Candidates came trotting up the stairs, and called to him, "Throk! A moment of your time, please. We need to discuss the troop dispatches to Morbis. Also, construction seems to be slowing down on Nefua."

The one called Throk made an impatient noise and followed the other Prime Candidate downstairs. This left the office open and unoccupied, and Welch wasn't about to squander the opportunity. He sidled in to see whatever there was to discover.

At first glance, there didn't appear to be much. The office

was as spartan in its contents as any of the others had been.
Just a desk with a computer terminal, and a couple of chairs.
Not so much as a picture on the walls or on the desk. But then
Welch noticed that the computer had been left on, and he
placed himself in front of the screen so he could study what
was on it.

What he saw caused him to go completely slack-jawed. It
was a good thing no one was able to see him, because if they
were, they would think that he looked like an imbecile.

Throk had been in the middle of juggling Prime Candidate
assignments, but it was the location of the assignments that
startled Welch. Lou was horrified to see, from manpower esti-
mates, that there were in excess of two thousand members
of the Prime Candidates, and it appeared from what he was
seeing that a sizable number of them were *not* on Centauri
Prime at the moment. These names that he'd heard since
arriving—Morbis, Nefua—they were outlying colony worlds.
Border worlds, worlds that wouldn't automatically be associated with the Centauri or, indeed, with any major power. And
those weren't the only worlds involved, either; there were at
least half a dozen more listed.

They were being used as mobilization sites.

Welch realized that he and Garibaldi had gotten it exactly
right. Xonos has been a red herring. The real action was happening at planets that were light-years from Centauri Prime.
They were developing weaponry. They were assembling
troops, undergoing training, all in the darkest secret. It was
easy enough to keep the secret, though, because the initial
talent pool at least was being drawn from the ranks of the
Prime Candidates. Young recruits who didn't attract much attention, and who could be relied upon for complete, unswerv-
ing discretion and dedication.

Essentially, the Centauri were moving from one colony
world to the next, leapfrogging as they managed to organize
forced labor on each one. There were no cries of conquest to
the Alliance, because the Centauri were basically conquering
themselves. Those colonists who had thought they had managed to build a new life for themselves by staking claims on

outlying worlds were discovering that they had been deluding themselves. The Prime Candidates, along with handpicked individuals from the ministry, were coming in and strong-arming them into aiding in a military buildup. Faced with the prospect of having support for their colonies yanked altogether, the colonists had no choice whatsoever but to comply. Thus was the Centauri government managing to build up its military muscle, all while flying below the radar of the Alliance.

It was possible that Londo knew nothing about this. Ministers Durla and Lione seemed to be running the Prime Candidates almost single-handedly. And Welch had the feeling that Londo had very little to do with day-to-day affairs of state.

Still, it didn't matter how much Londo knew or didn't know. Something had to be done about this, because Centauri Prime had had limits placed upon its militarization by the Alliance, and this was simply an attempt by the Centauri to engage in a buildup without detection. It appeared everything that had been whispered about the Centauri was absolutely true. They couldn't be trusted, even to the smallest degree.

Fortunately, as near as Welch could tell, the buildup still was in its preliminary stages. They had managed to catch it early enough that something could still be done about it. Once the Alliance was informed, they could shut it down before . . .

The shadows in the room . . . seemed longer than they had before.

Lou was certain he had to be imagining it. But there was something else; he felt a chill running down his spine, seizing it. He tried to turn his attention to the computer; however, he was unable to.

Something was happening, something was wrong, definitely wrong, but he had no idea what it could possibly be.

The chill seemed as if it were permeating his entire body, as if frost were developing on him and seeping right into his pores. He looked down at himself, but there was no change. Everything was fine.

Still, it was enough to convince him that it was time to get the hell out of there. He had a data crystal in his pocket, not by happenstance. He had hoped that he might stumble onto something useful, and he had come prepared. He shoved the crystal into the proper receptacle and downloaded as much information as possible. Then he pulled out the crystal, pocketed it, and turned to head for the door.

Throk was standing there, occupying the entirety of the door. He was going to have to wait until Throk got out of the way, because obviously he couldn't push him aside while he was invisible . . .

Except . . .

Except Throk was looking at him. Right at him.

Very cautiously, Lou moved to the left of the desk. Throk's eyes followed him. Lou looked down at the polished surface of the desk and saw his reflection staring back at him.

"You," Throk said, "should not have come here."

He had no idea what had happened, no clue how the mechanics of the cloak had failed him. But obviously they had. Still, Lou felt no real alarm. He was too old a hand at this, and wasn't one to panic easily. The thing to remember was, these were kids, playing at being officials. Whereas he was an adult and, as a representative of the Interstellar Alliance, he had just caught them at a breech of the agreement that restricted their military buildup. They were busted, and that was all there was to it.

From a psychological point of view, Lou Welch had the upper hand.

"All right, son," he said, dropping any endeavor to hide himself, since it obviously wasn't working. "Why not stand away from that door right now. We don't want any sort of trouble—"

"You," Throk said again, his voice sounding dull and empty, and even a bit resigned, "should not have come here." Even as he spoke, he reached into his belt and pulled on a pair of thin, flexible black gloves.

Then he came toward Welch. He approached with an economy of movement, as if he were in no hurry. Welch started to move right, but the room wasn't that big, and Throk easily continued to block his exit by sidestepping slightly.

"I'm warning you, kid. I'll break you in half. So don't try anything stupid." The one thing Lou had going for him was that Throk had made no attempt to call for help. Obviously he felt that he could handle this on his own. That, Welch knew, would prove to be his undoing.

Throk was within range now, and Welch went for him. Although he had received plenty of training as a member of EarthForce, Lou Welch was a barroom brawler from way back. He had the instincts and moves of a slug-out artist, and he used them now. He feinted with his left, then swung a quick right. It was a good swing, a fast snap from the hip.

Throk brushed it aside as if it were a punch thrown by a child. It barely grazed Throk's upper chest, and did no damage.

Lou swung again. Throk stepped slightly back so that the punch missed entirely, throwing Lou off balance, and before Welch could recover, Throk came in fast. The move didn't seem like anything, but it was so quick that it was like lightning, and Throk's punch shot in hard.

Lou tried to put up a defense, but Throk punched through it as if it were tissue paper. One punch doubled Lou over, and the second smashed in his face. Lou went down, blood fountaining from his shattered nose, and he felt an immediate swelling.

He tried to say something, tried to speak with bravado and say "Nice shot, kid," but he couldn't talk. He had the hideous feeling that the kid had just broken his jaw, but that the pain hadn't fully registered on him.

And then Throk grabbed him by his new hair, pulling him to his feet as if he weighed nothing, and Welch couldn't believe the kid's upper torso strength. The true significance hadn't fully dawned on him; he was still too busy being surprised by the power in his opponent. Throk got a firm grip on him, one hand holding him by the scruff of his neck, the other on the back of his belt, and he slammed Lou Welch into the wall, causing a crack in it. The impact was so violent that Lou literally saw stars.

For a moment he thought he saw Babylon 5 float across those stars in orbit, and then he felt nauseated, and decided that he was going to have to have that checked out later. Then he remembered that he was in the middle of a fight, except it didn't seem like much of a fight, but more of a slaughter.

*Fight back! Do something! Let this little punk know who's in charge!* Lou twisted free with an unexpected burst of strength, then turned and hit Throk as hard as he could in the gut. His fist connected with a stomach that felt as solid as rock. He thought that he might have broken a knuckle.

Then the room started to swirl. The exit suddenly seemed closer, and Lou tried to will himself over to it. At first his body didn't respond and then he was moving, a step toward it and then to . . .

. . . and then he was in the air. For one delirious moment he thought he was flying, and then he realized that Throk had lifted him clear of the floor and was holding him over his head. Then the floor was coming up to meet him with horrifying speed, and he crashed into it and lay there, the breath knocked out of him, unable to move. Everything hurt.

Throk's knee was jammed into the back of his spine and he felt hands on either side of his head.

*Guess you showed him who was in charge* was the last thought that flittered through Lou Welch's mind before Throk ruthlessly, but efficiently, snapped his head around and broke his neck.

Throk didn't move his hands until he felt Lou Welch's pulse cease. He found it interesting, from a clinical point of view, how the pulse kept going for some seconds after Welch had effectively died. He wondered if Welch was, in fact, already dead before the cessation of the pulse, or whether that was just some last, lingering reflex. In the end, it didn't make that much difference, he decided, as long as the result was the same.

He released his grip and stood, shaking out his hands. Then he turned and saw the grey figure in the corner of the room.

The figure that seemed to be part of the shadows, and then separate from them.

Throk stood paralyzed. While he was killing Lou Welch, his heart had barely sped up. He had simply acted in the defense of Centauri Prime, and had done so in as brisk and efficient a manner as he could. He had been so detached from it that he might well have been watching someone else perform the action.

What he was seeing now, though, struck at him. He felt an odd combination of fear . . . and . . .

. . . honor.

"Who are you?" Throk demanded in a loud voice, except that when he spoke it actually came out as barely above a whisper.

"Shiv'kala," said the grey creature. He reached down and lifted some sort of odd shroud from Welch's corpse. Speaking as much to himself as to Throk, he murmured, "This belonged to us. He should not have come by it. I do not know how he did. In the end, though, it could not protect him from me. I negated its effect so that you could see him, and you did the rest . . . very well. Our confidence was not misplaced." He looked at Throk with obsidian eyes. "You will probably want to remove the data crystal in his pocket."

"What are you?" said Throk. There was now no bravado in his tone at all.

Shiv'kala stepped forward and touched one hand to Throk's temple. Throk tried to move, but was unable to do so. "I," Shiv'kala said softly, "am simply a figment of your imagination."

Throk blinked, trembled slightly for no reason that he could recall, and looked at the empty office in front of him. Then he heard footsteps pounding up the steps behind him and he turned to face several other members of the Prime Candidates. They gaped in open astonishment at the corpse on the floor and then stared mutely at Throk.

Throk offered no explanation whatsoever. None seemed necessary. Instead he simply said, "Get rid of him." As an afterthought, he added, "And remove the data crystal from his pocket."

They did as they were told, removing the data crystal, tossing it on the floor, and grinding it underfoot. Within moments, Lou Welch's body had been shoved into a bag and dragged unceremoniously down the stairs, his head thumping rhythmically on each step as he was hauled along like a sack of vegetables. The Prime Candidates who had taken on the task made sure to haul the body to a site reasonably distant from their safe house, then tossed it into an alleyway. And there they left it.

Lou lay there for a time, passersby paying the lifeless heap no mind. And then a robed figure approached him. No one cared about the robed figure because somehow their eyes seem to glide right off him if they happened to look in his direction. He knelt next to the body, undoing the top of the sack and yanking it down so that he could have a clear look at that which he already knew he was going to find. The head was swollen black-and-blue where it had struck the wall, and dried blood had coalesced all over its face.

"Poor bastard," muttered Finian. "Vir's not going to be happy about this at all."

# — chapter 14 —

"I want him dead. Whoever did this, I want him dead."

Garibaldi was trembling with barely suppressed rage. He was standing in a Centauri morgue, where he had been summoned to come and identify the body of one Lou Welch, Human. Welch's body lay unmoving on the slab, surrounded by Garibaldi, G'Kar, and Durla, their faces grim. A coroner stood nearby, impassive.

"The emperor regrets that this has come to pass," Durla began.

"The emperor regrets. He couldn't be bothered to come here, is what you're saying."

"He had other things to which he needed to attend . . ."

"So did this guy!" snapped Garibaldi, stabbing a finger at Welch. "And he's not going to get to attend to them, because one of you bastards did this to him!"

"Mr. Garibaldi, I resent that phrasing—"

Garibaldi silenced him with a gesture. "Ask me if I care," he said tersely. "Let me make this absolutely clear, Minister. Whoever did this, I want his head on a platter with some nice garnish and a few lemon wedges, and I want it now!"

"Michael, this isn't accomplishing anything," G'Kar said softly.

"You know what, G'Kar? I don't care! If I keep silent, I still won't be accomplishing anything, so I might as well accomplish nothing at the top of my lungs!"

"Mr. Garibaldi, this is regrettable," Durla said, "but the simple truth is that Centauri Prime is no more immune from crime and random acts of violence than any other world . . ."

Garibaldi circled the slab and came right up to the minister. "This wasn't anything random. He found out something, and one of your people did this."

"Found out something. What would that be?"

"About what you people are really up to."

Durla's eyes narrowed. "If you have some specific charge," he said in a measured, deliberate tone, "then I suggest you take it back to President Sheridan. If you do not, then I will thank you not to throw around unsupported allegations, since they will do nothing to alleviate the tensions between our races. To the best of my knowledge, however, we have been quite forthcoming in answering all your questions, and proving to you that your accusations of military buildup have been groundless. As unfortunate as this situation is, what it most definitely does not need is to be complicated with unrelated accusations."

Garibaldi took all this in; then he leaned forward until he was right in Durla's face. When he spoke, it was so softly that Durla had to strain to hear. "If I find out," he murmured, "that you, or someone who answers directly to you, had anything to do with this . . . then I swear to God, Minister, I will kill you myself."

"I would not advise that," said Durla calmly. "That would create an incident."

"We've already got an incident," Garibaldi said, indicating Welch. "And someone is going to pay for it." His hands were opening and closing as if he was trying to find someone whose throat he could wrap them around.

And then a voice said sharply, "I don't think threats are going to help."

"Ambassador Cotto," Durla said quickly. "Your timing could not be better."

"Or worse, depending on your point of view," said Vir. He crossed the morgue, looking around uncomfortably. "Chilly in here," he said. Then he looked down in undisguised dismay at the body on the slab. That was one thing that Garibaldi genuinely liked about Vir. It was impossible for him to hide what he was thinking. Vir's face could be read more easily than a data crystal.

At least, that's what Garibaldi once would have thought. Now, though, he thought there was an air of inscrutability to Vir that hadn't been there before. Vir had changed in the time since he'd last seen him, Garibaldi realized, and he didn't think it was for the better.

Vir turned to the coroner, who was standing a few feet away. "Do we know the cause?" he asked.

It was Garibaldi who answered. "Yeah. The cause was that he was in the wrong place at the wrong time, and found out something he shouldn't have, and was killed for it."

"That's a serious charge, Mr. Garibaldi."

"Hey!" said Garibaldi. "It's not like Lou was picked up for jaywalking! A man is dead! As crimes go, they don't get much more serious than that. Serious crimes require serious charges—and serious punishment."

It was G'Kar who spoke up. "At the moment, Mr. Garibaldi, the one who is being punished is you. You are not responsible for Mr. Welch's death simply because you brought him here."

"Whose side are you on?" Garibaldi said, with a sharp look to G'Kar.

"Yours and his," G'Kar said promptly. "However, he is gone, and I don't think you'll be helping anyone with histrionics. There will be an investigation, but getting angry at the men in this room will not expedite it, nor will it create anything resembling the proper atmosphere for an investigation."

"Thank you for understanding, Citizen G'Kar," Durla said.

G'Kar fired him a look that froze the words of thanks in his throat. "I don't want, or need, your appreciation, Minister. What I want is your cooperation . . . and yours, Mr. Ambassador. If you desire the continuation of anything remotely approaching normal relations between your people and the Alliance . . ."

"Normal relations?" At that, Vir laughed bitterly. "Look, G'Kar, I hate to remind you, but at the moment 'normal' translates as 'We're watched for the slightest hint of aggressive behavior, so that people like you can be sent down to monitor us . . . and have something like this happen as a result.' " With that he indicated Welch's corpse.

G'Kar took a step toward Vir, studying him very carefully, as if dissecting him with his eye. "We are depending upon you to help us handle this matter, Ambassador. For what it is worth . . . I have always had a great deal of respect for you."

More harshly than G'Kar or Garibaldi would have expected, Vir replied, "Let us be candid, Citizen. You dripped blood at my feet to symbolize dead Narn, as if it were my fault. No one in this galaxy ever made me feel smaller than you did at that moment. So you'll excuse me when I tell you that your claim to have respect for me . . . well, that isn't worth much at all."

There didn't seem anything that Garibaldi or G'Kar could say in response to that. Instead, Garibaldi looked down once more at Welch, then rested a hand on his cold shoulder, and whispered, "I'm sorry, Lou." Then he and G'Kar left without a backward glance.

"Tragic," said Durla, shaking his head sadly. "Most tragic."

"Minister . . . I'd like to be left alone with him for a time." Vir glanced at Durla, then at the coroner. "If you wouldn't mind."

"Alone? Why?" asked the coroner.

"I knew this man," Vir said. "He was a friend, after a fashion. I'd . . . like to say some prayers. They're personal. I'm sure you understand."

"Of course I do," said Durla, who looked as if he didn't, but wasn't inclined to argue. "Will you be coming by the palace during your stay? Say hello to Mariel, perhaps?"

"Perhaps," said Vir. "Thank you."

The two Centauri exited the morgue, leaving Vir alone with Welch. He stared down at the dead man, shaking his head in silence.

"How did you get here so quickly?"

It was Finian who spoke, having practically materialized at

Vir's elbow. He was carrying a staff, which Vir hadn't seen him doing before. Fortunately enough, by this stage in Vir's life, it was becoming almost impossible to startle him. He merely stared at the techno-mage, and said, "Did the coroner see you enter?"

Finian gave him a look as if to say, *Oh, please.*

Deciding that pretty much served as an answer, Vir continued, "What do you mean, how did I get here so quickly?"

"I mean I sent a message to Babylon 5 only a short while ago, telling you what had happened. How did you manage to travel the distance so quickly?"

"I didn't get your message," Vir replied. "I . . ." Before he spoke more, he reflexively glanced around to see if anyone was listening. Then he continued, albeit in a lower voice, "I had already left Babylon 5. Mariel contacted me privately the moment she learned that G'Kar and Garibaldi were here. She felt it would be best if I was here while they were here. I think she was right, although I doubt she was expecting anything like this." He looked up at Finian. "So what happened? You wouldn't be here if you didn't have some idea."

"He had been using Shadow technology."

"Shadow technology?" Vir could scarcely comprehend it. "Where would he get that?"

"I don't know," admitted Finian. "Might have been happenstance. Most likely it was. He used a transparency web. It gave him limited invisibility. The use of it in the city drew me to him, and I arrived in time to see his body being hauled out of a building. I followed the people who were dumping him."

"What building? Can you take me to it?"

"Yes," Finian said distractedly. "It appeared to be a stronghold for those charming lads you refer to as the Prime Candidates."

Vir moaned. That was not news he had wanted to hear. The Prime Candidates—the servants of Durla, the pets of Lione. This was not going to be easy. "He found out something, didn't he."

"I expect that he did."

"I wish we could find out what it was."

Finian was silent for a moment, and then he said, "There . . . is a way."

"What? What way?"

Finian turned to him and said slowly, "The brain . . . is one of the greatest technological marvels of nature. Still, in the final analysis, it is simply a computer. And data can be downloaded from any computer . . . even one which has crashed."

"You can . . . you can extract that information from him? Even though he's gone?"

"In theory, yes. I've never done such a thing myself . . . but I know the technique. I simply . . . wish I didn't have to. Gwynn or Galen could do this with much greater equanimity than I could. But Galen has his own problems involving Captain Gideon, and Gwynn is attending to other business. So I'm afraid that I am it."

"Is it difficult?"

"A bit. I did bring a bit of help," he said, gripping the staff a bit more tightly.

"Is there anything I can do to help?"

"Yes. Keep the coroner out of here."

"Of course," Vir said matter-of-factly.

"This will take a few minutes. I don't need him in here."

"All right."

"Oh, and before you go, hand me that cutting tool, if you would."

Vir did as he was asked, then headed out to the coroner. The coroner, for his part, seemed perfectly inclined to head back into the morgue, and Vir did the first thing that occurred to him: he broke down in sobs.

"Great Maker . . . were you close with that fellow?" asked the coroner.

"I love him like a brother!" Vir cried out. He didn't even bother with the nearby chair; he simply sank down onto the floor, weeping piteously. Finding a source of tears wasn't all that difficult for him. All he had to draw upon was everything that had happened to him, and everything that he had done in the past several years, and the misery welled up effortlessly. Summoning tears was not a problem; for Vir, it was restraining them on a day-to-day basis that had been the challenge.

Consequently, Vir managed to keep the coroner occupied with finding a sedative that would calm Vir's nerves. The fellow finally located something and handed it to Vir, who popped it in his mouth gratefully and lodged it securely in his cheek so that he wouldn't swallow it. When the coroner turned away from him for a moment, Vir spat it into his hand and stashed it in his pocket.

"Are you feeling better?" the coroner asked him at last.

Vir nodded, but he still had that air of tragedy draped around him.

"I am so sorry you have to endure this," said the coroner. "You, Ambassador, are a soul in pain."

"Yes. I know," Vir said with utter sincerity.

"You need a drink. Come . . . I'll close early today, and we will go out and speak of happier things." At which point, the coroner rose and started to head into the examination room.

"No, wait!" Vir called out. "Uhm . . . stay here, just a few minutes, until the medicine kicks in!"

"You'll be fine, Ambassador. I'll just be a moment. I've already left the body out too long."

"But if you'd just . . ."

However, the coroner had already walked away. Vir felt his stomach lurching into his mouth. Finally, in a last ditch attempt to alert Finian that someone was coming, he called out as loudly as he could, *"But do you have to go back into the exam room? Do you really have to?"*

The next thing he knew, he heard an alarmed yelp from the coroner, and was certain that Finian had been spotted. He scrambled to his feet and ran into the examining room, not sure what he could possibly say or do, but determined that he had to do something.

When he got there, he found the room empty save for Welch's corpse and the coroner—who was white as a sheet. He didn't seem sickened; certainly he had seen far too much in his life for that. But his attitude was one of barely contained rage. "Who did this?" he demanded. "Who did this?"

"Did what?" said a confused Vir, and then he saw it.

The top of Lou Welch's head had been neatly removed. Sections of his brain had been meticulously and precisely removed and put into a pan nearby, and—Vir was positive that it was his imagination—just for a moment, they seemed to be pulsing as if with a life of their own.

Then whatever movement he saw, real or imagined, ceased, and he was left with his stomach wrenching itself around in fits of uncontrollable nausea. He knew he wasn't going to be able to contain himself. The best he could do was lurch to a nearby garbage can and thrust his head into it as everything that he had eaten in the past twelve hours made its violent return engagement.

The early evening air shored up Vir as he stood outside the building, leaning against the wall, his legs quivering. He had made his excuses to the coroner, which had not been a difficult accomplishment. The coroner, considering the circumstances, seemed disinclined to go anywhere, and he promised Vir a full investigation into the outrageous circumstances surrounding Lou Welch's mutilation.

"Vir."

He realized that his name had just been said several times, and it was only around the fourth or fifth time that he really, truly heard it. He turned and saw Finian standing just inside an alley, gesturing that Vir should join him. Fired by a cold fury, Vir immediately headed toward the techno-mage, joining him in the relative dimness of the alley. "How could you?" he whispered furiously, with such intensity that his voice came out gravelly.

But Finian was, at that point, totally without the casual calm that techno-mages so often affected. Indeed, he looked as shaken as Vir, and when he held up his hands they were specked with blood. "Are you remotely under the impression that was fun for me?" he demanded. "You had the luxury of becoming ill! I didn't. At least . . . not until I got out here." He leaned against the alley wall, looking shaken, and it was only then that Vir caught a whiff coming off Finian's breath. The techno-mage had been violently ill recently, as well. Nastily, Vir couldn't help but think that that was something he would have liked to see.

"There had to be some other way," Vir insisted.

"Oh, you know that, do you?" snapped Finian. "Your many years worth of training as a techno-mage has given you that insight, has it? I'm not a ghoul, Cotto. I don't derive any sort of sick pleasure from carving up the bodies of the dead. I did what had to be done. We've all done what we've had to do. Some of us are just less sanctimonious about it than others."

"I just . . ." Vir steadied himself. "I just wish you had warned me."

"Believe me, you would not have wanted to know."

Vir knew that Finian was right about that. If, during the time that he'd been working to distract the coroner, he had been thinking about what Finian was up to in the next room over, his ghastly imaginings likely would have hampered his ability to do his part of the job. Seeing that there was no point to pursuing or discussing the matter further, Vir sighed, "All right, so . . . so did you find what we needed?"

"Throk."

"Throk." Vir didn't follow at first, but then he realized. "Throk? Of the Prime Candidates? He's the one who killed Lou Welch?"

Finian nodded. "With his bare hands."

"Great Maker," Vir whispered. "I know him. He's . . . he's just a boy . . ."

"He's a young man whom I would not care to cross," Finian said.

"But why did he kill him?"

As quickly and efficiently as he could, Finian laid it out for him. Told him of the Centauri buildup, told him of the border worlds on which it was occurring, told him of the secret agenda that was being supported by the Centaurum. Throughout the recitation, Vir simply stood there, shaking his head . . . not in denial, but in overwhelming disbelief that all this could be happening to the world of his birth.

"My guess," Finian added, "is that there was a Drakh

involved in the murder, as well. I can't say for sure, because if there was, the creature didn't reveal itself while Welch was alive. But that would be the only reasonable explanation for Welch's technology having failed him when it did."

"So . . . what do we do now? We have to tell—"

"Tell who?" Finian asked quietly. "Tell what? There is no one in authority you can truly trust, and even if you do find someone . . . you have nothing you can really tell them. What would you say? 'A techno-mage extracted information from Lou Welch's brain and told me that Throk was responsible.' You have no proof, and the only verification that the Prime Candidates are likely to provide is that they'll make sure your corpse winds up next to Lou Welch's."

Vir nodded slowly. Once again, there was no point in denying anything that Finian was saying. He turned and paced for a moment, then paused.

"All right, then," he said finally. "My main job is to prevent this from getting any worse than it already is. And there's only one way to do that. But here's what I need you to do . . ."

He turned back to Finian and knew, even before he looked, that the techno-mage was gone.

"If he doesn't stop doing that, I'll kill him myself," muttered Vir.

Vir made certain to have Garibaldi and G'Kar at a safe distance from the palace when he told them. As it so happened, he had chosen the spot where Senna had, once upon a time, spent days studying with one of her teachers, gazing at clouds and wondering about the future of Centauri Prime. Vir didn't know that, of course, although the future of Centauri Prime happened to be uppermost in his mind, as well.

His more immediate concern, though, was that he needed to avoid having the outraged shouting of Garibaldi echoing up and down the corridors. Such an incident certainly would contribute very little to the cause of trying to make things right.

He needn't have worried. When Michael Garibaldi became as angry as he was at that moment, he tended to speak in a very low, whispered voice. "First," Garibaldi said, very slowly and very dangerously, "I want to know what you haven't told me."

Vir had to give Garibaldi credit. The fact was, Vir hadn't told him everything. He had said that the Prime Candidates had been responsible for Lou's death, but hadn't specified which one. He had told them about how Lou had died, but hadn't mentioned the possible involvement of the Drakh. And he had told them of the military buildup, but not how he had managed to find out about it.

"I've told you everything I can."

"Vir . . ."

"All right, fine," Vir said in exasperation. "A techno-mage sliced open your friend's brain and extracted the information that way. Happy?"

Garibaldi threw up his hands in exasperation, and turned to G'Kar. "You talk to him," he said to G'Kar, indicating Vir.

"Vir," G'Kar said carefully, "you have to understand: before we move on this information, we need to know—"

But Vir didn't let him finish the thought. "You can't move on it."

Both G'Kar and Garibaldi, who had spun back around, said, "What?"

"You can't move on it," Vir repeated. "I've told you about this as a show of good faith. You cannot—must not—do anything about it. The only one you can tell is Sheridan, and only if he likewise promises to make no move."

"You're insane," Garibaldi said flatly. "G'Kar, tell him he's insane."

"Well," began G'Kar, "I think if you study the . . ."

*"G'Kar!"*

"You're insane," G'Kar told him.

"No, I'm not," Vir shot back. "But I'll tell you what would be insane: letting the entire Alliance know what's going on, so that they can go after Centauri Prime."

"I don't give a damn about Centauri Prime," said Garibaldi.

"Yes, you've made that quite clear. But I don't have that sort of choice in the matter."

"And we're supposed to just let this go. Is that what you're saying?"

"I'm saying that I won't let it go. I'm saying that I'm going to do something about it."

"You are," Garibaldi said skeptically. "You. Vir Cotto. You're going to do something about it."

Vir stepped in close, and there was such cold fury in his eyes that Garibaldi reflexively stepped back. "I hear the condescension in your voice, Mr. Garibaldi. I know what you're thinking. You think I'm incapable of doing anything. That I'm inept. You think you know me.

"You don't know me, Garibaldi. These days, I don't even think I know me. But I know this: this is a Centauri matter, and it shall be handled in the Centauri way."

"And what way is that?"

"*My* way," Vir said. "Believe me, Garibaldi, you want me as an ally, not as an enemy. And I'm giving you the opportunity, right now, to decide which it's going to be. Choose."

Garibaldi bristled, clearly not pleased with having ultimatums shoved in his face. But before he could say anything, G'Kar put a hand on his arm and tugged slightly, indicating with a gesture of his head that Garibaldi should follow him. Working hard to contain himself, Garibaldi did so. They put a respectable distance between themselves and Vir before speaking in low tones.

"You're expecting me to go along with this? Just go along with it?" Garibaldi said, before G'Kar could even open his mouth. "Sheridan sent us here on a fact-finding mission. You expect me to go back and tell him 'Sorry, Mr. President. We lost a man and, yeah, we found out some stuff . . . none of which we can do anything about, because I didn't want to upset Vir Cotto.' For all we know, Vir's full of crap! For all we know, he's behind the whole thing!"

"Calm yourself, Mr. Garibaldi," G'Kar said. "You don't believe that for a moment."

Garibaldi took a deep breath. "All right . . . all right, maybe I don't. But still—"

"Lou Welch's passing was a terrible thing. I wasn't as close to the man as you, and I know you feel it your responsibility since you brought him in on this. But the truth is that, yes, we were sent here to find facts, and we have found them. Now we have to determine what to do about them."

"We tell Sheridan . . ."

"And what he, in turn, does with them will depend heavily on your recommendation. Before you give that recommendation, Mr. Garibaldi, I suggest you consider the following: The Alliance, and Earth, do not need another war at this time. Morale is at an all-time low, since no cure for the Drakh plague has yet been discovered."

"The *Excalibur* is working on it. Gideon says he's close," said Garibaldi.

"And he said the same last year. Perhaps he is. Or perhaps he is trapped in what your people call Zeno's paradox, where he perpetually draws half the distance closer to his goal, but never reaches it."

"What are you saying?"

"I'm saying that more bad news, of this significance, is not necessarily needed."

"You're suggesting we cover it up?"

"I'm suggesting that we accede to Vir's request that he be allowed to handle it. If we provide that, then you and Sheridan will have a valuable ally within the royal court. He will be a useful source of information. Plus, you have to consider the long term."

"The long term." Garibaldi shook his head. "I'm not following."

Lowering his voice even more, G'Kar said softly, "That man is going to be emperor one day. So it would behoove you to lay the groundwork now for a solid relationship. Vir Cotto is the future of Centauri Prime."

It took a few moments for Garibaldi to fully process what G'Kar was saying. "The future of Centauri Prime." He chucked a thumb at Vir, standing a short distance away, idly pulling on his fingers. "Him. That guy."

G'Kar nodded.

"And would you care to tell me, great mystic, how you happen to know that?"

Unflappable, ignoring Garibaldi's tone of voice, G'Kar said, "One evening, when Vir was rather in his cups, he told Lyta Alexander of a prophecy made by one Lady Morella . . . a Centauri seer whose veracity is well known, even on my Homeworld. Lyta and I have spent a good deal of time together in recent days, and she told me."

"So let me get this straight," Garibaldi said. Despite the flip nature of his words, he did not sound remotely amused by the notion. "You're telling me that you heard thirdhand that some Centauri fortune-teller predicted Vir would someday become emperor, and I'm supposed to let Lou Welch's killer, plus an entire secret war movement, slide, based on that. Her 'veracity is well known.' I never heard of her. How am *I* supposed to know if she's so wonderful."

"Lady Morella also predicted that Londo would become emperor, years before it happened."

Garibaldi didn't reply immediately to that. Instead he scratched the back of his neck, then looked around at Vir, who hadn't budged from the spot. "Lucky guess," he said finally.

G'Kar's gaze fixed upon Garibaldi, and when he spoke next, Garibaldi understood how this man had forged himself a place of leadership on his Homeworld. His words were quiet, direct, and filled with utter conviction.

"Michael," he said, dropping the formal surname for the first time that Garibaldi could recall, "there is something you must understand . . . and perhaps you already do, on some level. You and I, Vir, Londo, Sheridan . . . we are not like other men."

"We're not." He wasn't quite sure how to react to that.

"No. We are not. We are creatures of destiny, you and I. What we say, do, think, feel . . . shapes the destinies of billions of other beings. It is not necessarily that we are that special. But we were born at a certain time, thrust into certain circumstances . . . we were created to act, and accomplish certain things, so that others could live their own lives. It was . . . the luck of the draw. And as creatures of destiny, when that destiny is previewed in whatever small amounts it chooses to reveal itself to us . . . it would be the height of folly for us to turn our backs on it, disregard it. Indeed, we do so at our extreme peril.

"There is enough peril in the galaxy right now, Mr. Garibaldi, that I do not think it necessary to add yet more."

Garibaldi stood there for a moment, taking it in. Then, without looking at Vir, he gestured that the Centauri should join them. Vir quickly walked over to them, a look of quiet concern showing clearly on his face.

"So you want to keep this matter in-house, as it were," Garibaldi said. "Keep it quiet. Hush it up, so that the Alliance doesn't come down on you with all guns blazing, and pound you flat into nonexistence . . . just as you tried to do with the Narns."

"I could have done without that last part, but yes, that is essentially correct," Vir said dryly.

"All right," Garibaldi said. "We play it your way . . . on one condition."

"And that would be?"

"You're asking for a hell of a leap of faith here, Vir. I'm not a leap-of-faith kind of guy. I tend to look before I leap. You want me to have faith? You give me something to look at. You understand what I'm saying?"

"I . . . think so . . ." He nodded his head, but then shook it. "Actually, I'm not entirely sure, no . . ."

"Someone killed Lou Welch. That someone has to pay for it, to my satisfaction. You know who it is, don't you."

"Yes," said Vir.

"Then I want him delivered up. I don't care what you have to do, what paths you have to clear. I want it done."

"What you're asking is impossible," Vir told him.

"So is what you're asking. Me, I try to do at least one impossible thing a day. I suggest you practice the same goal, and start today. Understood?"

Vir was silent for a very long time, and then he said, "If I manage justice for Lou Welch . . . you will keep the Alliance away from Centauri Prime."

"For as long as humanly possible. You'll have the opportunity to ride herd on it. But you've got to show me you're capable of doing so. I don't care how you get it done. Just do it. Do we have a deal?"

He extended a hand. Vir, however, did not shake it. Instead he looked down a moment, and then said very softly, "Yes. I will keep you apprised."

And then he turned and walked away, leaving G'Kar and Garibaldi looking at each other in silence.

"He'll never get it done," said Garibaldi. "He'll cover for the guy. Or he'll give us more excuses why he can't be brought to us."

"I think you're wrong," G'Kar told him.

"In a way, I hope so. I'd like to see Vir succeed. I think, at heart, he's the best damned man on this planet. And in a way, I hope not . . . because I'd like the chance to find the guy who killed Lou . . . and do to him what he did to Lou Welch. Sounds like a win-win proposition to me."

He smiled, but there was nothing except pain in the smile.

# — *chapter 15* —

The evening hours were stretching toward the late night as Throk approached the entrance to the Prime Candidates' safe house. There was another, main headquarters that was used for recruitment and to hold up as a symbol of all that was great and wonderful in the Prime Candidates organization, but the safe house was their true home. Indeed, he spent more time there than he did at his own residence.

Two others of the Candidates, Muaad Jib and Klezko Suprah, strode along briskly next to Throk. They were newer inductees to the organization, people whom Throk himself had brought aboard. He regarded them somewhat as protégés, and looked forward to guiding their training as members of the most glorious and farseeing group in all of Centauri Prime.

Muaad and Klezko had been a bit shaky the previous night when they'd been asked to dispose of the Human's body. But since then, Throk had had a long talk with them, and they seemed much calmer now. That was certainly a relief. They were Prime Candidates, after all. The Candidates watched out for each other, and covered each other's backs. They were working hard to adopt the same stoicism and determination that Throk so ably displayed, and he was quite sure that they were going to come along very nicely.

And then something separated itself from the shadows ahead.

Throk slowed, his eyes narrowing, and Muaad and Klezko likewise reduced their pace. For a moment, Throk had an odd

feeling of déjà vu. A figure stepping forth from darkness . . .
why did that seem familiar to him?

Then he saw who it was.

"Ambassador Cotto?" he said. "Is there a problem?"

Vir smiled widely and spread his hands in a manner that
was both subtle and overt. The gesture looked cool, routine,
and friendly; by the same token, it went to show that there
was nothing of any danger in his hands. "Just wanted to talk
to you for a moment, Throk. Can you spare the time?"

"Of course," said Throk. He wasn't particularly concerned
about Ambassador Cotto—the man was a bumbling idiot, an
amateur pretending to be a diplomat. His appointment to
Babylon 5 was a waste of time, for Babylon 5 was inhabited
solely by enemies of the Centauri Republic. Since the Alliance already hated the Centauri, Vir could hardly do any
further damage. And he had lost his woman to Minister Durla
in a card game. How utterly pathetic was that? The ministers
seemed to have some regard for him since, for some reason,
Durla did. But Throk knew him for what he was: an oaf. Still,
even fools should be humored every now and then.

He nodded to Muaad and Klezko, who proceeded into the
building. Throk then approached Vir slowly, and said, "How
may I be of assistance?"

"I know you killed Lou Welch."

Throk prided himself on his unflappability. He had worked
long and hard to maintain an air of such detachment, and no
one, and nothing, could ever throw him off guard or off balance. But Vir's words, coming as they did from that pasty, in-
sipid face, were the equivalent of a club to Throk's skull. And
one word, one unfortunate word, slipped unbidden from between his lips.

"How . . ."

The moment the word was out of his mouth, Throk wanted
to kick himself. That was the absolute last thing he wanted to
say. But it wasn't for nothing that Throk was one of the fore-
most leaders of the Prime Candidates. Barely half a second
had passed before he recovered his wits.

". . . could you think such a thing," he continued, the pause almost imperceptible.

Almost.

"Oh, come now, Throk," Vir said, as if they were long-lost friends. "How could you think I *wouldn't* know? Centauri Prime has no greater protector of its interests than the Prime Candidates, and there is no greater Prime Candidate than you. The coroner said that someone killed the Human with his bare hands. That being a figure of speech, of course. The killer wore gloves. Those uniforms of yours come with gloves, by the way . . . don't they, Throk?"

"Many people wear gloves," Throk said. "The night air is quite cool."

"Yes, yes. That's so true," Vir commiserated. "Plus, it makes it next-to-impossible to get good DNA traces off the victim."

"Ambassador, I don't know what—"

"Of course you don't, of course you don't," Vir said. He draped an arm around Throk, and Throk stiffened. "Look, Throk . . . despite appearances, I'm not an idiot. I see which way the wind is blowing. I know what the future of Centauri Prime is, and I can tell you this: it's not having the Humans hovering over us and watching our every move. It's the people like you, the Prime Candidates. You are the movers and shakers; you are the next generation of greatness. Some day," and he laughed and patted Throk on the back, "you're going to be running things. You're probably going to wind up being my boss. So I figure the best possible thing I can do is get on your good side now, right? Right?"

"Right," Throk agreed slowly, still a bit confused but trying not to show it.

"So you see what I'm saying, then."

"You are saying," Throk guessed, analyzing each word thoroughly before he released it, "that if I did have something to do with the demise of . . . what was his name?"

"Welch. Lou Welch."

"That if I was involved with Mr. Welch's demise . . . you would not care."

"It's us against them, Throk," Vir said, leaning in even closer. It was at that point that the Prime Candidate caught the whiff of liquor hanging on Vir's breath. The man was drunk. It was likely that, come morning, he wouldn't even remember the conversation. "Us against them. And me . . . I want to be us. Let them be them . . . and we're us. United we stand, divided we fall. Right? Right?"

"Right," Throk said again.

Vir nodded, staring at him a time longer, staring into his eyes so intently that Throk felt as if Vir were trying to locate some treasure inside his skull. Finally Vir released him, and said, "You, Throk . . . are going places." Then he turned and, with a slight stagger, wobbled away into the evening.

Throk watched him go, the pitiful shell of a Centauri with aspirations toward . . . something. Throk couldn't be sure what. If he truly believed that he had some place in the future of Centauri Prime, then he, Vir, was woefully kidding himself.

Shaking his head, Throk entered the safe house and strode into one of the meeting rooms. Klezko and Muaad were waiting for him, as were several others.

"What did he want?" asked Klezko.

"To make a fool of himself," Throk replied, smirking. "In that, he was quite successful." Then he frowned. "But he knew that I killed Welch. We have to find out how he knew . . . and once we have . . . we will probably have to dispose of him, as well."

Vir sighed heavily as he looked at the small cylinder in his palm. It looked like nothing. It seemed so insignificant. Yet he was holding his future, right there in his hand.

He had looked squarely into Throk's eyes when he had stated that Throk had killed Lou Welch. Vir had become quite adept at being able to see what people were thinking, spotting any hint of duplicity, just by looking in their eyes. Perhaps he had simply gotten a lot of practice by being with Londo for so long.

So when he mentioned Welch's name, he had watched Throk's eyes, his face, for some sign of innocence. Some sort of confusion as to why Vir would be saying such a thing.

Instead he had seen it plainly. Throk had been momentarily confused, but it was the confusion of guilt. He had started to say "How," and then he had paused, obviously reconstructing the sentence that would have continued "did you know?"

But Vir had known. Vir was sure. Terribly, horribly sure. He was sure that Finian had not lied to him. The techno-mages had been many things, but deceivers they most certainly were not. They seemed to have a greater love of truth than any beings he had ever encountered.

Still . . . he had to be positive, beyond even the slightest shred of doubt. Because Vir knew himself all too well, and if one fragment of uncertainty remained with him, it would haunt him forever.

And so he listened, via the device that was now in his ear. Listened carefully, and Throk—in his arrogance—wasted no time in telling him what he needed to know. "But he knew that I killed Welch."

There it was . . . the evidence right there. All Vir needed to publicly . . .

To publicly what?

Throk came from too solid, too powerful a family. The house of Milifa was tightly allied with that of Durla's . . . Mariel had confirmed that for him, even though he had already been reasonably certain of it. Plus Throk was one of the first of the Prime Candidates, and was destined for greatness. The death of one nosy Human wasn't going to stop him from fulfilling that for which he was intended.

Of course, Vir could press the matter. He could go straight to the emperor. But he had every reason to believe that Londo would never stick his neck out, not at this point in time, be-cause there were too many people out there who were inter-ested in severing that same neck. Particularly if he were perceived as acting in a manner that was contrary to the best interests of Centauri Prime.

Furthermore, if Vir did desire to press the matter . . .

. . . he was a dead man.

That was beyond question. If the emperor couldn't cross the powers that be, certainly Vir's prospects were nil. He would be accused of operating in opposition to the grand and glorious destiny of Centauri Prime, as personified by Throk and his associates.

So if he did seek punishment for Throk through proper channels, he would most assuredly fail, and his life would be forfeit. He would have to lock himself into his quarters on Babylon 5, and never set foot out again.

The alternative was to turn the matter over to Sheridan. But then the entire matter would become known to all. The entire Centauri Homeworld would be at risk. Who knew how many thousands, hundreds of thousands, might die in the resultant chaos?

Vir turned it over and over in his mind.

He had sought out help. He had gone to Rem Lanas, who had proven to be something of an electronics expert. He had gone to Renegar, who had been pegged to oversee the dig on K0643 because he had familiarity with demolitions. He had been in touch with them somewhat regularly since the debacle on K0643, and they had learned from that disaster: They had learned whom to trust. They had learned that some of the underpinnings upon which the movements of Centauri Prime were based were, in fact, built upon sand.

Vir had brought them along slowly, building his own foundations, brick by brick. And Lanas and Renegar had begun speaking to others. Others who had survived K0643 and were disenchanted by the Centauri brain trust that had organized what had amounted to little more than a paid death camp. And others still, freethinkers who had been driven underground or exiled.

Now, though, matters had come to a head, a bit more quickly than Vir would have liked. He was a careful, methodical thinker, and he did not desire to act precipitously. He had to act at this point, though. He had to do something. Centauri

Prime was simply not ready for a war, and he was not ready to
roll over and let his world be assaulted again.

Garibaldi would not be satisfied with anything less than
justice.

"No choice," whispered Vir.


"You should have seen him," said Throk with amusement.
"Draping his arm around me. Acting as if I were his son. He—"

Muaad's eyes suddenly narrowed. "Wait a minute," he
said. "Turn around."

Throk looked puzzled. "Why?"

"Just do it."

Throk did so, and Muaad's fingers ran questingly over
the back of Throk's uniform shirt. "There's something here,"
he said. "A small lump . . . some sort of a device."

"He put something on me?" Throk's fury was mounting
immediately. "How dare he! What is it?"

"Some sort of transmitting device," said Muaad. "He was
eavesdropping on us."


Vir had known that eventually deaths would be necessary.
He had wanted to minimize it.

"I am a good man," he said.

His finger quivered.

"I am a decent man."

He thought about Cartagia, crumbling, with an astounded
look on his face and a heartful of poison injected by Vir.

"I am a moral man."

He thought about the Drakh he had killed when he had
blown up the Shadow base.

"I am an ethical man."

His voice was becoming increasingly soft as his hand
shook.

Throk had killed Welch. The others had helped remove the
body, and had stayed silent. They were guilty, all guilty, of a
crime that had brought Centauri Prime to the brink of war and
possibly total annihilation.

"I have no choice," he said.

* * *

"I'll kill him!" said Throk. "Enough is enough! How dare he plant a voice transmitter on me! He—"

Then he remembered something else.

Vir had patted Throk on the head as well.

His hand flew up. He felt the hard round disk, hidden by his high crest of hair. He pulled at it. It was attached via adhesive.

Vir flipped open the end of the cylinder. There was a small button on it. There was water dripping onto it, and he realized belatedly that it was his own tears.

He had found and read that book. The one about how all boys grow up, except one. He, Vir, had to grow up, his childhood ending with one stroke of a button.

"To die . . . would be an awfully big adventure," he whispered. "I'm . . . I'm sorry."

He closed his eyes and pushed the button.

*"Seňna!"* Throk cried out.

And then his head erupted in flame.

The windows of the safe house blew out, shattered glass flying everywhere. Passersby, completely unprepared, screamed and ran, momentarily convinced they were under assault yet again by the Alliance. Seconds later, the entire front wall collapsed, and the small structure tumbled down, while flames licked hungrily at it. There was more screaming, more running, and everyone was looking skyward, trying to see from where the next shot would originate.

Because all attention was directed to the heavens, no one would even have noticed if Vir had been nearby. He wasn't, however. He was several blocks away, leaning against a wall, while sobs racked his body so violently that he felt as if he would never be able to stand up again on his own. By the time rescue teams arrived to pull bits and pieces of the Prime Candidates out of the rubble, Vir was long gone.

* * *

Garibaldi stood on the balcony at the palace, watching the activity in the city some distance away. The entire area had been brightly illuminated, lights rigged to allow the rescue teams to do their job.

There was a chime at his door. "Come in," Garibaldi called, and G'Kar entered with that brisk stride of his. He went straight to the balcony and stood next to Garibaldi, who hadn't taken his eyes off the emergency scene. "Manage to find out what's going on?"

"Nothing definite," said G'Kar. Sardonically, he pointed to himself, and added, "It's not as if this is a face that is going to set Centauri tongues to wagging. You?"

"It's not as if anyone's big on Humans either," he admitted ruefully. "The only thing I've managed to pull together is that no one seems to think it's an accident. I'm not sure if anyone is dead . . ."

"Yes. Some are dead."

G'Kar and Garibaldi turned to see that Vir was standing in the doorway. He had not bothered to ring the chime. He looked haunted.

"Who? Who died?" asked Garibaldi.

"Several of the Prime Candidates." He paused a moment, and then added almost as an afterthought, "And me."

"What?" Garibaldi shook his head, uncomprehending. "I don't underst—"

Then he realized. It all hit him with the intensity of a burst of white light.

And Vir could obviously see in Garibaldi's eyes that he understood. He nodded in silent affirmation.

"G'Kar," Garibaldi said. "I think that we'll be leaving tomorrow."

"We will?"

"Yes. We will."

Then G'Kar comprehended, too. "Oh," he said. "Yes. Of course we will."

Vir nodded once and started out the door. He stopped only when Garibaldi said, "Vir . . . thank you."

He turned and faced Garibaldi, and said, "Both of you can go to hell. And me, too." Then he walked out without so much as a backward glance.

# — *chapter 16* —

"You should have let me do it."

Renegar spoke in a low voice as he sat in Vir's quarters on Babylon 5. Vir was staring at his own reflection in a bottle of liquor, and didn't seem especially inclined to respond.

"Vir," prompted Renegar. "Did you hear what I said?" The remarkably beefy Centauri seemed to take up more than his fair share of the space in the quarters. "You should have let me do it. It was my explosive charge."

"But it was my responsibility," Vir replied. They were the first words he had spoken in an hour.

It had been days since Vir had returned to Babylon 5. And one by one, the various individuals he had summoned were assembling. Soon they would be in this one room, which was not Vir's customary quarters. He had rented a separate facility on Babylon 5, under a fake name, paid for with funds pulled from a blind account. He was taking every possible step to be cautious. He was all too aware that that was how it was going to have to be for him for, quite probably, the rest of his life.

"Vir . . . look . . . you tried to warn me of things that I wasn't willing to pay attention to before," Renegar said. "I owe you for opening my eyes. I would have—"

"Renegar," Vir said slowly, "we are going to do everything we can . . . to spare lives. We are going to be as careful as possible. But I'm not an idiot. I'm not naive. I know that, sooner or later, people are going to die. Perhaps innocent people. I will do all that I can to avoid it . . . but it may very well happen."

"What are you saying?"

"I'm saying that I'm no longer going to be able to keep my hands clean."

"So you figured you'd get them dirty all at once."

Vir nodded.

"All right," Renegar said with a heavy sigh. "But if you're going to get this worked up and distraught over people dying . . . you may very well be in the wrong line of work."

"Don't think that hasn't occurred to me," said Vir.

Finally, the last of them arrived.

Vir looked around at the people gathered in the room. A dozen had been able to make the trip; that had been all that seemed judicious at the time. He had chosen them so carefully because one wrong move meant the end for all of them. If he missed a bet, if he brought a spy into their midst, he was signing their collective death warrant.

There was only one person missing . . . and, moments later, the door hissed open and he entered. Vir actually smiled when he saw him. He was the oldest individual in the room, certainly, and yet he moved with a spring in his step that evoked an old warhorse being pressed into service.

"Hello, Dunseny," he said.

The former valet of Londo Mollari bowed his head slightly. "Hello, good sir."

There were nervous, suspicious glances from several of the others in the room. Rem Lanas voiced the worries that were going through all their heads.

"This man worked for House Mollari for his entire life. Is it wise to have him here?"

"I still work for House Mollari," Dunseny promptly replied. "And the interests of House Mollari are not served by the bastards who are presently in power." He bowed slightly to Vir. "What small skills I can provide are yours, Ambassador, as you may need them."

"Gratefully accepted," Vir said.

He studied the men gathered around him. They waited for him to speak. He couldn't recall the last time people had sat in such anticipation, waiting for him to open his mouth. He wondered if G'Kar felt the same way when the Narn gathered around him and waited for him to bestow new pearls of wisdom upon them.

"All right," Vir said slowly. "There is much that needs to be done, and much we have to do. Centauri Prime is proceeding down a road that it must not be allowed to follow. And we have to do everything we can to forestall it. Even as we speak, there are installations, buildups underway on colony worlds whose very purpose has been corrupted. They have been forced into the service of an escalating war machine. We have to stop it."

"You're speaking of sabotage," one of the Centauri said.

Vir nodded. "That is exactly right, yes. All of you have had cause to suffer under the current regime. All of you are free-thinkers, or have had your eyes opened by various circumstances that you could not have anticipated . . . but now that they have happened, you cannot turn away. The Centaurum is propelling our beloved Homeworld toward certain destruction, and we have to do whatever we can to head it off."

"But isn't it a delaying action?" asked Rem Lanas. "By engaging in sabotage, we're not putting a halt to anything. We're just slowing things down. Isn't it possible that, sooner or later, Centauri Prime will still be pulled into the center of a war?"

"Yes. It's possible," Vir admitted. Then, his voice strong, he continued, "It is also possible that, if we provide sufficient resistance, we will be able to get people—both those in charge and those who are disdainfully thought of as the commoners— to reconsider what they're doing. It doesn't matter how small the insect is; repeated stings will bring a body down.

"I cannot emphasize enough the danger that's involved. You are not all of the individuals involved in this effort. I did not feel it wise for any one person, outside of myself, to know everyone who is involved in our little endeavor."

"That way if any one of us is captured, he cannot turn in the entire underground at one time," Dunseny said.

Vir nodded. "Ideally, of course, if any of us is captured—

Great Maker forbid—he will not turn in any of us. Death before dishonor."

There were affirming murmurs from throughout the room.

It was so easy to say, of course. So easy to believe that death would be embraced before the names of any coconspirators would be turned over.

But he had no choice now. He had gone too far. *It* had gone too far. He had no choice but to see it through.

Despite Londo's assurances to the contrary, Vir Cotto had never felt less invincible in his entire life.

"All right," Vir said. "Here's what we're going to do . . ."

**EXCERPTED FROM**
*THE CHRONICLES OF LONDO MOLLARI.*
**Excerpt dated (approximate Earth date)**
**January 18, 2271.**

Durla told them all it was an isolated event. At least, that was what he said publicly.

Privately he sang a very different tune, and promised a full investigation into the destruction of the Prime Candidates safe house, which had not proved to be so safe. Howling the most loudly was Milifa of the House Milifa, the patriarch who had lost his son in a hideous explosion that people still speak of in hushed voices, even though it happened months ago.

After all this time, Durla's investigation continued to turn up nothing concrete, only supposition. He told any and all who would listen to him that there was an underground movement brewing, a group of saboteurs who had been responsible for the killing of the handful of Prime Candidates, and who would undoubtedly make more strikes against us if given the opportunity. The problem is that relative peace causes complacency, and because there were no further assaults, Durla's theories soon lost credence.

That has all changed, however.

Today we received word that there were attacks on two of our colony worlds. And not just any attacks. The munitions plant—my pardon, the educational facility—on Morbis was blown sky high. The weapons development center—my pardon, the health facility—on Nefua is now a pile of rubble. Both blasts happened within a day or so of each other. It was a clear message to us that we are not simply dealing with happenstance or an isolated instance. This is nothing less than war . . . a war being waged from within.

Durla, however, is managing to work the situation from both sides. He cannot seem to make up his mind. Sometimes he claims that the attacks are part of an internal underground of saboteurs and protestors. Other times he states that the Alliance is behind the attacks. Occasionally he blends the two, stating that there is indeed some sort of rebellious crew of saboteurs, who are being supported and funded by the Alliance. No one appears to notice the fluidity of Durla's sentiments. Either that, or no one wishes to point it out, for fear that Durla will not react well.

It is hard to dispute Durla's success, however. Minister Vallko has been holding up Durla as an example of all that is well and good in Centauri society, and they have formed a formidable team. I worry for the direction that matters are presently taking.

And here I sit, feeling increasingly frustrated and helpless . . . but simultaneously feeling very much in control. With all that is going on, the presence of the emperor has almost gone unnoticed by those who are vying for power. They are making such noise in battling one another, that one cannot help but feel that they will end up drawing fire upon themselves. And when all that fire is burned away, then with any luck, I shall be the only one left. And would that not be the ironic, final laugh upon them all.

The one bit of good news to come from all this is that Dunseny has returned to my employ. With the passing of Throk—and good riddance to him—I was left without a valet. Apparently Durla had matters of greater importance to worry about than who should be at my side to help me on with my coat or whisper in my ear about matters that do not seem to have much in the way of great consequence for Centauri Prime. Truthfully, I do not know if I should be relieved or insulted.

I have not seen Vir recently. I should send him a message to come to Centauri Prime so that we may chat once more.

I certainly hope he is keeping himself out of trouble.

# — *chapter 17* —

It had been ages since John Sheridan had set foot on Mars, and somehow he never tired of it. As he sat in the meeting room at Edgars/Garibaldi Enterprises, drumming his fingers absently on the table, it seemed to him that it almost didn't matter how many far-off worlds he had traversed. There was still something about the mystique of Mars. Perhaps it was all the old literature devoted to it, turning it into a mysterious place of strange canals, exotic multiarmed creatures, and a haven for invaders of all sorts who wanted nothing but to attack the hapless Earthlings and steal away with their women.

"President Sheridan." A voice came over the large screen, set into the wall to his right. "There is an incoming message for you."

"Put it on," he told the voice's invisible owner.

Within moments the screen flickered to life, and there was Delenn, with David by her side.

He was a remarkably handsome boy, David. A real head-turner, even at his relatively young age, if Sheridan did say so himself. Towheaded with a ready grin, and a snapping sense of intelligence and cold amusement in his eyes, both of which he got from his mother. Sheridan couldn't help but feel that David actually was more charming than his father and more intelligent than his mother. It made for a very formidable combination.

David was also, however, old enough to feel chagrin at any sort of open display of affection. Delenn, who doted on him—too much, Sheridan thought privately—had an arm draped around him, which was causing him to squirm right on-screen. He did not, however, voice protest. He knew better than that, particularly where his mother was concerned.

"I just wanted to remind you," Delenn said, "that you promised you'd be home in time for David's moving-up ceremony in school."

With a slightly plaintive voice, David said, "I already told her it doesn't matter, Father. She keeps insisting anyway."

"You promised you would be there, and I simply want him to know that a promise from his father remains a promise."

"Don't worry," laughed Sheridan. "I just have this final meeting on Mars, and then I'll be able to come home."

"You're meeting with Michael, I take it?"

"Yes. And . . ." His voice trailed off.

Immediately Delenn was obviously on the alert. "And who?" she inquired.

"Well . . . it turns out that the new Centauri prime minister is in the area. When he learned that I was here, as well, he requested a get-together. I didn't see how I could refuse him."

"A new prime minister?" She frowned. "I had not heard of this. When did the Centauri elect a new prime minister?"

"Quite recently. His name is Durla."

"Durla." She wrinkled her nose. "I know this one, John. I've read of him. Trusting any Centauri is problematic enough, but this one . . . he is a dangerous one. He is Londo, without the conscience."

"Considering I'm not sure just how much of a conscience Londo ever had, that's a rather frightening assessment," said Sheridan.

David shifted uncomfortably on the screen. "Do you need me for this anymore, Mother?"

"No, no. You can go. Tell your father you love him."

For response, David rolled his eyes and then moved quickly off-screen. Delenn reflexively took a step toward the screen, as if somehow she might be able to step through and be there with him.

"Delenn," Sheridan said thoughtfully, "a real-time connection between Mars and Minbar is not an easy thing to put together. It's complicated and it's not cheap. Did you really do this just to remind me of his moving-up ceremony?"

"It's silly," she said, but there was nothing in her demeanor that seemed to indicate that she truly thought it silly. "I have been having . . . concerns lately, John. Strange dreams . . . unlike others that I have had. I am wondering . . . whether someone is trying to tell me something."

"What sort of dreams?" asked Sheridan. He wasn't about to dismiss the concerns out of hand, even though they sounded a bit odd. After all, the Minbari often had their sensibilities informed by everything from prophecy to souls, so he wasn't about to ignore anything.

"I keep . . . seeing Centauri. I see Londo. And . . . an eye . . ."

"An eye? What sort of eye?"

"Watching me. Just an eye. Nothing more than that, and then the other night, I had a dream that it looked right through me, as if I wasn't there, and straight at David. I don't know what any of it means."

"Neither do I, but I have to admit, you're making me nervous as hell," said Sheridan.

"John . . . come back as soon as you can. I know as president of the Alliance you have responsibilities, but . . ."

"I will. As soon as I can, I promise. And Delenn . . ."

"Yes?"

"I'll keep my eye peeled."

She sighed and made no effort to hide her annoyance with him. "Sometimes I don't even know why I bother," she said, and then the screen blinked out. He realized with some frustration that he had forgotten to tell her he loved her. He hoped that she wouldn't hold it against him.

The problem was, now all he could picture was an eye staring at him.

"Thanks a lot, Delenn," he muttered.

Garibaldi was already in the conference room, chatting with Sheridan, when Prime Minister Durla arrived. Next to him walked a fairly stunning Centauri woman whom Sheridan recognized immediately.

"Lady Mariel, isn't it?" asked Sheridan. "A former wife of Londo's, correct?"

"Actually," said Durla, "the Lady Mariel is, in fact, my wife now. We married several weeks ago."

"Congratulations!"

"Thank you, Mr. President," Mariel said softly. She seemed far more reserved, far less flirtatious than the last time Sheridan had encountered her. He supposed that it was only reasonable for a newly married Centauri woman to be more restrained. Still, he couldn't help but feel that there was something more to it than that. Almost a distant melancholy, as if she had lost something, rather than gained a husband.

"And of course, I remember Mr. Garibaldi," continued Durla. "He came to visit us the year before last, as I recall. Matters were in something of a disarray at the time, I regret to say. We are getting things more solidly in hand, however."

Durla took a seat opposite Sheridan and Garibaldi. Sheridan saw that the Lady Mariel was standing, and gestured for her to take an open chair. But Mariel shook her head, gently but firmly. "I prefer to stand," she said.

"All right," Sheridan said with a shrug, and turned his attention to Durla. "So . . . Mr. Prime Minister . . . how may I be of service?"

Then he saw Durla place a small object upon the table. "May I ask what that is?" Sheridan inquired.

But before Durla could respond, it was Garibaldi who answered. "It's a recording device," he said. "I was wondering if he was going to produce it or keep it hidden."

"You knew I had it?" Durla asked, clearly surprised.

"You don't walk into the headquarters of a former chief of security without a few scans being done on you, without your knowing," said Garibaldi, sounding remarkably blasé.

"Very good. Very, very good. As you can see, though, I intend to keep this meeting open and aboveboard. Do you mind if I record it, Mr. President?"

"As long as security-related matters aren't being discussed, not at all," said Sheridan gamely.

"Very well, then. In truth, Mr. President, I only have one question, and then I will take up no more of your time."

"All right. What would that question be?"

Durla leaned forward, and there was a hawklike expression on his face. "When will you be calling off the attacks on our colonies?"

Sheridan blinked in confusion. "I'm sorry . . . what? Attacks? I'm a bit unclear as to what you're talking about . . ."

"Are you." Durla, for his part, didn't seem remotely puzzled. "Then I will clarify for you. Agents of your Interstellar Alliance have been secretly attacking various Centauri outposts. You see that we are endeavoring to build ourselves up, to make ourselves great again . . ."

"Now just hold on," snapped Sheridan, his temper flaring.

Durla steamrolled right over him. ". . . that we are attempting to purse the glory and respect that is due the Centauri Republic . . . and you snipe at us, and you endeavor to tear us down. Six months ago, there were attacks on the worlds of Morbis and Nefua. Since then, there have been more, on other worlds. Either attacks or sabotage of existing works for the purpose of slowing them down or eliminating them altogether."

"That is a complete fabrication."

"And is it a fabrication to say that certain members of your Alliance will never rest until Centauri Prime is wiped from the annals of galactic history?" Durla's voice was rising, and Sheridan felt as if the man were making a speech right from the board room.

"It most certainly is," Sheridan told him flatly.

"Is it a further fabrication to say that your Alliance has been trying to undermine the security of Centauri Prime, infiltrate it with its own people or else try to obtain influence with certain Centauri who might be amenable to disposing of the current regime?"

"This is ridiculous. Mr. Prime Minister, you requested this

meeting and I agreed to it. I did not agree to having baseless accusations hurled at me."

"And when we agreed to peace, Mr. President, we did not do so with the intent of signing away the Centauri soul. He rose abruptly from the table. "I suggest you keep that in mind in your future dealings with Centauri Prime . . . lest we feel the need to deal with you in the future in a way that will make it clear just who, and what, the Centauri are."

With that, he turned and headed for the door. Mariel said nothing, barely glanced in their direction, as she silently followed Durla out of the room.

Garibaldi and Sheridan stared at each other for a moment, then Sheridan said, "You want to tell me what the hell that was all about?"

"Notice he took the recorder," said Garibaldi, and sure enough, it was gone.

"Yeah, I noticed. Are you thinking the same thing I'm thinking, Michael?"

"Grandstanding."

Sheridan nodded. "He's trying to make himself look good to the folks at home. So he records this meeting, tough-talks me, and then screens it for the Centauri so he can show them that the Alliance isn't going to have Centauri Prime to kick around anymore. Lots of huzzahs for him, boos and hisses for me . . ."

"And another step for stoking the fire of war."

Sheridan fixed a steady gaze on Garibaldi. "You really think that's what he's up to?"

"Don't you?"

"Yeah. Yeah, I do. Problem is, I can't do anything about it . . . thanks, in no small measure, to you."

"To me?" Garibaldi said in obvious surprise, apparently thinking that Sheridan was kidding.

Except that Sheridan was most definitely not kidding. "Look, Michael . . ." and he sat down next to Garibaldi, leaning on the table. "You asked me to keep quiet the things that Vir told you. I did. You said he begged for the chance to handle it internally."

"And he's doing the job," Garibaldi pointed out. "That whole thing Durla was complaining about, the bombings and such . . . that has to be Vir's people. It has to be. And if Durla came in here to bitch about it, you know it has to be because Vir is hurting him. If it were just momentary setbacks, Durla wouldn't waste his time, even if it meant getting brownie points with his people."

"The problem with letting Vir attend to it, however, is that he *has* done a good job. Or at least apparently so."

"What do you mean?"

"I mean, Michael," said Sheridan, looking impatient, "months ago, years ago even, the Alliance governments were ready, willing, and able to do whatever was required to hold down Centauri Prime. But time has made them complacent. People have a short memory, Michael, even when war is involved. Try to tell them now that Centauri Prime might be on a road to buildup, and you're not going to get the Alliance off its collective ass to do anything about it. It's a time of peace, Michael, and people want to keep it that way. I can understand it. But it's damned frustrating. Because it means that I can't get anyone to do anything about it until Centauri Prime has engaged in a buildup so massive that it's literally going to be coming down people's throats. At that point, it may well be too late."

"Perhaps you want to call a meeting . . ."

Sheridan shook his head. "Why? I'll just learn from the Alliance members what I already know, and the Centauri can hold it up as another example of anti-Centauri warmongering. Won't that be fun."

"So you're saying we do nothing. We just stand by and let it happen."

"We watch," Sheridan said. "We wait. And we keep our fingers crossed."

"Keeping our fingers crossed," Garibaldi said with unbridled sarcasm. "Is that a military strategy now?"

"One that I'm learning to depend on more and more as time goes on," said Sheridan, holding up crossed fingers on both hands.

## EXCERPTED FROM
### *THE CHRONICLES OF LONDO MOLLARI.*
### Excerpt dated (approximate Earth Date) April 18, 2273

I almost died today.

This past year . . . it has been referred to as the "Year of the Long Knives." At least, that is what they have called it in private. In public, they simply refer to it as the Time of the Great Loyalty.

Ever since his election as prime minister, Durla's reach has been everywhere. Ghehana is no more. He has sent soldiers through there, through the seamier side of Centauri Prime, with a mandate to rid it of all the undesirables. They are, after all, the most likely to plot against those who are the holders of the status quo. Who, after all, is more envious of those who have everything . . . than those who have nothing.

All the upper echelon naturally cheered this plan.

Then Durla came for the upper echelon.

Oh, not for all of them, of course. He only came for those who would not swear undying fealty to Durla, and he already knew in advance whom it was he wanted on his side. There were some who were able to purchase their loyalty, prove it that way.

But there were others—men who served before me, proud men, accomplished men—who did not like the way that Durla did business. Men who stood up to him, who spoke their mind. Who had watched Durla's people come in, month after month, until all in power answered to Durla, and who decided they could be silent no more.

Sanctimonious fools.

They were perfectly happy to be silent as long as they thought Durla was going to leave them alone. Once they realized that they were not safe, then and only then did they begin to rattle their sabres . . . at which point, Durla severed their sword arms.

He desires to do more than solidify his power, you see. He wishes to make certain that he controls the hearts, minds, the very soul of Centauri Prime. And he has systematically eliminated all those who might oppose him.

Today he came for me.

I was there in my throne room. Senna was with me. We spoke, not for the first time, of finding a husband for her. I am concerned that I might not be able to protect her forever. "I do not need protection, Highness. I am a grown woman now. I can care for myself," she said. The proud boasts of youth. How charming it is to hear it. How little she knew, as the doors burst open and Prime Minister Durla entered, swaggering and confident. He was accompanied by a small entourage of followers.

"To what do I owe this honor?" I asked calmly.

He came right to the point. "There are those who challenge your loyalty to Centauri Prime, Your Highness."

"I do not doubt it," I said. Senna looked apprehensively from Durla to me.

"It is important that the people of Centauri Prime know that their emperor is to be trusted implicitly. That their emperor is not in the grip of enemies of our Homeworld."

"I agree with that as well," I said.

"I wish to head off accusations that challenge your loyalty, Highness."

"Indeed. Very well."

Without hesitation, I turned to a guard and gestured for him to come near me. He did so, a look of confusion on his face. "Give me your dagger," I said, pointing to the ceremonial blade he wore on his hip.

The guard looked to Durla silently. Durla, clearly a bit confused, nevertheless nodded. One of my guards seeking approval for one of my orders. That alone should make clear the sort of world we live in.

So the guard handed me the dagger, and I examined the blade. "Tell me, Durla," I said softly, "do you believe in the Great Maker?"

"Of course."

"Good." Then I suddenly gripped Durla's wrist and brought his hand to the hilt of the blade. Before Durla could fully grasp what I was doing, I put the point to my own throat and closed my eyes. "Then let the Great Maker himself judge my loyalty, and guide your hand."

Then I stood there and waited.

For I knew one thing, you see.

Durla was a coward.

He loved to posture. He loved to preen. He loved to allow others to do his work for him, and maneuver behind the scenes while people suffered from his machinations. But he did not like getting his hands dirty. Ever.

He was hoping that I would cry out in protest, or fear, or lose my temper, or in some way give him something with which to maneuver. Instead I put it into the hands of the Great Maker . . . and into Durla's.

He wanted to show all the witnesses who were present that I was weak. That I would grovel before a subordinate. Instead I made a direct appeal to our Supreme Being. Durla was to be his vessel.

The Great Maker, as I suspected, had other things to worry about and did not weigh in on the subject.

Durla lowered his blade and said, in a most subdued voice, "Perhaps . . . we should speak of this later, Highness."

"I remain always at your service, Prime Minister," I replied with a deep bow, whereupon Durla and his people cleared out of my throne room.

Senna let out a long, unsteady breath of relief. "I thought . . ." she began to say.

But I waved her off. "Do not think," I told her. "It is an entirely overrated pastime."

I recently put forward the first major decree I have issued in months: I have banned any and all foreigners from this world. Any who are found here face imprisonment or worse. I have done so supposedly as a show of strength, to indicate that Centauri Prime is officially turning its back on the rest of the galaxy and stating that we wish to be left alone.

In point of fact, I do it as much for off-worlders as for ourselves. I would spare them any unpleasant fates that might befall them should they come here under the misapprehension that they are dealing with a civilized society.

It is evening now. I am alone in my study, alone with my thoughts . . . or as alone as I am ever allowed to be. The weather has been quite temperate lately, but I am beginning to sense a coldness in the air. If I were fanciful, I would say that they are the winds of war, sweeping toward us.

But I am not a fanciful person. For my reality is so ripe with madness, that to imagine flights of fancy would surely be a comedown.

The shadows grow longer, and they reach for me. I go to them quietly this night . . .

. . . but perhaps for not much longer.

Prepare
yourself for the
senses-shattering conclusion
of the Centauri trilogy, *Legions of Fire*.

## *LEGIONS OF FIRE*
## *OUT OF THE DARKNESS*

### by Peter David

### Based on an original outline
### by J. Michael Straczynski

*Coming this fall!*

*Del Rey proudly presents a five-book set of definitive episode guides to the smash-hit SF TV series!*

# Babylon 5: Season by Season

Book 1, **SIGNS AND PORTENTS**, features: a foreword by actor Michael O'Hare (Commander Sinclair); two introductory essays—"Getting *Babylon 5* into Orbit" and "*Babylon 5*'s First Season"—by author Jane Killick; a complete synopsis of each episode, from the pilot, "The Gathering," through the climactic season finale, "Chrysalis," followed by an in-depth analysis.

# Babylon 5: Season by Season

Book 2, **THE COMING OF SHAD-OWS**, includes: Killick's essays "By Any Means Necessary: Making *Babylon 5* on a Budget" and "*Babylon 5*'s Second Season"; a complete guide to and analysis of the season's twenty-two episodes, including "Points of Departure," "Hunter, Prey," and "The Fall of Night."

Book 3, **POINT OF NO RETURN**, begins with a fascinating look at how this groundbreaking series pioneered a new special-effects frontier. Then Killick's essay "*Babylon 5*'s Third Season" presents a thrilling summation of the series' major turning point—the culmination of the Shadow War. And episode-by-episode summaries cover all of the third season's twenty-two shows, including the stunning finale, "Z'ha'dum."

Published by Del Rey Books.
Available wherever books are sold.

# Babylon 5: Season by Season

Book 4, **NO SURRENDER, NO RETREAT**, sums up the spellbinding fourth season: Captain Sheridan being pronounced missing and presumed dead on Z'ha'dum, Delenn feverishly rallying support for an all-out offensive against the Shadows, internal strife among the Centauri erupting in a shocking and violent betrayal, and Garibaldi resigning as security chief and plotting against his comrades. From "The Hour of the Wolf" to the shattering finale, "The Deconstruction of Falling Stars," Jane Killick's summaries and analyses capture all the action and intrigue of Babylon 5 circa 2261—"the year everything changed."

Published by Del Rey Books.
Available wherever books are sold.

# Babylon 5:
# Season by Season

Book 5, **THE WHEEL OF FIRE**, covers the last season of the history-making show as the action reaches the boiling point and the stage is set for the follow-up series, *Crusade*. Episode by episode, Jane Killick looks at Byron and his rogue telepaths' demand for a homeworld, Elizabeth Lochley's assignment as head of Babylon 5, Sheridan's inauguration as president of the new Alliance, G'Kar's unwilling ascension to the role of messiah, and the clandestine political intrigue on Centauri Prime.

The
**BABYLON 5 SECURITY MANUAL**
is the next best thing for fans who wish
they could really be there!

This definitive manual details everything there is to know about maintaining security aboard the Babylon 5 space station. Here, Chief of Security Garibaldi and his successor, Zack Allan, reveal vital, highly sensitive information necessary for keeping the peace, including:

•Complete descriptions of Babylon 5's structure, technical operations, personnel, and population

•Portraits of more than forty key types of life-forms from throughout the galaxy

•Full technical illustrations of weapons, crafts, uniforms, and accessories

•Comprehensive maps of every deck, level, and section of Babylon 5

•And much more!

Published by Del Rey Books.
Available wherever books are sold.

**Look for all the *Babylon 5* books.
Published by Del Rey Books.**